I0748751

Published by Bent Spine Media
Los Angeles, CA

Book design and cover illustrations by Paul Beveridge
paulbeveridge.com

ISBN: 979-8-9945844-0-8

Printed in the United States of America

First Edition

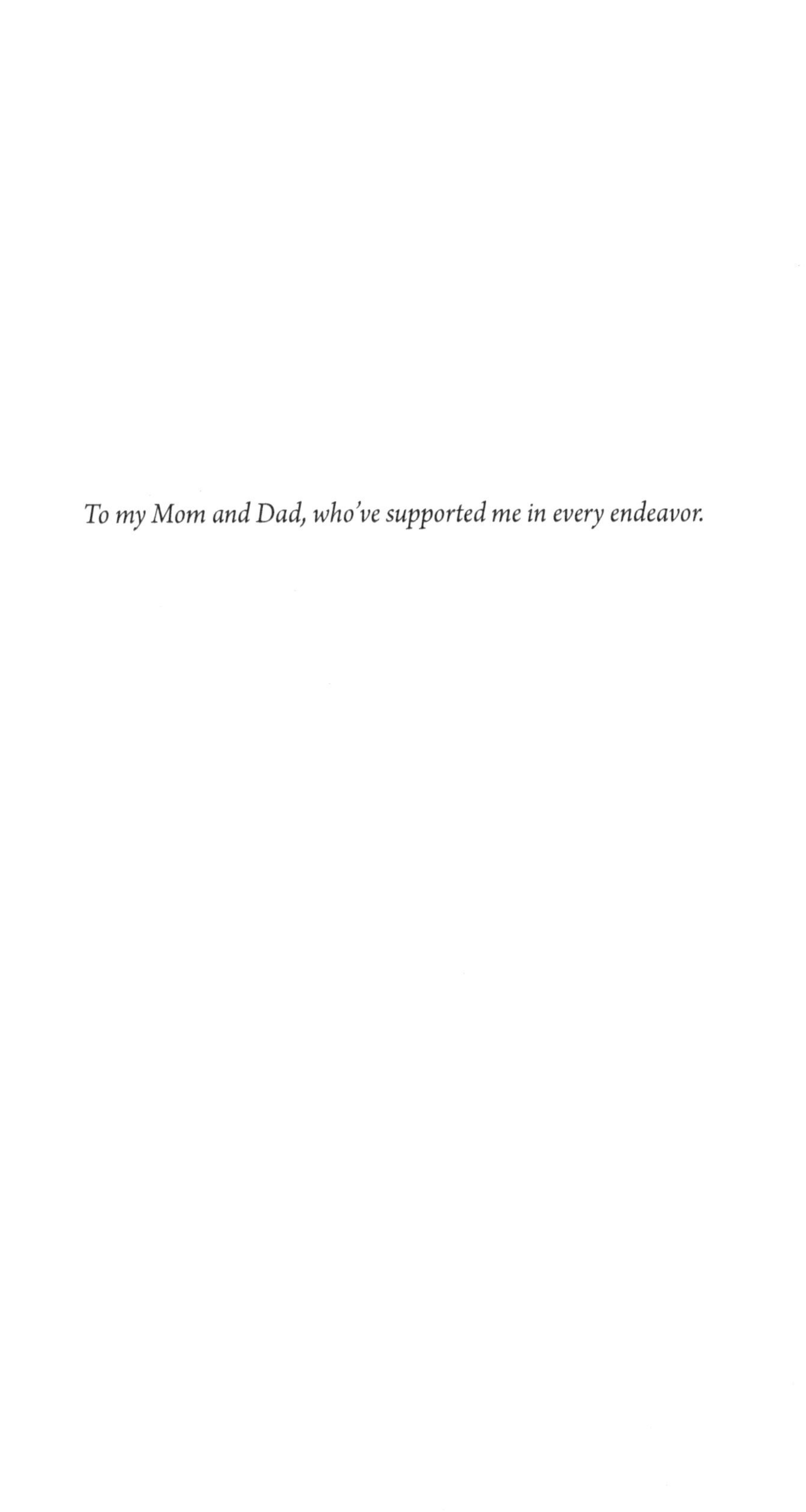

To my Mom and Dad, who've supported me in every endeavor.

AN IAN SHARP NOVEL

FROM *The* ASHES

THE FIRST NOVEL IN THE WHISPER TRILOGY

ROBERT J. WATSON

NOVELS IN THE

WHISPER SERIES

CONTENTS

PROLOGUE

Luis Quadros sat in the back of a black Lincoln limousine, his chubby fingers of his right hand dug into the leather upholstery while the other drummed a silent tattoo against the knuckles of his wife's intertwined fingers. Staring out the window, he saw nothing but a rush of distorted lights and blurred figures—passing phantasms obscured by the tempest of troubled thoughts raging through his head.

"...Every year we're seeing the Amazon cleared away by these big soybean producers," a nasally squeak penetrated the outer edges of his consciousness, "and if this keeps pace like it is then that'll mean Brazil will corner the market for soybeans in a matter of years..."

Snapping back to the present, Quadros nodded politely at the gentlemen opposite him: the distinguished senator from South Carolina, his host for the evening. This particular American was a perfect extraction of crude oil painstakingly distilled into the finest legislative lubricant the autocrats could manufacture. He had slicked black hair, lacquered skin, and a Southern drawl that made the hardest of consonants land upon the ear like the gentle cooing of a blue jay.

"...I don't know if you know this," the senator said sweetly, "but soybeans have become a major crop in South Carolina. It would be a shame if our farmers were pushed out of this market. Many lives would be destroyed," his face scrunched tightly, feigning remorse. "Now I can't let that happen. So I came up with this idea. I know how much you treasure the Amazon—would like to see it protected."

"That's true," Quadros mumbled, half listening.

The senator thrust forward testing the elasticity of the seat belt. His hands fluttered before him as he spoke. "I'll pull some strings and get the whole US Senate body to put pressure on President Rousseff. Force her hand to sign an environmental protection treaty prohibiting further development into the Amazon in exchange for a more lucrative trade agreement between us and Brazil. You get your precious forest and we keep our soybeans competitive." His lips curved into a triumphant smirk. "Now how does that sound?"

"I'll bring it up to her," Quadros offered perfunctorily. He was not in the mood for politicking at the moment. His time in the United States had done much to wear him down and its effects were clear to see upon his features. His once boyish chipmunk cheeks fell into pug-like jowls; his irises disappeared into black holes; and his sinewy body sagged off the bone. He appeared nothing more than a shell of the man he had once been. Exhausted, all Quadros wished for was rest.

Beside him his wife, Anir, sensed that Quadros's aura had darkened in hue—the vibrant chartreuse dimmed to a despondent juniper. Concerned, she squeezed his fingers. He glanced her way and smiled, it failed to reach his eyes. Anir scanned his face for any hint of what might be going on in his brain, but all was shrouded in the muted haze she was more than familiar with whenever Quadros disappeared deep into his thoughts. She knew not to prod otherwise he might retreat even deeper into himself. Thus, she smiled in return waiting patiently for the haze to clear.

The limousine pulled up to the curb.

Quadros forced a cheerful façade and exited the car. Anir followed, her hand tethered tightly to his, while the senator brought up the rear.

A battalion of patrons stormed the lone double doors of the theater where two red vested doormen braved the assault. They scanned tickets with a hurried air, afraid that any delay might see them trampled by the invading force. A cacophony of discordant revelry rang out like a triumphant battle cry.

The senator leaned into Quadros's shoulder and said something Quadros couldn't make out. He merely nodded and followed the senator into the breach. As they advanced a barrage of shoulders knocked into Quadros, forcing him off balance and sending him into the patron before him. Someone with two left feet kept clipping his heels. A thick scent of aftershave stung his nostrils. Quadros's jaw clenched, fending off the brunt of this onslaught.

One night, he recited silently to himself, *one more night.*

The senator flashed his tickets, the doorman scanned them, and they filed into the foyer. Yet, here too Quadros failed to find any solace: patrons filled every inch of floor space from wall to wall. The assault upon Quadros's senses resumed. He inhaled deep and followed the senator into the fray.

"What do you think?" The senator shouted over his shoulder, his chest puffed up like some nobleman passing through his serfs.

"It is a marvel," Quadros declared lamely. Though the gold art deco sunbursts and crystal chandeliers might have inspired awe in him once, he dismissed them as nothing more than gawdy. Yet, he knew his role for the night—that of an ever appreciative guest—and so sought out praise he could lavish upon his host, but his heart just wasn't in it tonight. To make matters worse, the gross violations of his personal space only further rendered him incapable of doing so. He breathed, "uhmmm."

Luckily, Anir came to his rescue, "Very elegant. If only Brasilia had a theater as beautiful as this one, I'd go every weekend."

The senator beamed with delight, "I know a few donors who have deep pockets. Let me pull a few strings and see what I can do about that."

Quadros rolled his eyes. *Pull a few strings*—the senator's hollow turn of phrase wore thin quick.

One more night.

At the staircase the senator stopped and turned fully toward his guests. "You two go on up to our seats. I'd like to get something to wet my whistle before the show starts. Would you like anything?"

Quadros shook his head. "No, thank you."

"Please, it's my treat," he insisted.

Again Quadros politely refused.

Just as graciously the senator relented and said, "Alright, I'll see you up there." And into the crowd he disappeared. Relief washed over Quadros.

The senator's private box was a low lit compartment covered in red velvet. Three matching upholstered chairs lined the railing overlooking the stage. Quadros pulled one of them out and bowed low playing the part of an overzealous servant eager to please. Anir matched her husband's humor with a deep curtsy before sitting down.

Seated, their hands dangled between them, their fingers entwined. They watched in silence as the patrons in the orchestra scrambled to their seats. Anir grew jittery as the clock ticked closer to curtain. Her excitement caused her to bounce in her seat. She glanced at Quadros and beamed with delight. Quadros couldn't help but smile in return, her enjoyment was infectious.

But the feeling didn't last long. From the darkness of his mind a shadowy tendril slithered out and snatched him away, roughly four thousand miles away where trouble was brewing. As much as he wished to be back in Brazil he knew he was not to have the rest he yearned for. Instead he'd have to act the moment he touched ground and snuff out some smoking kindling before it reached a flashpoint. He needed to act—act now—but first…

One more night, he pleaded to the shadowy tendril advancing upon him, *then on to Pernambuco.*

"What's the matter?" Anir asked, noticing once more her husband's darkening aura—now a frightful phthalo.

"Nothing," he muttered. "A little homesick is all."

"Me too. All this travel has worn me out. I miss home." Her words shone a powerful light, casting the tendril back into the darkness.

He squeezed her fingers as a tiny spirit of happiness revived his good nature. "I'm glad you came along. Couldn't have done it without you."

"Oh please," she dismissed, blushing. "I was a total bore."

"Yes you were," he teased, "A wonderful bore. I've been running around from one social gathering to the next and you've been there every step of the way. So patient and supportive. I never had the chance to thank you."

Her eyes locked onto him, two brown laser-focused question marks.

Quadros observed the patrons below. "Why do you think we're here?"

"Because that wind-bag of a senator invited you. As a guest you know you can't ref…" Her words faded into silence when Quadros began shaking his head. She pursed her lips together and waited.

"For you," he declared.

The light in her eyes rivaled the sun and her jaw fell into her lap.

Quadros slouched. "You know I don't care for the theater—I would have refused the senator immediately when he asked. But I know how much you enjoy it, and well…it is our last night here after all. So… enjoy."

The words tumbled out of Anir's mouth all at once forming an incoherent jumble of syllables. Collecting herself, she closed her mouth, breathed a moment, then leaned over the armrest to plant a kiss on his cheek. She nudged her chair closer and nuzzled her head in the nook between his shoulder and neck. Quadros felt at ease.

The shadowy tendril returned. As Quadros lovingly braced his wife, it slithered out from the darkness and into his thoughts. *Poverty-stricken farmhands …Private militia…Bullets flying through the air…*

blood staining the dirt... Eldorado de Carajás... I can't let that happen... not again.

"Made it just in time," the senator twittered, falling into his seat and jolting Quadros out of his thoughts. "And what a view. Wasn't easy to get these seats, you know. It's a sold out show. But I pulled a few strings." He took a swig of his drink, the ice clinked together.

Quadros shuttered.

The senator split the distance between them and inquired in a softer tone, "So have you given my proposal any thought?"

Quadros could smell the alcohol on his breath. "I'm sorry?"

"About the soybeans and preserving the Amazon," the senator reminded him. "It'll be a good deal between us, build some mutual respect. What do you say?"

"Ah yes," he feigned recollection, "However this isn't something that can be agreed upon in a night. There are a lot of factors that need to be discussed first, and a few people who I must consult with. But it is a very intriguing proposal."

The senator accepted Quadros's reply at face value and backed off. "Fine, fine. Just don't take too long. Opportunities like this don't happen often, Mr. Quadros." He downed another gulp of his drink. "There are upcoming elections to consider after all."

An epiphany struck Quadros like a thunderbolt: *I best hire a bodyguard when I get back.*

The tendrils directed a wave of concentrated paranoia right at the fear center of his brain. The levees were no match for its terrible power—the wave crashed into them and splinted them like toothpicks. His thoughts flooded with suspicion.

Death threats were nothing unusual for those in public service, but Brazil had two means of functioning: the first concerned the traditional rigmarole that is government bureaucracy, and the other a craven submission to those positioned high in the upper echelon of society. Quadros had planted himself right in the center where any slight shift in footing could send him teetering into an abyss. And there were plenty on the sidelines all too willing to offer a kindly push.

"Welcome ladies and gentlemen to tonight's performance..." the pre-show announcements bellowed through the house. The chatter faded. Anir excitedly squeezed Quadros's hand. He replied with a lame distracted smile.

Once the announcement finished the lights dipped to black and footsteps shuffled across the stage. A cold blue spotlight revealed a man in uniform marching atop a lone piece of barren scaffolding flanked on either side by two metal staircases. Black curtains hung behind it.

The man stopped, leaned against the railing, and peered into the darkness.

A voice off-stage inquired: "Who's there?"

The uniformed man countered: "Nay, answer me. Stand and unfold yourself."

"Long live the King!" Another man stepped on stage dressed also in a uniform.

"Barnardo?"

Shakespeare's greatest drama had begun.

Quadros settled into his chair, readying himself mentally for the next three hours. *One night.*

Not too long into the play, he inhaled an impatient breath and began to fidget in his seat. His hands fluttered incessantly till Anir could endure this no longer. She detached herself from him and perched her arms atop the railing, her chin resting on her folded fingers, completely enthralled.

His restlessness quickly spread to his leg which thumped noiselessly against the floor. Without looking Anir swung a hand back and clamped his knee still. Quadros, doing his best to appease her, occupied his mind by reciting his mantra over and over again through his head: *one night, one more night.* This kept the tendril at bay like a lullaby soothing an errant beast.

"To be, or not to be—that is the question."

Quadros sat up; he recognized the quotation. On stage Hamlet stepped forward, stared deep into the audience, and lingered silently as he thought. Madness tinged his eyes.

"Whether 'tis nobler in the mind to suffer

The slings and arrows of outrageous fortune,

Or take arms against a sea of troubles,"

Quadros latched onto those words. Though he was familiar with Hamlet—having read it in school—he had never heard them ring so true before.

Hamlet fell back to the metal stairs and ascended the scaffolding. His timbre subdued.

"And by opposing end them? To die: to sleep—

No more; and by a sleep to say we end

The heart-ache and the thousand natural shocks"

Quadros arched forward, mesmerized by Hamlet's morose pontification. Though he didn't understand the language entirely he felt its meaning pierce his core. As if Hamlet were offering important advice directly to him. He listened on:

"That flesh is heir to. 'tis a consummation

Devoutly to be wish'd. To die, to sleep;

To sleep, perchance to dream: ay, there's the rub!"

Suddenly, a tight pinch in Quadros's chest flung him back into his chair. He gasped then fell silent. Any tightness in his muscles eased, and his body went limp. His head slumped down to his chest. His hands dangled at his sides. The tendril dissipated into nothingness. He didn't move, nor breathe.

Quadros went out in a whisper.

Anir swirled her head but found only her husband there relaxed, asleep, in his chair; his aura now unreadable. She shrugged, and returned her attention to Hamlet's monologue:

"For in that sleep of death what dreams may come
When we have shuffled off this mortal coil,
Must give us pause."

PART 1

BRASÍLIA

Come let us weave our freedom.
Strong arms that tear the ground,
Under the shadow of our courage,
Unfurling our rebellion,
And plant in this land as brothers/sisters!
Come, let us fight fist raised!
Our Strength leads us to build,
Our country free and strong.
Built by people power!

- MST ANTHEM

FAMILY MAN

Ian Sharp sat in the driver's seat of his 2006 Ford Escape. He was parked in the driveway of his new home twirling a plain golden ring between his fingers. For the last six years that ring had held firm to his left ring finger, yet in the last few weeks it's seen the bottom of the cup holder more often than naught. The thought of that alone weighed heavy upon his soul. Sharp breathed a sorrowful sigh, slipped the ring back onto his finger, and heaved himself out of the car.

His feet dragged behind him as he walked the short pathway to the porch of his monstrous house, a schizophrenic eyesore disfigured by the 2008 housing crash. It had been caught in the middle of major renovations when the previous owners were forced to rush the project and sell it for way less than market value. Everything clashed: windows didn't match, wood buttressed stucco, and Art Deco overpowered the original Victorian architecture. It was ugly and Sharp wasn't sure if he could ever turn this deformed house into a home.

At the door he riffled through the keys on his chain, selected one, and tested it in the lock. It failed. His shoulders slumped and the light in his eyes dimmed as he commenced attempt number two.

His third attempt proved successful when he heard the satisfying click. In that moment, he expelled any apprehension and anguish he had in his heart and forced a smile. The door creaked open announcing his arrival.

Before he could fully cross the threshold they were already on him. They latched tightly onto his legs with their hands and feet.

"Daddy!" they cried in unbridled excitement.

"Oh! What do we have here?" Sharp inquired playfully, examining his two twin daughters, barely six years old. Their matching blue eyes fixed on him. "Do I see some monkeys on a monkey tree?"

"No!" they teased, burying their faces into his pant legs.

"I think I do." Sharp managed a stilted step, then another, all the while vocalizing exaggerated grunts. "And they are stuck on tight pretty well, there's nothing that could shake these monkeys from the monkey tree, now is there?"

The girls giggled and tightened their grip around his legs.

"Not even the storm that's approaching!" He waddled through the foyer and vocalized the sound of wind with his mouth. "Oh no, it's getting stronger. Better hold on tight!" He shook one leg then the next.

"No, don't!" The girls pleaded between joyous fits of laughter. "Go away, storm!"

"Uh oh, the wind's picking up." He swooshed a hand through their dirty blond hair.

"Stop it."

"It's starting to blow things all over the place. Watch out, it's carrying an anthill right towards you." His fingers scurried over their necks and back, they squirmed under the torment but refused to let go. "There's ants everywhere."

He stopped. "What's this? It looks like...Snakes!" His arms slithered down their backs and wrapped around them.

"No, not the snakes!" the girls yelled.

"Ants and snakes and wind, can the monkeys stay on the monkey tree." Sharp poked and prodded and tugged and tickled till the girls' tiny hands could hold no longer. They collapsed to the floor. Kneeling, Sharp continued the assault as his girls writhed on their backs, flailing their hands and feet around, trying, in vain, to bat away the ants and snakes. All the while laughing wildly.

"Stop it! Stop tickling me!" they begged. "Stop!"

"Only if you promise to get ready for bed."

"I promise, I promise."

Sharp relented and stood up, his six foot frame towering over his girls. "Good, now go upstairs and brush your teeth. I'll be up soon to tuck you in."

They fumbled to their feet and scurried up the stairs. Sharp watched them disappear into their room. Just then a new thought popped into his mind, *how much am I going to have to hide from them?* His fatherly pride dissipated, replaced by a lingering concern. Keeping secrets from them won't be so hard, but his wife was a different situation entirely.

Passing the conclave of boxes stacked about the dining room, his shoes clopping against the hardwood floor, he crossed into the kitchen. It was a cozy space with tiled counters and wooden cabinets tightly encircling an island stove. To its right stood Katelyn over the sink, her hands hidden in soapy water.

"Hello," Sharp announced.

Her blue eyes locked onto him. "Hello," she replied curtly. Still dressed in her bank teller outfit, she looked haggard, as one gets after a long and exhausting day of customer service. Dark smeared remnants of make-up hollowed her eyes. Her skin sagged and her hair frizzed at the ends. Mechanically, she set a plate onto the drying rack and picked up another. "Didn't think I'd see you tonight."

Sharp stepped to her. "Sorry, another long day at work." He planted a kiss on her cheek. A whiff of perfume struck his nostrils, reviving an old memory that had since grown worn and thread-bare over the years. Yet before he had a chance to travel down memory lane, he peeked at her naked wet hands and his thoughts were rent asunder.

"Where's your wedding ring?" he demanded.

"I don't wear it when I do the dishes," she explained matter-of-factly. "I put it right there, see?" She nudged her head toward the windowsill above the sink.

"Katelyn, you could easily lose it that way." He scolded. "If you'd just use the dishwasher then you wouldn't—"

"I haven't lost it so far." Katelyn interrupted matching his overbearing insistence with cool assurance. "I have a system—you got to trust me. Okay?"

Sharp pressed onward. "How many times—"

"If you want it done your way then you've got to be here to do it."

Sharp sputtered into silence, but refusing to concede, he suggested, "At least put a bowl there or something. That's all."

"Alright," she relented, "that can be done." Setting the plate aside she grabbed the ring and slipped it on. "Oh, that's right!" She declared as if an epiphany had struck her, "I'm supposed to be faithful and lust after no other guy. Would have forgotten that without this." She feigned relief with a swipe of her hand across her forehead.

Sharp rolled his eyes.

Sensing Sharp's sour mood, Katelyn lifted herself onto her toes and planted a kiss on his cheek. "Don't worry, you're not losing me anytime soon. You've at least got me for another twelve years—once the girls leave for college."

"Oh jokes on you," he countered, "that's if they go to college."

"The odds are more in my favor in that aspect," she volleyed as she sauntered out the kitchen. Sharp trailed behind her. "But the odds of you being home for dinner? Now that's something I wouldn't bet money on."

Sharp sighed, "not tonight please. I'm still just getting my bearings there, it'll take some time for me to adjust."

She proceeded through the dining room and ascended the stairs. "You promised me this would be a nine-to-five when we moved to San Diego." Her words contained not a trace amount of irritation, she merely stated the facts. "I'm not seeing that. Since we moved you've barely been here. And then there's the months away spent 'training.'"

"It's the new job." Sharp's jaw tightened, he still felt uncomfortable discussing anything job related to her. "Still getting settled in. Once I do, I'll be able to help around the house more."

The validity of that statement didn't matter so much to Sharp; he knew he had to say something encouraging.

Katelyn ignored him and continued, "Have you even touched a box since we moved?"

"Yes," he scoffed defensively, "I think so. Someone had to get them off the moving van."

Katelyn marched into the bedroom. A hastily unpacked collection of boxes cluttered every inch of floor space. The bed lay on the ground without a frame and a rivulet of crumpled sheets hung over the edge.

She slid open the closet door, pulled out a hanger, and shrugged out of her clothes. "You've told me repeatedly how you want to be there for Beth and Susie, the way your father wasn't there for you. You still want that, right?"

"Yes, I do," he insisted. "But I'm committed to the Navy. Whatever they command me to do I have to do. The situations are completely different between my dad and me. And, besides, taking this job was the best choice for our family, right?"

Rather than answer, Katelyn diverted the conversation elsewhere. "When was the last time you visited him?"

Sharp thought for a moment. "It's been a while. But I will when I can. It's not like he's going anywhere." He ignored the pang of apprehension pulsating in his heart. His father was a sensitive subject that he preferred left buried. It made things easier that way.

"You know Harry Chapin's got a song you should hear," she needled, perhaps a bit too harshly.

"It's not going to be like that, honey." He asserted and plopped onto the bed. "We both knew this wasn't going to be easy when we got married. You knew full well that we weren't ready to have kids."

Katelyn paused at the closet, inhaled a breath, then exhaled. She spoke as she changed into a pair of sweats and a casual T-shirt. "I know, but we didn't need to get married either. But now we've got to keep up appearances." Approaching him, she gazed longingly into his emerald eyes. "And I know everything you're doing has been with good intent. But, honey, you don't have to bear the brunt of it alone."

Sharp jerked back slightly. "I don't know what you're talking about."

Katelyn fell to her knees in front of him and fiddled with the buttons of his Summer White uniform. "Honey, you have to admit that the whole reason why you've been running around is because you're afraid you won't be able to support us." She striped the uniform off exposing his white undershirt and tossed it across the bed. "However, we're supposed to be partners. My job at the bank helps support this family too. You don't have to act like the sole breadwinner anymore."

Sharp barely mounted a defense. His lips fluttered but they refused to form the words he wished to say. A heavy silence ensued.

Katelyn filled the void. "I'm just worried moving to San Diego is only going to be more of the same."

"It's not," Sharp breathed in a whisper. Rising off the bed, he went over to the closet, undid his belt, and slipped out of his pants. In a firmer tone he said, "Everything is falling right into place. And as soon as I get back I should be—"

"Get back?" Katelyn's whole demeanor shifted to the offensive.

Sharp froze in the middle of putting on his pajama bottoms. His hands clenched so tight his knuckles turned white. Internally he cursed himself for this careless slip. Slowly he straightened up, tied the ribbon of his pajamas, and stared Katelyn right in the mouth—the closest he dared venture to her eyes. "Yes," he rasped in a muted hiss.

Katelyn crossed her arms and leaned forward. "What was that?"

Sharp swallowed. "I received an assignment today. A big one. I head out tomorrow. Probably be back in a week."

An incredulous laugh burst from Katelyn's mouth. She rose up to her full height and began pacing the floor space available. "It's like you're trying to prove my point. What's so big about this assignment?"

"I…I'm—" *investigating an assassination* "—evaluating the efficiency of information gathering of our Brazilian department." He twisted the truth. "The admiral himself personally chose me. I couldn't say no."

Sharp girded himself for another of Katelyn's tirades. Something he had grown well accustomed to after the multitude of rash decisions he had made without consulting her first. Yet her tirade never came. Though the veins in her neck spasmed and her pupils turned to daggers, her stance shivered merely a fraction as she stifled the volcano erupting within her.

Is this it? Sharp worried. Dread bubbled in his chest. He waited too frightened to say anything lest he set her off. After what seemed like an eternity, Katelyn finally dropped her head to her chest and sighed. A forlorn sigh that seemed to drain her of life. She whispered in defeat, "alright."

Taken aback, Sharp studied that one word, analyzing it for any deeper meaning. He came up short wishing instead that she had exploded.

"Alright?" He prodded for clarity.

She simply nodded and repeated, "Alright."

"Good," he said, still on edge. "It'll only be for a week. And when I get back I'll see about moving Mom down here so she can babysit the girls…while you're in class," he added, testing a possible olive branch.

Katelyn flinched. "In class?"

"Yeah," Sharp offered a smile. "We've talked about you going back to college to get your programming degree."

A slight glimmer of hope flashed across her eyes before reality snuffed it out. She shook her head. "No, there's so much still to do.

We aren't even fully unpacked yet. And I still haven't found the right school to enroll the girls in. And I haven't been in a classroom in years."

"Honey." He put his hands on her shoulders. "Just give it some thought, okay?"

She lowered her head. "I don't know."

With a finger he raised her head by the chin, and peered into her eyes. "I promise when I come back, things will be different. I love you."

Katelyn collapsed into his embrace and nuzzled her face into his chest. "Fine, but you're going to have to tell Susie and Beth you're leaving."

"Of course." Sharp squeezed her tight and breathed in her perfume.

Before the girls' bedroom door, Sharp waited a moment to collect himself. *How long will I be able to hold this up? Can't tell anybody what I've joined, or about my new identity: Ian Sharp. God forbid any of them ever finds out.*

Casting such thoughts aside, Sharp turned the doorknob and entered.

Susie and Beth's room was a compact space, made even tighter with twice the furniture: two beds, two writing desks, and two nightstands. The single dresser pressed against the far wall acted as the demarcation between the girls' side of the room. Most of the contents of their moving boxes were scattered across the floor.

"Daddy!" Susie shouted. She hopped off her bed and ran towards him. "Can we go to the beach tomorrow?" She pleaded with the most sincere puppy dog eyes.

"I'm not the one to ask, honey," Sharp dodged—best not to make things worse with Katelyn. "You'll have to ask your mother."

Beth groaned and flung her head back against her pink pillow. Her body prostrated across the bed. "We always have to ask her!"

"I'll do it!" Susie blurted and nearly rushed out of the room if Sharp hadn't caught her by the arm in time.

"No, wait. I'll ask her, but later. I want to tell you two something." He picked Susie up and plopped her down next to her sister. "I'm going on a business trip tomorrow. Miles away. I'll be gone for a week at most. Which means it'll just be your mom, and she'll need you two on your best behavior. Understood?"

"We already know that, Dad," Beth whined. "We've always got to be on our best behavior when you're away. Which seems like always."

Her comment struck him deep like a dagger to his heart, yet Sharp tried his best to brush it off, but the damage had already been done. "Then I expect you to act no different this time. Now, snuggle into bed and I'll read you a bedtime story."

Susie and Beth didn't move. They stared at him pouting.

"What? What is it?" he inquired, scrutinizing their mischievous faces.

Susie spoke up, "We don't want you to read a bedtime story to us."

"Oh, then what do you want me to do?" He asked, certain of the answer already.

Beth leaned over to the CD player atop their dresser and pressed play. The tune of one of their favorite songs emanated from the speaker. One Sharp knew well. It came from the latest princess movie they'd seen months ago. The girls were obsessed with it; listening to it non-stop. And, every now and then, they insisted Sharp dance with them to the song called "The Lullaby Waltz."

Sharp stood to his full height and looked down at Susie. He bowed low and she replied in kind. A melodic tinkle faded in, followed by a lone violin. Susie planted her feet atop his and raised her hands for him to hold. They twirled slowly to the music. The princess sang:

Welcomed sleep, whispered dreams.

Enter a world where nothing is false,

And life is eternal or so it seems,

Once you begin the lullaby waltz.
Let the melody fill your saddened soul,
And mend your heart of that love-shaped hole,
Till you forget of all your faults;
While dancing the lullaby waltz.

Beth hopped off the bed and tapped Susie's shoulder. Susie stepped aside. Sharp bowed and Beth did the same. Her turn to dance.

Sleep away the fits and flurries,
And dream of times once happy and gay.
Let the lullaby ease you of your worries,
Till morning brings another day.
Don't be afraid when you awake.
Just clasp your hands and let it take.
For the music is playing inside your thoughts,
Where you'll hear the lullaby waltz.

Sharp wrapped an arm around Beth and raised her up to his chest, then swooped up Susie in the other arm. Their little arms enfolded his neck as he spun around in place.

Sleep away the fits and flurries,
And dream of times once happy and gay.
Let the lullaby ease you of your worries,
Till morning brings another day.

The orchestra faded out, leaving only the tinkle once more. The princess sang her last refrain:

And feel the love within your heart
Of when you danced the lullaby waltz.

Over all too soon, Sharp lowered the girls and commanded softly, "Alright you two, it's time for bed."

Beth and Susie groaned. "One more! Can we please have one more dance, daddy? Please."

He shook his head. "I'm sorry, but I only do one dance a night. Now get into bed."

Susie and Beth sulked to their respective beds and mumbled disappointment as they settled under the covers. Sharp planted a kiss on their foreheads and whispered, "Goodnight, I love you."

"Love you too," they replied.

At the door, Sharp snapped one last mental picture of his girls snuggled in their beds before turning out the lights.

The alarm clock went off early the next morning and Sharp slapped it with the palm of his hand. He arose groggy. Forcing himself out of bed, he staggered to the bathroom to begin his morning ritual. A good shave and shower woke him up.

He slipped into a dark blue suit and collected his duffle bag he had packed the night before. As he did, he heard the sound of shuffling behind him. He turned and found Katelyn sitting up in bed, staring at him. Hoisting the strap over his shoulder, he said, "You won't even notice I'm gone."

"Still plenty of time for you to not help finish unpacking the house," she quipped.

"You've done such a good job so far; wouldn't want to disrupt anything."

They shared one last kiss. "So long."

"Have a nice flight," she said. "I love you."

"I love you too." And with that he left.

Outside, Sharp threw his stuff into the trunk of the car and settled into the driver's seat. He examined the ugly house one last time before he slipped the golden ring off his finger. *Ian Sharp is a bachelor,* he reminded himself, and dropped it into the cup holder.

THE MISSION

Sharp settled into his window seat of the airplane receiving a great blow to his ego. He'd expected to fly first class—just like all the other spies he imagined—but expectations have a funny way of clashing with reality. Instead he was thrown into the economy class that stirred awake a gremlin of disappointment within Sharp's psyche. It rampaged across his thoughts with a fury, tearing apart any hopeful fantasies of what this job might entail. *Had I truly made a mistake accepting this transfer?* Not even the sweet lullaby of reason could soothe the gremlin 's rage: he was a federal agent now, meaning he had to work on a federal budget.

As the plane ascended into the air, Sharp reached between his cramped knees for his bag. He ruffled through it and pulled out his mission briefing. Sharp's objective was to find and, if possible, apprehend the person who assassinated Luís Quadros, the Minister of Agrarian Development of Brazil. There were no clues or leads to follow, except an order to connect with the commander of Brazil Branch and learn if they had uncovered anything in the passing days. Sharp hoped they had something for him, otherwise his first mission might end in failure and he was not going to let that happen, no matter what.

The gremlin plowed on, disrupting his attention. As much as he tried to read further, a haze spread across his eyes and a restlessness inhabited his legs. His mind contorted into a narrow sieve till only droplets of concentration fell far and few in between. Surrendering, Sharp scanned the cabin for nothing in particular as the file fell onto his lap. He stared off into oblivion till his wandering mind transported him back in to time to that fateful day aboard the *USS William Jefferson Clinton.*

He stood atop the gangway observing the crowd of families on the dock below. A pair of sailors ran past him and were greeted with a chorus of cheers and an exchange of warm hugs with everyone gathered. From Sharp's vantage point it appeared to be a jubilant reunion—he wished he could feel the same level of excitement as them.

As he watched the revelry from afar, he noticed someone step into his peripherals.

"Good, I thought I'd find you here," the captain declared. Sharp offered a salute and he returned it in kind. They stood together observing the merriment below. "You're not alone you know."

"What do you mean, sir?"

"I find the hardest part of any tour is returning to land. Civilian life seems like a foreign concept to me at this point. That's why I don't tell anyone when I've returned anymore, I just show up. I don't need any of this pageantry."

"Oh no, sir," Sharp awkwardly explained, "I'm just looking out for my wife."

"Right," the captain barked unconvinced, the bristles of his mustache twisted to one side. "Anyways, there's someone here who wants to talk to you. Privately. You can find him in my quarters."

"Who?" he inquired.

The captain shrugged. "You'll have to find out for yourself."

"Yes, sir. Thank you." He saluted once more, then traversed the labyrinthine corridors down into the belly of the ship.

The captain's quarters was nothing more than a giant cold lifeless box of gunmetal gray walls complete with a gunmetal gray desk and a gunmetal gray bunk. A single ray of light shone through the porthole.

At the desk sat an officer with almond shaped eyes and a Summer Blue uniform. He wore silver oak leaves on his collar, a few ranks higher than Sharp's single gold bar.

"Hello," Sharp greeted, "I'm Ensign—"

"Yes, I'm familiar," the officer interrupted, his face an indecipherable mask. His slender fingers shifted through a file of documents resting on the desk.

"Master's degree in History, fluent in Spanish, top of your class at OCS," he read mechanically, "high marks in close quarters combat. Weapons proficiency could be a lot better," he stated as coolly as a chef stating that a stew needed more salt. "And you prevented a sailor from committing suicide. Impressive."

He inspected Sharp's frame carefully till they reached his unnerved facial expression. Sharp struggled not to break contact from this officer's black depthless gaze. "You'd make a valuable candidate for our agency."

"Agency?" Sharp asked.

He nodded slightly. "Yes, my superior believes you'd make a valuable addition to our team."

"Really?" Sharp couldn't help but feel flattered, even though the officer's piercing stare still left him off kilter.

"Please, if you are interested in a transfer to our agency and want to hear more," the man stated, "close the door and have a seat."

Sharp didn't hesitate. He did as he was told like an obedient pup and sat down on the barren mattress. The springs creaked.

"I'm Commander Tansoag, the Chief of Operations for Sector Seven."

Sharp titled his head. "Sector Seven? Never heard of that."

"Good," Tansoag replied stoically. His face appeared ageless, not a wrinkle to be found as his lips moved minimally around the words they formed. "We are a covert agency for the DCS."

"DCS?"

"Defense Clandestine Services—the intelligence arm of the Pentagon." Sharp leaned forward, his interest piqued. Tansoag continued, "Based on your research skills and clear interpersonal capabilities you'd prove effective as an agent in the field. With proper training you'd be a prime candidate for vital intelligence gathering missions."

A half concealed grin split Sharp's lips. "You want me to be a spy?"

Tansoag's ridged face revealed nothing. "If that's what your ego would prefer, certainly."

Sharp checked himself, and leaned back. A tingling sensation raced through his spine and settled in his heart where it morphed into a twisted ball of apprehension. "Can I hear more about what this transfer would entail?"

Tansoag's ageless face swung from side to side like a pendulum in a grandfather clock. "I can't devolve anymore information until I get your acceptance. Otherwise, we will shake hands, depart ways, and never meet again. And, of course," he added, "you'll forget all about this conversation."

Bit extreme, Sharp thought. "But I should know a little bit more before I commit, at least. Why should I accept?"

Tansoag leered at him unblinking—in fact Sharp wasn't sure if had blinked once this entire time. He offered, "It'll be an opportunity to travel the world..."

Sharp's brow arched—he'd been a rover in his younger days before his girls were born.

"...You'd have a direct hand in protecting the United States from any foreign schemes..."

The edges of his lips bent downward impressed. It'd give him purpose.

"...And there's plenty of downtime between missions."

The clincher: he'd finally be able to keep a promise.

"I accept," Sharp declared, eagerly offering his hand and sealing the deal with Commander Tansoag.

Sharp's legs ached for movement. He shuffled his feet across the thin carpet—a minor relief—while also straightening his back and rotating his shoulders. He wished for nothing more than to be in Brazil already, but the gremlin let him hang in limbo a little while longer.

Why was I even chosen for this mission? His mind sought a distraction.

Early yesterday morning he found a slip of paper on his desk ordering him to the tenth floor of Sector Seven Headquarters. It had no signature, but everyone in headquarters knew the office number attached to the note—the director of Sector Seven himself.

Nervous, Sharp walked the pale yellow hallway toward the foyer where the director's personal secretary sat at a metallic desk. She wore a nice republican cloth coat while her feathered hair fell in waves like that of Farrah Fawcett. Her youthful buoyancy marked her as a genuine All-American woman with an untamed spirit harkening to the days of Rosie the Riveter: she served her country, and she served it proudly.

"Good morning," Sharp said, his voice shaky. A placard on her desk identified her as one Beverly Harris. "Miss Harris. I hope I'm in the right spot."

Miss Harris smiled warmly. "And you are?"

"Ian Sharp." The name still sounded foreign to his ears as it left his lips.

"Ah yes, our newest candidate," she recalled cheerily like a zealous PTA mother welcoming the newcomers. "How is everything going? Adjusting well?"

"Yes, I am," Sharp nodded. "And I was told the director wanted to see me."

She brightened. "Oh. Must be something important if he's called for you directly. You may go in. He's waiting for you."

"Thank you." He turned toward the double doors. They were just as unprepossessing as everything else at Headquarters, but as Sharp stared at them apprehension consumed his being. He was paralyzed.

From his fellow coworkers he heard the stories about the man on the other side of these doors. They recounted how the director had taken on a battalion of Vietcong in the jungle of Vietnam, alone, after the wind had set him down miles away from his drop zone; How he personally hunted down and executed his own best friend of so many years once it was discovered that he had been passing information to their enemies; That he'd received the Purple Heart, along with several other prestigious awards, four times when he refused to abandon his troops during the invasion of Grenada (the amount of appendages he lost that day varied depending on who was telling the story).

If that weren't enough, much about him still remained a mystery. They knew nothing of his hobbies, his interests, whether he was married or not, or even his name. Because of this, everyone referred to him simply as "Sir."

Sharp swallowed down his apprehension and reached for the door handle. The moment he glimpsed the office on the other side the gremlin of disappointment stirred half-awake.

Expecting opulence, Sharp instead encountered an office of utilitarian grayish-blue walls absent any decoration. Atop the light brown metallic filing cabinet rested a lone fake rubber plant. The cheap wooden desk, devoid of any personal effects, took up the center of the room while the lowered white blinds shielded the occupants of any natural light.

On the couch was Tansoag, his stone-like countenance on full display. He sat straight up with both legs planted firmly on the floor and the palms of his hands perched atop his kneecaps.

Behind the desk sat a four star admiral who, Sharp presumed, was Sir. Unlike the stories Sharp had heard, it turned out Sir still had both eyes, a fully intact, though lopsided, nose, thin lips around bristly teeth, and two perfectly functioning hands. His uniform contained a once athletic build that had grown rather stocky since becoming a desk admiral.

Sharp noted that Sir still displayed a rather impressive visage nonetheless. He approached the admiral, his chin up chest out, and spoke with as much military confidence as he could muster: "Ensign Ian Sharp. You asked to see me."

"Course," Sir replied, the word low and gravelly. His body remained perfectly still as if carved out of marble. He merely stared at Sharp, an elbow crooked atop the armrest and his chin planted between his fingers. "Have a seat."

Sharp settled into the lone office chair stationed before the desk.

"How's the new name doing you?" Sir asked.

"It's fine, Sir," Sharp replied, "though it's not one I would have picked myself."

"Shame, thought it was a good one when I came up with it," he remarked flatly.

Sharp bit his lips. "It's a good name nevertheless."

"Anyway, I have a mission for you." The statue came to life. Sir bent a little to the side and produced a file from a drawer.

"What do you know of Brazil?" Sir asked as he inspected the file.

Sharp shook his head. "Not very much, Sir. My focus was on U.S. History."

Sir glanced at Tansoag for a fraction of a second then locked onto Sharp. "But you know Spanish, correct?"

Sharp nodded. "Yes, fluently. There had been a time I hoped to move to—"

"Excellent," Sir smirked proudly at Tansoag, "then that should help you in Brazil."

"They speak Portuguese," Tansoag reminded him unemotionally.

The smirk wilted a fraction before he dismissed Tansoag with a shrug. "They're practically the same thing, it'll still do him some good there."

Sharp opened his mouth to correct Sir, but decided otherwise. Instead he asked, "What's in Brazil?"

"You haven't heard?" Sir inquired. "It's practically taken over every news cycle for the last week. We might be going to war with Brazil."

"What?" Sharp jolted forward, surprised.

"Relax. A trade war," Sir amended, "which could possibly lead to a real war if things spiral any further out of control. And this is where you come in."

"Me?" A weight crashed heavily on Sharp's shoulders.

Tansoag briefed him, "Less than a week ago, Luís Quadros, the Minister of Agrarian Development of Brazil, was assassinated here in the United States. He had been invited to watch a performance of Hamlet. At some point during the show a .223 Remington bullet struck him, he died immediately. Nobody noticed until the performance was over."

"Jesus, didn't think Hamlet was that bad," Sharp joked. Receiving no reaction, he lowered his head and cleared his throat.

"He was a foreign dignitary, Sharp," Tansoag continued. "Minister Quadros was a very popular public figure in Brazil, specifically among the landless. Been their standard-bearer ever since the *Abertura*." He didn't bother trying to pronounce the Portuguese word correctly. "His supporters practically forced Quadros onto President Rousseff when she won the presidency last October. Now that he's been assassinated Brazil is in an uproar."

"Makes sense," Sharp commented. This reminded him of the American Revolution. When colonists soon after the Boston Massacre cried out for British blood. "Emotions are high right now, but in time once that energy's been spent it'll die down and everyone will move on."

"That's what we thought too," Tansoag cautioned. "However, at 8am Brazilian time yesterday President Rousseff acted on this public outrage, forcing our hand."

"What did she do?" Sharp's brows knitted together.

"Yesterday morning she held a televised speech blaming the United States for the assassination of Minister Quadros—calling it a major lapse in security protocols. Then advanced the notion that we were in fact aiding the assassin due to our inaction. Which isn't true. We are doing everything we can to track down this killer. Either way, President Rousseff believed it important to send a message that further delay will not be tolerated. She gave us an ultimatum: deliver the assassin or any vital information that might lead to their arrest, or Brazil will be forced to undertake drastic measures."

"What measures?"

"Sanctions, hopefully," Sir offered, "Brazil doesn't have the military capacity to fight an actual war—it's all posturing. But for them even treading down this path could lead to major consequences. Their democracy is rather fragile, teetering on the edge of chaos every day. Should this blow up in President Rousseff's face then this might instigate a military coup, and establish yet another dictatorship. And who knows what they'll do to unify the nation—perhaps declare war for the hell of it. We'd prefer that it didn't happen."

"So we pretty much are going to bow down to Brazil's demands?"

"I'd say we're more maintaining good international relations with our sister nations to the south."

"We've been given a week to deliver anything we can to the Brazilian authorities."

"A week?" Sharp sputtered in surprise.

"Yes. You leave tomorrow for Brazil. We have a suspicion that his death originated somewhere in his home country. And I want you to investigate that possibility. Everything you'll need is in the folder. Once you touch down in Brazil, the Brazil Branch commander, Lieutenant Braasch, will pick you up at the airport. The Lieutenant will brief you on any recent developments."

A knock at the door interrupted them.

"Come in," Sir replied.

In walked a man resembling a narrow beanpole draped in a loose lab coat. His skin was a thin papery white and a sharp widow's peak bisected his scalp. His health was clearly a nonexistent concern for him. A jovial grin split his thin lips. "Hope I'm not too late," despite his sickly appearance his voice exuded life.

"You're actually on time for a change," Sir stated. "Did you bring what I asked for?"

"Yes, yes." He stepped further into the office, his shoulders naturally slumped. "You know I always deliver." He noticed Sharp and his eyes lit up. "This must be Mr…I'm sorry, what was it again?"

"Ian Sharp."

"Ah yes. Mr. Sharpie, it's good to have you aboard. I'm Dr. Derek." He extended a bony hand and they shook. "Now, I've got a few things for you on your mission." He reached into his pocket and pulled out a tiny stack of cards. "Here you are."

Sharp received them and turned them over in his fingers. They were his new calling cards embossed with a sleek border encircling his name and a phone number. His job title merely said: Consultant. Vague enough to mean anything.

Dr. Derek explained, "now that's the agency's special phone number, specifically for you, and whatever mission you're on. Just tell one of our operators how you'd like them to respond and we'll make it so. Adds a good amount of credibility to whatever cover story you're using out in the field."

Sharp acknowledged the new information with a nod, then pulled out his wallet to slip them into place.

"Take this as well." Dr. Derek produced a smaller item no bigger than a thumb. "Since *Jefe* here refuses to take any of my recommendations, our agents don't know how to hack into anything. So to fix this I created this little doohickey." He palmed it off to Sharp. It looked like an ordinary flash drive. "Insert that into any USB, then call up the R&D department here and we'll do the rest. There's someone standing by at all hours of the day. So give us a call when you need to hack into any computer."

"Thanks, I'm sure it'll come in handy." Sharp pocketed it.

A shock of turbulence knocked Sharp out of his reminiscence. Fishing the flash drive out from his bag, he twirled it between his fingers. As he did, he couldn't help but notice the faint white outline of skin on his left ring finger. A clump of guilt plopped onto the bottom of his heart and settled there. He put the drive away and stared forward at the back of the seat before him. And wondered what awaited him in Brazil.

THE COMMANDER OF BRAZIL BRANCH

Sharp felt his face shrivel like a raisin the moment he stepped out of the Brasília Presidente Juscelino Kubitschek International Airport. Sweat plastered his forehead and stained his collar. He wiped the perspiration away with the back of his hand and waited by the curb for his contact to arrive.

Fortunately, a woman dressed in a bright Summer Blue uniform approached him almost immediately. Her blouse accentuated the curvature of her body while prominent cheekbones sharpened her face. She had striking blue eyes, thick black brows, and full red lips.

"Hello," she greeted, her demeanor one of disinterest, "I'm Lieutenant Heather Braasch. You must be Ian Sharp." She extended a hand, but Sharp stood frozen. He stared blankly at her—he hadn't expected his contact to be a woman, nor one so beautiful.

Braasch noticed the hesitation in Sharp and her brows arched slightly. A slow dawning reddened her cheeks. She treaded lightly, "Hello?" Retracting her hand she went for the folder wedged between her left armpit and examined it. She glanced from the folder to Sharp then back to the folder. "You are Ensign Ian Sharp, correct?" She inquired.

Hearing his new name snapped him out of his momentary daze. He stammered a jumble of nonsense before regaining his powers of speech. "Ah yes, I'm Ian Sharp. Sorry, long flight...and the sun's already got me cooked." He played it off. Swallowing, he found his throat had suddenly grown very dry. He offered a hand. "Heather Braasch. Did I hear that correctly?"

"Yes, that is correct." They shook hands. She held a firm grip, again surprising Sharp. "Now that I've found you, let's get out of here." Lieutenant Braasch spun around and pressed through the crowd. Sharp followed behind lugging his bag over his shoulder and ignoring the strange flutter he felt in his heart.

Braasch led him into the parking garage and towards a well-maintained gray Lincoln Continental. Sharp threw his luggage into the trunk and situated himself into the passenger seat. Braasch revved the engine to life, maneuvered out of the garage, and onto the streets of Brasília.

His eyes widened in wonder as he glimpsed a cityscape completely alien to him. From afar he noticed the jaw-dropping edifices that were without rival in the entire world. Giant white structures testing the limits of human imagination brilliantly designed to incorporate the curves reminiscent of Brazilian women; cold concrete contrasted against man-made pools of warm reflective water; and distinctive pillars created the illusion of suspension off the ground. Then there were the streets themselves. Designed for automobiles, the capital housed no traffic lights and few sidewalks. Wide thoroughfares prevented traffic jams. Braasch and Sharp cruised at a steady pace without ever needing to stop—a Californian's paradise.

As Sharp marveled at the beauty of the capitol, something off in the distance caught his eye. He squinted but still could not fully comprehend what he saw. It appeared to be a gathering of some sort on the neighboring street—a farmers' market maybe, or festival perhaps. Though he couldn't gauge its size it had to have been large if Sharp could spot it at this distance. And it seemed to stretch for blocks and blocks without end the further their car drove parallel alongside it. Pointing, he asked, "What's going on there?"

"The reason why you're here." She replied without taking her eyes off the road. "It's a vigil for Luís Quadros scheduled for tonight. There are several of them happening throughout Brazil. The largest is at the Ministry of Agrarian Development where he worked."

Sharp huffed out a breath impressed. "I've never known a minister to have such a huge following."

"Quadros was a rare type of politician," she explained. "Don't think he had an enemy in the world. Especially with how difficult agrarian policy can be." Braasch turned left and the gathering disappeared from sight. "His death sent shockwaves through the country."

"Yes. Sir told me about the situation. He said the President gave us only a week to find the assassin."

"Less time now. We've got only six days left," Braasch corrected. "And this isn't a fight we want to have. Brazil's been angling to establish their own hegemony in South America for a while now, but our dominance in the Western Hemisphere has prevented them from achieving that. They need something drastic to unite the continent together against us. I wouldn't be surprised if Quadros's death was homegrown right in the Presidential Palace."

"You think that's really a possibility?" he asked incredulously.

Braasch shrugged, "Once you eliminate the impossible, whatever remains, no matter how improbable, must be the truth."

Sharp couldn't help but smirk. "I see you've watched some Sherlock on the BBC as well. But this isn't a television show."

"It still stands," she declared with unyielding conviction, "We've got to accept every angle here, no matter how absurd. Politicians have made careers out of a single disruption like this—manufactured or not. Whether this is good happenstance or intentional, Rousseff is taking advantage of it and we have to be cautious."

Sharp rubbed a hand against his chin and reflected on what he had learned about Richard Nixon. He successfully fear-mongered his way to the Vice Presidency by stroking the fears of communism during the Cold War. *Would Rousseff do the same?*

Braasch cut through his thoughts. "And no."

"Sorry, no what?" He asked.

"I don't watch television. I've read the stories. Multiple times. That just so happens to be one of my favorite quotes."

"I see, yes." Sharp lowered his head and fell quiet. He didn't know how to respond to her—or what to say next—and so let the conversation die. An awkward silence carried them the rest of the way to their destination.

Brazil Branch Headquarters sat on the corner of a long boulevard and resembled a giant upright mirror with five slender columns shaped like airplane wings racing down the length of it. A reflecting pond encircled the building at ground level and bounced sunlight onto the reflective façade. It glimmered and sparkled in the early afternoon sun.

Braasch guided the car into a parking structure and took the spot reserved for the Commander of Brazil Branch. Without a word they stepped out and rode the elevator up three flights before arriving at her office. Much like Sir's, it was devoid of any personal effects and contained the bare essentials: filing cabinet, desk, and chairs.

"Have a seat." She waved a perfunctory hand at one of the empty chairs. Then sat down behind the desk and pressed a button on the intercom with a finger. She spoke into it, "Lieutenant Estrella, could you come to my office, please."

"Roger that," a voice confirmed.

Sharp sat in the chair offered to him—the thin layer of padding as cushiony as a block of wood—and suddenly came to the realization that function overshadowed comfort here; it seemed to be the rule at Sector Seven.

He asked, "Who's that?"

Braasch leaned back in her chair with ease. "He's the Division Commander for Brazil."

"Division Commander?" Sharp tilted his head. His understanding of Sector Seven's chain of command still eluded his full comprehension.

"He oversees operations in Brazil."

"Isn't that what you do?"

Her face reflexively scrunched together at the question as if she were reacting to a sudden whiff of rotten eggs. "My title is a misnomer. My real jurisdiction is the member countries of Mercosul. Columbia Branch handles the rest of Latin America. We just happen to be named based on the country our headquarters are located in, thus the confusion. I'm in the process of changing our titles for better clarity."

Just then a man appeared at the door. He was a medium sized figure with a face creased by pronounced laugh lines around his eyes and mouth. His uniform looked ragged as if he'd been wearing it nonstop for the last several days. Silver bars hung from his collars, signifying his rank as a Lieutenant Junior Grade, one pay grade above Sharp's.

"You rang, master," he announced gleefully, his lips breaking into a wide toothy grin. Then he noticed Sharp and the grin expanded unnaturally bigger. "Ah I see you found a playdate. *Hola, soy* Manuel Estrella. *¿Y tú? Mi amigo.*" He offered a hand to Sharp.

Sharp matched his enthusiasm. "*Soy* Ian Sharp. *Mucho gusto.*"

"Oooh." Estrella feigned flattery, "*El gusto es mio.*"

"Enough," barked Braasch. Her brows furrowed.

The grin never left Estrella's face. He simply shrugged and took the seat next to Sharp. Reclining, he let the backrest thud against the wall so that only the balls of his feet touched the ground.

Braasch began, "Ensign Sharp is here to help with the Quadros case."

"Is he now?" Estrella gave Sharp a once over with his brown lively eyes, the only part of him that exuded youth. The rest looked as worn out as his uniform. "How so? What do you know?" he questioned.

Sharp answered honestly, "Not much actually. This is my first mission."

Estrella nodded. "Good. Good. A neophyte; just what we wanted during a time sensitive case. Always like a challenge. And did the big man himself send you with anything? New information? A lead, perhaps?"

Sharp shook his head.

Estrella glanced over at Braasch. "Defective. Gotta send him back to the factory. Maybe we can get our money back."

"Enough."

Sharp suspected that she used the word 'enough' a lot when it came to Estrella. He was the undisciplined dog and she the taut leash.

Braasch stated, "Doesn't matter. He's to observe only."

Blindsided, Sharp exclaimed, "What?"

"You're too inexperienced," she said half candidly and half chafed. "You'll shadow me, take notes, observe, and do *nothing*." She emphasized.

"But I'm here to assist —"

"I don't need assistance," she cut him off, her voice stern. "You're here only because of Sir. And nothing I said would change his mind. So…I'm stuck with you, for a week at most. You do everything I command and stay out of our way, and I'll put in a good word for you. Is that clear?"

Sharp demurred, "Crystal, ma'am." The gremlin of disappointment snarled.

Braasch smiled. "Good. Now," she turned her attention to Estrella, "status report."

He threw out his hands in defeat. "Your guess is as good as mine. We interviewed everyone we could find that might have had a motive and even his worst enemies are in shock."

"Someone's lying," Braasch declared. "He's got to be tied up in something. Maybe this wasn't political."

Estrella shook his head. His chair leveled to the floor and his feet fell flat. His precociousness evaporated. "Quadros was a pretty squeaky clean guy: couldn't be bought, no mistress, no drug habit, not even a single parking ticket. No skeletons in his closet whatsoever."

"There's something," she exclaimed, refusing to budge. "There has to be. Any word yet on his wife?"

"Nope."

"Damn. She could be the key. We have to find her."

"What happened to her?" Sharp piped up.

Estrella answered, "Anir Quadros boarded a plane two days after the assassination and when it landed she wasn't on it."

"Do you think she was involved?"

Estrella scoffed. "No, they were madly in love. She would never betray him. At best she'd give us an important lead."

Braasch stared up at the ceiling and thought aloud, "Quadros has been ruffling feathers for years now, and there had never been an attempt on his life before. The wealthy landowners threatened action should he be confirmed as Minister of Agrarian Development, but that proved to be an empty threat. Until now. Why now? Why the United States?"

"We're just circling squares here, Braasch," Estrella admitted. "If we had the time we might be able to do the proper footwork, but we don't. If we hit too many dead ends then we're screwed."

"Might I offer something?" Sharp ventured.

"What is it?" Braasch exclaimed.

"He was killed in the United States, right?" he began. "The day before he was to return home. If he was assassinated so that he could be replaced then they could have killed him whenever they wanted. But he was killed in the US, why? Could it have been to manufacture an international crisis? Maybe." He waved to Braasch. "I know, Braasch, that's what you think. But if the government did do it then it would have been brought out to light already. Someone in government would have talked by now—we'd have a lead. Yet, we don't. Plus, the President would be the first person we'd investigate. If they did do it, then they were only setting themselves up to get caught."

"Then why do you think he was killed?" Estrella inquired.

"Someone—not in government—wanted chaos. And they knew that Quadros was positioned exactly in the center where if he were killed it would spark the most amount of chaos. He would be the perfect catalyst."

"Catalyst for what?"

Sharp shrugged. "I don't know. The briefing file didn't offer that much information in that regard."

Silence descended on them as Braasch and Estrella contemplated Sharp's observation. When it finally clicked, Braasch's chair creaked as she came level with her desk. She offered tepidly, "You might have a point."

Sharp brightened, the corners of his lips twisted excitedly. "I do?"

She ignored him as she mentally fit the pieces together. "Could it be for the sanctions? Maybe a full blown trade war. That's the angle." Newly energized, she snapped her sights on Estrella and commanded hurriedly, "Send out a request to all our Subdivisions for information of any recent agricultural developments. See if there are any major trade negotiations going on right now. I want to know what major crops the United States imports from here, and how sanctions might affect them. Get me a list of the largest domestic producers of foodstuffs as well. Let's see what that shows us."

"Got it," Estrella replied and jumped out of his chair.

Another thought struck her and she blurted out, "And who's in charge of the Ministry right now?"

Estrella halted at the door and wracked his brain a second. "A guy named Victor Geisel."

"And he checked out alright?"

"Yes, ma'am. A typical pencil pusher who rose up through the Ministry to become second in command."

"Then we'll have to set up a meeting with him," she muttered to herself.

"And what would you like me to do?" Sharp asked.

Braasch looked at him as if suddenly remembering he was there. "What?"

He mustered his nerve. “Surely you need my help. A fresh perspective. That’s probably why Sir sent me down here.”

“Still doesn’t mean I need your assistance.” She brushed him aside. “But you might be good to have around.”

Sharp didn’t know how to react. Her comment left him confused more than anything. Luckily, Estrella came to his rescue.

“Knowing her, that’s a compliment, rookie.” He clapped Sharp on the back. “Maybe by the end she’ll let you get coffee for her.” He laughed.

“Enough, Estrella.” The leash still as taut as ever. Estrella eased into a muffled smile. Braasch pulled the phone from its cradle and pressed it against her ear. “I’m sure you’d like to unwind some after your flight. Let me call you a cab to take you to—”

“Hey Lieutenant,” Estrella interrupted her, “why don’t you let me take him? I can fill him in on the situation here and make sure he gets something to eat. What do you say?”

She gave this a thought then directed the suggestion to Sharp. “Well?”

“Why not?” he replied. “Sounds like a splendid idea.”

“Fine,” Braasch relented, placing the phone back into its cradle. “Once you’ve sent out that message, Estrella, you’re free to do whatever you want with him.”

Estrella clapped his hands together and rubbed them enthusiastically. “Perfect. Come on, Sharp. Let me show you around town. You’ll enjoy it, trust me. See what Brasília’s really like.”

THE OTHER HALF

"Ever had Brazilian food before?" Estrella asked as he strode through the parking garage. His keys jingled in his hand with every step.

Sharp shook his head. "No—er—I don't know. I know I've had Cuban food but not Brazilian. I usually go wherever my wi—friends take me." He corrected himself just in time.

Estrella gave Sharp a mischievous glance. "Well then, now's your chance to taste some authentic Brazilian food. And I know just where to go. Come on." He rounded a mud splattered red Chevy Hatchback and eased himself behind the steering wheel.

As they cruised through the streets of Brasília, Sharp soaked in the city's beauty once more. The sleek architecture still struck him with awe. Completed in 1960 Brasília stood as the country's crowning achievement. It still stands today as the symbol of President Juscelino Kubitschek's declaration of "fifty years of progress in five," encapsulating Brazil's self-sufficiency, innovation, progress, hope, and democracy. Brasília's founding ushered the nation into a new era. Yet for many it remained a promise left largely unfulfilled.

The further they traveled, Sharp noticed a sudden and stark change in the scenery. Gone were the slender skyscrapers; replaced now by crowded weather-beaten single-level stucco structures. The wide magnificent avenues narrowed into poorly maintained surface streets. The brilliance of Brasília transformed into a slum.

A frightened nervousness rattled Sharp. "Where are we?" He asked.

"Ceilândia," Estrella replied. "When Brasília was completed it attracted all kinds of people. Thousands flocked to the new capital. However, Brasília wasn't ready to accommodate that many people yet. And it wouldn't be good to have a bunch of *favelas* spring up around it. So, in a span of nine months, they built Ceilândia."

"I see…" Ceilândia reminded Sharp a lot of the neglected areas of San Diego, the ones where you do your best to avoid or drive through without ever stopping. "And why are we here?"

"Cause there's a good restaurant I want to take you to," Estrella proclaimed. "None of that manufactured pomp and circumstance crap they serve out to tourists. But real down-to-Earth homemade food. And that can only be found here, outside, on the outskirts."

"I would have been fine with manufactured pomp and circumstance if I'd known you were taking me here. I'd prefer to survive the night."

A laugh burst from Estrella's lips. "Oh, you and your first world sensibilities. Can't stay in your middle class bubble all your life."

"That's not what I meant," Sharp shot back.

"Right. Anyways…" Estrella switched gears. "We won't find what we're looking for in Brasília proper."

"What do you mean?"

"I've been thinking about what you said earlier—about Quadros being a catalyst. And that got me thinking."

"And?" Sharp prompted.

"If we're going to crack this case then you need to learn a little something about the MST."

Estrella spun a hard left and jerked the car onto a dirt road. Sharp's entire body shook at the sudden turbulence. Easing down on the brake, they slowed to a stop. "We're here," he announced to a shaken Sharp.

The restaurant looked completely abandoned. Graffiti stretched far across the façade and a wide piece of plywood boarded up one of the windows. Above the entrance a sign read: '*Celebrações das Favelas.*'

Sharp got out of the car and swallowed at the disconcerting prospects of what he'd find inside.

"This place grows most of their own ingredients," Estrella explained as they entered. "So you know it's fresh."

The inside was just as dingy as the outside. An aroma of sewage, burnt wood, and exotic spices assaulted Sharp's nostrils. A layer of grease coated the walls and a tinny whine of Brazilian music strained to be heard over the static of the speaker. Fake plants attempted to liven up the place in vain. A few people milled about, keeping mostly to themselves. Nothing looked pleasing to Sharp.

A teenaged hostess walked up to them wearing a tight stained black shirt and ripped jeans.

"*Olá, ¿Quantos*?" She asked.

"*Dois*," Estrella replied.

She led them to a barren square table with flimsy wooden chairs. Sharp and Estrella sat down and the hostess offered each their own menu. Sharp perused his options but quickly realized he couldn't read anything; certain Spanish cognates popped out at him but not enough to allow for comprehension. Therefore, he abandoned the menu and laid it down on the table. He eyed Estrella, waiting.

When Estrella set his menu down, Sharp leaned in whispering, "You couldn't at least have picked a place that had a chance of passing a health code inspection?"

Estrella gave out a hearty laugh. "Let the germaphobes worry about the health code."

"Then what about structural integrity?"

"Meh, everyone's got a time to go. If it's my time then so be it."

Sharp rolled his eyes. "But you don't have to take me with you."

Estrella laughed again at Sharp's discomfort.

The waiter, a significantly older gentleman with plenty of missing teeth, arrived at their table. He placed two glasses of water in front of them then asked if they were ready to order. Estrella asked for a dish called *Beiju;* Sharp seconded the dish for himself. The waiter nodded and left without writing anything down.

Resting his elbows on the table, Sharp said, "Alright, you brought me here to teach me about the…what was it?"

Estrella took a sip of his water before jumping into his lecture. "The MST: *Movimento dos Trabalhodores Rurais Sem-Terra.* Otherwise known as the Landless Worker's Movement. It came into existence during the *Abertura,* when Brazil transitioned from a military dictatorship to a democracy. In 1981 a man nicknamed Natalino pitched a tent at the intersection of Road 324 in Rio Grande do Sul as a protest for land reform. News spread throughout the country of what he was doing, and soon hundreds of landless, starving, citizens flocked to him. At its peak the occupation had over six hundred families, totaling 3,000 people.

"Naturally, the military regime tried to shut down *Encruzilhada Natalino,* as the occupation came to be called. At first they offered land in the Amazon, but the occupiers refused. So, they brought in military 'specialist' Colonel Curió to apply a little more pressure to the camp. He increased the number of soldiers bordering the occupation, intensified interrogations, diverted food trucks, and unleashed spies and troublemakers. He oversaw a war of attrition. Yet the morale of *Encruzilhada Natalino* never diminished. It thrived and endured his disruptive tactics.

"After four weeks, Colonel Curió gathered his things and departed. *Encruzilhada Natalino* had won! Soon afterwards the Catholic Church mediated a resolution between the encampment and the regime: the redistribution of 1,870 hectares of unused land to 164 families. Their success gave birth to the *Movimento dos Trabalhodores Rurais Sem-Terra* which is now one of the most influential and widespread movements in Brazil today."

Sharp listened attentively. "How does this relate to what's going on now?"

"Minister Quadros was a powerful figure for the MST. If you're correct that his death was supposed to trigger something, I think it was to awaken the anger of the MST, not incite some international crisis; that's just a bonus."

"You think this is possible?"

"The MST doesn't have a standard bearer anymore. His death created a power vacuum. We're already seeing President Rousseff angling to fill it, but there are others. They're trying to appeal to them and only one can succeed. So who will it be?"

Sharp stroked his upper lip with the palm of his hand. Something clicked in his brain. He raised an inquisitive brow. "You've got a lead, don't you?"

"I've made a few inquiries," Estrella stated causally, though his eyes darted around the place, suspicious of anyone listening in.

Sharp pressed harder, "And what did you find out?"

Estrella leaned in closer to him and whispered, "Leonel Stedile."

"Who's that?"

"Senator Leonel Stedile." He repeated. "He's offering up the best message to Quadros's supporters. Ever since being elected to congress he's worked closely with the Ministry of Agrarian Development, and has built a career off of labor issues. He's our best lead right now."

"And he's here?"

Estrella nodded. "He's giving a speech tonight not too far from here."

"If this is true why would he—why would anyone want the support of the MST? What purpose is there?"

Estrella shrugged. "That's what we'll have to find out."

"Have you told Braasch about this?"

He shook his head. "She's too stubborn for me. She's hung up on the idea that this had to be some sort of power play between the United States and Brazil. She's playing geopolitics, when the answer's been in front of her this whole time. But you—" he flung out his hands toward Sharp "—you convinced her in minutes to investigate a different line of inquiry. It was impressive. And, if it turns out that there is something here, I'm going to need your help to convince her again. What do you say?"

Sharp replied without hesitation. "Of course."

Estrella's cup of joy overflowed. He could barely contain his excitement.

The waiter cut the revelry short, however, when he arrived carrying two plates of *Beiju* to their table. *Beiju* was a Brazilian delicacy similar to a pancake or crepe. Made from tapioca starch and dry gum, it's often cooked on a griddle and stuffed. Sharp's nostrils inhaled a familiar aroma that reminded him of home: a ham and potato dish his mother used to make. Cutting into it and shoveling a forkful into his mouth, the texture at first proved rather tough and flavorless, but then, as he chewed, a mixture of sweetened ham and rich tapioca drowned his taste buds in delicious flavors. Sharp melted, gushing over his plate. It was the best meal he had had in a long time.

Scarfing down the last bit of his *Beiju,* Sharp leaned back and released a full and hearty sigh. "Now that was good," he exclaimed.

Once the bill had been squared away they left the establishment and walked a block or so to work off their meal. In the distance Sharp could already see a huddled mass gathering for that night's vigil.

The gathering was located in a small local park where a makeshift stage and podium had been erected. People milled about claiming their spots and hundreds more arrived the closer it came to the main event. Some had the foresight to bring blankets to sit on while others fiddled with folding chairs. Several news station vans hung back with their antennae extended high in the air ready to broadcast at a moment's notice. Onstage a rotund figure spoke, mostly ignored by the gathering, they weren't here for him. Eyeballing it, Sharp estimated that there must have been around 300 men, women, and children present.

Sharp and Estrella stood in the back. The mood was somber, restless, and yet rejuvenating. Hundreds had come to share in their sorrow and partake in a sense of community. When the sun disappeared and blackness took the sky, several candles flickered to life and their flame hung in the air, creating their own constellation of stars here on Earth.

When it came time for the main event, a man stepped to the podium, spoke a few words, then began his introduction: "I have the great honor of introducing not only a great senator but a dear friend. May I introduce to you: Senator Leonel Stedile."

The crowd jumped to their feet and cheered wildly as a slender man appeared onstage. He waved a hand to greet the cheering audience as he strutted to the podium. "Thank you," he shouted into the microphone over the applause. "Thank you all for coming." The cheering refused to relent. "Thank you," Stedile repeated and let out his hands hoping to settle down the crowd. A repartee that lasted for several seconds until the gathering finally grew tired of applauding and fell silent.

"It is such a great honor to be here," Senator Stedile yelled into the microphone. "This year is a momentous year. We're celebrating the thirtieth anniversary of the founding of the *Movimento dos Trabalhodores Rurais Sem-Terra.* Founded when brave landless farmers gathered together and challenged the military regime. And their legacy continues on to this day—in each and every one of us. But, friends, on a night we should be celebrating, we are mourning instead."

Stedile's beak of a nose wafted from side to side like a weathervane as he spoke. He sounded aggrieved. "We lost a close friend and an ever vigilant soldier. He'll leave behind a giant hole in our hearts that no other will ever be able to fill. Whoever was behind this thought that by silencing Quadros they would also silence us. But we have to prove them wrong. We must speak up and be louder than ever before." His voice revved to a near shout and his beady eyes narrowed. "Let this be a turning point in our struggle for equality and land reform. Otherwise what happened six days ago, or even thirty years ago, will have all been in vain."

The gathering seconded his sentiments with applause. Observing the impact of Stedile's words on his listeners, Sharp leaned over to Estrella and whispered, "You think he was behind this?"

Estrella shrugged without taking his eyes off of Stedile. "I'm not sure. Quadros and Stedile were good friends—practically brothers. They rose up through the MST together. But that still isn't reason enough *not* to be suspicious of him. Cain still murdered Abel after all."

Sharp gave this some thought and, as he did, he watched the crowd eat up the senator's speech. They hung on his every word; hungry for consolation in their time of grief. That's when something caught his eye: the back of a blue hoodie shoving others aside rather aggressively to get closer to the stage. Interest piqued, Sharp parted his lips to say, "Hey, Estrella," but the words never came out.

The explosion was all consuming.

THE CHASE

A wail of screams stirred Sharp awake. His eyes flicked open, but all he saw was a haze of colors; of black silhouettes dancing before a backdrop of orange fire. For a moment he didn't recognize where he was—the blast had thrown him hard against the grass and knocked him unconscious.

Disoriented, he propped himself up onto all fours. His arms wobbled like a house of cards during an earthquake. He spat the taste of grass out of his mouth.

Sharp's senses came back to him. The cries of bloody murder pierced his eardrums. A stampede of shoes dashed through his field of vision. A burning heat rubbed against his skin.

When the world stopped teetering so violently, Sharp raised his head and observed what was happening. A roaring fire raged where the stage once was. From there a scene of carnage spilled out across the grass. The fallen cried out pleading death rattles. The sight produced a surge of bile from Sharp's stomach and into his throat. He resisted the urge to vomit. Instead, he willed himself to concentrate only on standing up.

Once on his feet, he watched the pandemonium play itself out around him. Everything was a frantic blur. The frightened scattered through the streets while the brave comforted the injured. Sirens wailed in the distance. Car horns blared. And yet what stuck out from the madness for Sharp was the casual stride of someone in a blue hoodie; gliding across the street as if out for a casual Sunday stroll. Something clicked in Sharp's mind and he instantly remembered what he saw right before all went dark. *He threw it.*

A rush of adrenaline coursed through his veins. His mind snapped into focus and he knew that he had to apprehend that person. He charged forward.

But a hand latched onto his shoulder disrupting his launch.

"Sharp! Finally up, that's good." Estrella exclaimed relieved. "How are you doing? Are you hurt?" His watery red eyes, blinking like a hummingbird in flight, scanned Sharp's frame for injuries. "So much for the vigil, huh? God. I can't believe—"

"He's..." Sharp rasped, his vocal cords felt rusty. "He's...He's over there."

"Who?" Estrella's relief transformed into concern. "Who's over there?"

"The guy who threw it. The bomb. He's there. He threw it." Sharp shrugged away from Estrella's grasp and stumbled forward. His sights locked onto the hoodie.

"Really?" Estrella bounded forward, closing the gap between them. "You sure?"

"Blue hoodie. Saw him throw it right before the explosion."

Estrella eyed the scene. "I see him," he confirmed, "Are you sure about this?"

Sharp nodded.

Together they plunged into the chaos. Weaving in and out through the cars proved easy enough, but the sidewalk on the other side was jam packed with people. Sharp and Estrella had to push their way through just to keep their suspect in view. The suspect never once looked back, he merely pressed through the growing mass of curious bystanders who flooded the sidewalk to observe what was going on.

A firetruck inched through the stalled traffic sounding its horn as firemen hung off its metal frame waving arms and shouting commands. The cars before it maneuvered awkwardly out of the way. One even hopped the curb and eased into the bystanders. They shuffled back to give it space and, as they did, the bomber slipped past them without breaking his stride.

The further they traveled away from the epicenter of the commotion the more Ceilândia seemed to return to normal. The noise dissipated into casual nighttime quiet and the huddled onlookers thinned out to a trickle on the sidewalk. Darkened windows marked a city drifting off into sleep. And all that remained of the explosion was a faint cloud of black smoke wafting through air above stout stucco buildings.

A horn announced the arrival of a white car cruising down the now nearly empty street. The bomber stopped, eyed the oncoming car, and positioned himself at the lip of the curb.

"That's it," Estrella breathed. "Come on, if we're quick they won't see us coming. You go for the suspect. I'm going for the driver." He booked it across the street before Sharp could respond.

Sharp's heart beat nervously in his chest as he approached the suspect. Taking in deep controlled breaths, he tried to remain calm and remember his training. Anticipation numbed the tips of his fingers.

The white car pulled up before the bomber. He reached out a hand for the car door handle.

Inhaling one last time, Sharp leaped into a sprint and, with all of his might, he charged at the suspect and slammed his shoulder into him, knocking the bomber off his feet and onto the cement. He lay there momentarily dazed.

Before the driver could react, Estrella ripped open the car door and grabbed ahold of him, but the belt held him in place. Estrella went for the buckle. The driver swatted him away as he shouted something in Portuguese. His foot slipped off the brake pedal and the car lurched forward. It jostled the driver, presenting Estrella an opportunity to release the belt. A soft click proclaimed his success.

That's when the unseen man in the backseat swung himself out of the car and grabbed Estrella. Tearing him away from the driver, the man threw Estrella into the street. They locked eyes.

The driver spouted some more words in Portuguese but the man ignored them. He advanced on Estrella.

On the other side of the car, Sharp towered over the downed suspect. Bending over, he reached for him but the bomber snapped out of his daze and propelled the heel of his shoe into Sharp's shin.

"Ah," Sharp grunted through gritted teeth. He fell to one knee. The suspect went for a jab to his jaw, but Sharp leaned back just in time and countered with a succession of blows aimed at the bomber's abdomen. The suspect collapsed to the ground, curled into the fetal position, and nursed his wounded midsection.

Satisfied, Sharp stood up, careful not to put too much weight on his aching shin.

The white car peeled away from the curb, its tires screeching, and revealed Estrella duking it out with another man in the middle of the street. They circled like two lions posturing for dominance, growling out taunts and swiping their claws.

Sharp instantly spotted the telltale signs of exhaustion in Estrella's form: short gasps of air, shoulders slumped, hands wavered. If Sharp didn't act quickly then that would be the end of Estrella.

Click.

Sharp's heart jumped at the sound. He raised his hands to his shoulders and silently cursed himself.

The suspect staggered to his feet, his finger tight around the trigger. His body bent forward with his free arm nursing his stomach. He shouted in Portuguese at the combatants in the street:

"*Ei! Eu tenho seu amigo aqui. Se você quer continuar lutando, eu posso matá-lo agora.*"

Estrella jerked his head toward Sharp. His body slumped in defeat.

"*Que pena. Eu estava apenas me aquecendo.*" Estrella remarked haughtily. The man he'd been fighting laughed, prompting Estrella to challenge him. "*Não acredita em mim? Se o seu namorado aqui não tivesse interrompido, eu o teria caído em segundos.*"

"*Cale-se*!" The bomber barked, but Estrella refused to obey.

"*Você só está ferido porque foi espancado por uma criança. Não pode vencer uma batalha com os punhos como um homem de verdade. Tenho que recorrer a uma pistola.*"

"*Cale-se*!" he shouted, his face turning an angry red.

Sharp wasn't sure what exactly Estrella was saying, but he could see the effect. The suspect was growing ever more agitated.

Estrella taunted. "*Pelo menos o seu amante aqui sabe como lutar. Ele é o dominante aqui neste relacionamento agora não é?*"

"*Eu falei cala a boca*!" The suspect exploded. He swung the pistol toward Estrella, offering Sharp his window of opportunity. He flung himself at the suspect and slapped his forearm. The pistol fired wide of its target. Wrapping his fingers around the bomber's hand, he wrested the weapon away.

A fist connected with Sharp's cheek, stumbled back while the bomber fled.

"Estrella," he called out. "He's getting away."

"Forget me, I've got this guy!" Estrella shouted as he once again engaged the other man. "Get after him!"

Sharp nodded and hurried after the bomber. He bounded easily from curb to street to sidewalk, block by block, gaining on his target.

Sharp reached out his hand, the tips of his fingers brushed against the back of the blue hoodie. He nearly had a firm grasp. But at the last second he heard a car horn wail and noticed the flash of headlights careen right toward him. Instinctively, Sharp jumped out of the way just in time to miss becoming roadkill.

The white car swerved uncontrollably across the empty street, the tires screeching as it did. It barreled down the lane, running a red light and turning out of sight.

Sharp breathed a sigh of relief then quickly resumed the chase.

They ran another series of blocks before the bomber rounded another corner. Sharp followed before skating awkwardly to a stop. A grateful smile formed around his heaving breath. They stood at the entrance of a residential parking lot surrounded on three sides by tall black security fencing. The suspect had cornered himself.

The suspect hurried toward the nearest door and tugged on it, but it refused to budge, a combination lock held it secure.

From behind, Sharp closed the gap between them, and put a hand on his shoulder, "Time to give—"

The bomber spun round in the blink of an eye and planted a fist in Sharp's stomach. Sharp fell back, groaning, his hands cupping his gut. Only then did he realize he was still holding the pistol. In a flash he shot out his arm and the bomber backed into the fence, raising his hands.

"Good," Sharp wheezed between breaths. "Now you're going to stay there…till help comes." With his free hand he pulled out his cellphone, tapped the keypad, then put it to his ear. It rang three times before Estrella answered.

"This is Estrella. Did you get him?"

"Yeah, just need someone to come pick us up. We're in a residential lot at the corner of—" He stepped back out of the entryway and read the nearby street signs aloud.

"Roger that."

"How about you?" Sharp asked, never taking his eyes off the bomber. He displayed a posture of defiant resignation.

"Guy had a mean uppercut," Estrella assessed, "but wouldn't rank him in my top ten of best fights I've been in."

"Been in that many, huh?"

"Tell you all about them once we get these guys in custody. Okay, give me a sec to call headquarters. They should be there in about twenty minutes."

"Copy." They hung up and Sharp put his phone away.

The suspect spoke up, "You no stop us." He pronounced the words in a thick Portuguese accent.

"Us?" Sharp inquired.

A sly smile curved the corners of his mouth. "Nothing stop Pope's plans, *Santidade* rise again."

"And what's his plans? This pope?"

He shook his head. "You get nothing from me. I no talk."

"Fine." Sharp shrugged feigning indifference. "But you will once we start the interrogation. I'm sure you and your buddy will tell us everything we want to know."

The bomber peeled himself off the fence, straightening his back. A calm serenity filled his eyes. "No," he spoke softly, "I never talk. I die first before talk." He stepped forward.

"What are you doing? Stop!" Sharp tightened his grip on the pistol. "I'll shoot." A slight tremble in his outstretched hand belied his hesitation. He raised the palm of his other hand to the butt of the gun for added stability. An old nightmare of a memory flashed across his eyes. His jaw tightened.

The bomber slowly wheeled his left foot forward and planted it firmly on the asphalt. In his broken English he proclaimed prophetically, "You no understand. Pope's plans. He want fire. Death by fire. Then life! Nothing stop him."

"I said stop." His muscles turned to stone. "Don't take another step." A finger wrapped around the trigger. His breath grew shallow. He struggled to beat back the memory.

The bomber ignored him and swung out his right foot. His eyes now pierced through Sharp. "Death mean life."

"What did I tell you!" Sharp yelled, boiling anxiety consumed his heart.

"Pope bring fire to the world. And from fire he create a world new. It not be stopped."

"Stop right there, I said," His voice squeaked.

"Shoot me." He pressed his chest up against the barrel of the pistol. "But that no stop the *Santidade*."

An unexpected tear welled in Sharp's eye and sailed down his left cheek. Sharp couldn't do it. He couldn't bring himself to pull the trigger.

If he hadn't spotted the slight flick of the bomber's pupils glancing over his right shoulder, Sharp might have been done right then and there. But that flick gave him enough warning to jump to his left just in time to escape the rush of the white car while the bomber leaped the other way.

The car screeched to a halt and the bomber scrambled into the backseat. Sharp scurried to his feet and fumbled for the door handle, it flapped in his fingers uselessly. The car jolted backwards, ripping the handle from his hand, and careened into the street. Running after it, Sharp raised the gun in a futile attempt to stop it. The white car sped away and disappeared from sight.

Sharp fell to his knees as the gremlin of disappointment hovered over him, grinning. He wiped the tear away from his cheek.

Despite how late it was, a flurry of activity roared through the police station when Sharp arrived. Among the rows of plastic waiting chairs sat Estrella, a cup of coffee in his hands. Seeing Sharp enter, he bolted out of his chair and crossed to him. "Sharp," he greeted. "Thought you'd never make it. So where is he?"

"He got away," Sharp lamented with a lowered head. "I had him cornered and I let him get away."

Wrapping an arm around Sharp's shoulders, Estrella led him to a chair and said, "Can't get them all. At least we've got one of them. And the police'll make him sing like a bird in no time." They sat down. "Don't beat yourself up over this, Sharp. Everyone screws up from time to time. Take it from the master here. This won't be your first nor your last."

"Yeah, I guess." Sharp felt a little lighter until he saw Braasch barge into the station. Dread overcame him.

She looked exactly the same as she did earlier in the day but the skin around her eyes was darker and heavier. Spotting Sharp and Estrella, Braasch charged at them. "What happened?" She barked.

"Lieutenant!" Estrella jumped out of his chair. "Wasn't expecting you."

"Got a phone call. Heard you and Sharp here—" She nudged her head his way "—called headquarters for backup. Told me that you apprehended some suspects and had them brought here. I'd like to know what happened."

Together, Estrella and Sharp traded off retelling the events of the night. Sharp relayed how the suspect managed to escape, but with a few details left out. He wasn't exactly sure why, but he had the inclination to withhold the information he had retrieved from the bomber. For now, he decided to file away the mention of the Pope and the *Santidade* for a later time. And the moment he did, somewhere deep in his subconscious there was a haughty howl, like a wolf praying to the moon.

When they finished, she commented, "Sounds like we can leave this to the police to handle."

"What do you mean?" Estrella asked, taken aback. "They killed Stedile, a close friend and partner of Quadros. You don't find them related?"

"This is unfortunate, but ancillary. Stedile's assassination is, as of right now, a domestic issue. Which means it doesn't concern us."

Estrella scoffed at the idea, but decided it was better to bite his tongue.

"As for you." Braasch snapped her sights on Sharp. He straightened. "You need to do better."

Her rebuke struck Sharp like a baseball bat to the chest. "What?"

"Go to your hotel and get some sleep." She ordered without further comment. "We've got a meeting with the Acting Minister of Agrarian Development tomorrow."

"If I may," Estrella found his voice, "I'd like to come back here tomorrow and learn what the police have gotten out of our guy."

Braasch sighed. "It'll be a waste of—"

"We should hear what he has to say," Sharp jumped in. "Stedile and Quadros were both leading voices for land reform. I believe what happened tonight only further proves someone is trying to stoke outrage here."

"But how does his death—"

"I don't know," Sharp replied before she could finish. "But I wouldn't put it past President Rousseff to use Stedile's death to rally the Brazilian people behind her. Strengthen her standing at home so when she confronts the United States…" He let Braasch's imagination fill in the rest.

Her face twisted in thought for a moment, then relented. "Okay, fine. Do what you need to, Estrella."

"Thank you," he replied courteously.

"Now, get some sleep," she restated. She rubbed her eyes as if the very word 'sleep' had only now reminded her of how tired she was herself.

"Yes, Ma'am," Sharp and Estrella said. And with that Braasch turned and left.

Estrella looked at Sharp knowingly. "See, she listens to you."

"That's cause I gave her a good reason to, you should give it a try someday." He quipped.

Estrella laughed. "She'll twist herself into knots before she'll accept anything I say. But thank you for backing me up… Come on. I'll drive you to your hotel."

ACTING MINISTER GEISEL

The *Eixo Monumental,* Monumental Axis, is the central avenue of Brasília and, much like the National Mall in Washington D.C., is the civic and administrative center of Brazil. At its apex there's the *Praça dos Três Poderes* (Plaza of the Three Powers), where the Presidential Office, National Congress, and Supreme Federal Court reside harmoniously. On the opposite end, there's the *Esplanada dos Ministérios* that consists of seventeen architecturally identical ministry buildings laid out like two rows of squat reflective dominos. The farthest from the *Praça dos Três Poderes,* and closest to the Cathedral of Brasília, houses the Ministry of Agrarian Development.

On this day, weather-beaten men, women, and children dressed in ragged clothing and red ball caps packed every square inch of the lobby. A portion held flowers or candles and wept in solemn mourning. Others beat upon the Ministry's windows and stomped their feet in unruly protest. Security guards futilely corralled the growing throng that spilled out onto the street. News reporters scrambled for the best coverage as the events unfolded. A chorus of chanting filled the air: "*Ocupar, Resistir e Produzir*!" "*Ele será vingado.*"

Sharp and Braasch waded through the sea of red ball caps, and red shirts, and red flags; emblazoned on every one of them was a crude drawing of a woman standing straight-backed while a man behind her held a machete in the air, both ready to march into the heat of battle together in arms. A green outline of Brazil encased these stoic figures as the words *Movimento dos Trabalhodores Rurais Sem-Terra* wrapped around the image.

The elevator doors pinged open and the two of them practically fell in. "Let's just get this over with," Braasch groaned when the doors closed.

Stepping out of the elevator several levels above, Sharp and Braasch found themselves in the center of a ministry scrambling as they conducted damage control: a hundred conversations overlapped one another, a stampede of shoes thundered against the office floor, and phones cried out to be answered. They passed through the tempest like invisible specters, none bothering to acknowledge their existence, and approached the Minister's secretary. Braasch spoke to her in Portuguese. She smiled courteously and gestured for them to enter.

It was an office-shaped office with furniture-shaped furniture, and a long wide window. The acting Minister sat at the desk, his head lowered and a phone pressed against his ear. He was an older gentleman blessed with youthful black hair coiffed conservatively with a tinge of white edging his sideburns. However his jawline had collapsed long ago leaving only a cleft marking where his chin had once been. Darkened sunspots ravaged his cheeks and nose.

Minutes passed before he hung up the receiver and exhaled a long exasperated breath as he fell back into his chair. His thin frame already sagged from exhaustion. Then he remembered his guests and sat up straighter. He welcomed them, "Olá, I'm Victor Geisel, Acting Minister." The Americans introduced themselves.

The creases around his eyelids deepened as he spoke. "What happened last night has everyone on edge." His words were devoid of any emotion—he couldn't muster the energy.

"Yes, we saw the commotion downstairs," Sharp related. "There are a lot of angry people."

Braasch eyed him, a silent reminder: *shadow and do nothing*. Sharp received the message, but hadn't decided if he was going to obey or not. The defiant howling in his subconscious grew louder.

The minister reclined in his chair. "Stedile was an important figure for the MST. He worked with the Lula administration for about two years before he made a run for Senate. Practically cruised to a victory on a wave of MST support." He flung out a hand towards the window behind him, "and might have made it to the presidency. But now, with both Minister Quadros and Senator Stedile dead, the MST is lashing out without any guidance. President Rousseff's handling it the best she can, but…" He changed the subject. "Now, what can I do for you?"

"Actually," Lieutenant Braasch began, "we wanted to ask you a few questions about Quadros. As you may know the President gave the United States only a week to find Quadros's assassin."

The Minister nodded, the chicken fat of his neck wobbled as he did. "Yes, it was awfully rash, in my opinion." He combed a hand through his hair. His tone grew reflective. "I'm not sure exactly how much help I could be to your investigation."

"We've talked to everyone we could think of who might have had something against Quadros—political rivals, disgruntled constituents, those types. And nobody seemed to have a bad thing to say about him. But, perhaps you might be able to shed some light here."

The Minister glanced up at the ceiling in thought, a meaty hand scraped across his lips. "Quadros was a master of persuasion. You could have him in a room with fourteen different people with fourteen different perspectives on something, and after an hour Quadros would have convinced them all that he was on their side. Though I would say his biggest obstacle would be trying to reign in the MST; they never made it easy for him." He exhaled heavily.

"How so?" Sharp asked. He heard the wolf growl softly.

The minister rested an elbow on his desk and planted the cleft of his remaining chin on his knuckles. "Ever since the massacre of Eldorado de Carajás in 1996, the MST has had significant political clout when it comes to agrarian development. President Cardoso yielded to their demands and established the Extraordinary Ministry of Agrarian Issues. That was before it was renamed the Ministry of Agrarian Development." He added. "Then when Lula wanted to focus on family agriculture instead of land redistribution, the MST would have none of it. A rift opened between them, and Quadros was caught in the middle. He never really recovered from that battle. Shame Quadros died before he could mend that trust between the government and the MST. Something I strive to finish when I'm officially sworn in."

A barely perceptible buzzing caught Sharp's attention as the minister talked. In his peripherals, he saw Braasch slip a hand over her pocket, purse her lips, and carry on with the conversation.

"When you're sworn in?" She repeated curiously. "So the rumors are true that you're going to replace Quadros."

The Minister peered down a little coy. "It's not official yet, but it is expected that I will be nominated." A glint of pride shone in his eyes. "We're waiting for the commotion to die down first before making the announcement."

"Why do you want to be minister?" Sharp mumbled absentmindedly, momentarily oblivious that he'd spoken loud enough to be heard. Two pairs of eyes honed in on him. He straightened in his chair, realizing his mistake, and fumbled to sound professional. "Just that it seems like being the Minister of Agrarian Development is a very hazardous position right now. Are you prepared to continue that fight?"

Through willpower alone, Sharp kept his focus on Minister Geisel, refusing to even peek at Braasch. He was sure she was shooting daggers his way with her eyes.

The Minister dismissed Sharp's concern with a wave of his hand. "I wouldn't have gotten into politics in the first place if I wasn't ready to face the risks of making tough decisions. True, land reform has become something of a controversial subject here," he admitted, "but if we don't do something about it, then nothing will ever get done."

Braasch's pocket rumbled again. She adjusted herself playing deaf to its low cry.

"Yes," Sharp nodded, with Braasch momentarily preoccupied he decided to venture further. "You mentioned earlier that you promised to mend the rift. How are you going to go about doing that?"

"I don't think that's—" Braasch interjected, but bit her lip when her pocket once again rumbled to life. Concealing her irritation, she rose out of her chair. "If you'll excuse me. I have to take this." She let herself out.

Once the door closed behind Braasch, the Minister considered Sharp's question. "Now you asked what I was going to do to mend this rift, Mr. Sharp. Well, right now this ministry has a bill in the works that would settle this land issue once and for all in Brazil. It's ambitious, but the political climate right now might ensure its passage with overwhelming support."

"Really?" Sharp expressed intrigued. "What's the bill about?"

"It's a proposal to rectify the massive concentration of land here in Brazil. We've tried to relieve this by legalizing 'squatter's rights,' reducing fraud, purchasing unused land, and so on. It's worked to a degree, but the problem is that the amount of unused land is starting to dwindle, and soon we'll have to start redistributing excess hectares of large plantations regardless of whether they're being used or not. You can imagine the uproar this is going to cause among the landowners. So, this bill would set forth a timeline for this process and allocate oversight of reclamation and redistribution to INCRA."

"What's INCRA?" Sharp inquired.

"*Instituto Nacional de Colonização e Reforma Agrária*. The institute preserves the national registry of rural properties and manages public lands. If this bill passes then this will be but a starting point. One, I hope, everyone will see as the best path forward for all parties involved."

"That is awfully ambitious." Sharp commented. *Great way to court MST support.* He mused. *For himself, or for someone else?* He leaned forward, deciding carefully what he'd say next now that he was alone with the minister. "Yet, there has been one thing that's been bothering me. I hope you can help me out here, Minister." Sharp expressed an air of hesitant concern.

"What is it?" The Minister prodded.

"It's just that…I was at the vigil last night."

"Really?"

"I wasn't too far from where the guy threw the bomb, and I heard him shout something."

"What did he say?" The minister asked, his curiosity piqued.

"Now my Portuguese isn't that good, but he shouted something like 'For the *Santidade*,' or 'Long live the *Santidade*.' Either way it ended with 'the *Santidade*.' What can you make of that?"

"Are you sure he said that?"

Sharp nodded.

The Minister waved his hand away brushing the remark aside. "Perhaps he was a religious fanatic. Retribution for violating one of his Holiness's most sacred commandments. Stedile was caught having an affair a long time ago, and that might have turned many of his supporters away from him. The guy must not have forgiven him."

"Seems pretty extreme to go that far just because of an affair, don't you think?" Sharp reasoned.

The Minister shrugged. "People have done worse for less."

"Maybe," he relented, then attempted a much more direct approach. "But Stedile was a champion for land reform. Is there any relation there?"

The minister rattled his head from side to side. "Let me see." A click of his tongue proclaimed his success. "Yes, now I remember. There was something about the *Santidade* in the books I had to read while at University. It was nothing more than a footnote really, but it mentioned that the *Santidade* had been a group of rebelling runaway slaves. Or at least believed to be."

"What do you mean?"

"There's so little known about it that it's mostly considered gossip. Stories of Indians and African slaves escaping bondage and banding together to overthrow their Portuguese rulers. Though there are some accounts of actual slave rebellions, none if any related to the *Santidade*. I doubt he shouted that as a reference to this."

Sharp couldn't be too sure about that. He was familiar with the fear mongering of the antebellum south in the United States and the tales told to frighten white slave-owners. They'd relay stories of Nate Turner, Gabriel Prosser, and Denmark Vessey as a way to ensure the owners remained ever vigilant of any possible slave uprising. Then there are the modern American social movements who have a habit of adopting monikers harkening back to deeply rooted historical events for added relevancy—such as the emergence of the "Tea Party" the year before. Perhaps the *Santidade* had been revived.

Shaking his head, the Minister concluded, "You'd have a better chance connecting him with Antônio Conselheiro than the *Santidade*. No, this guy was a religious extremist and nothing else."

Sharp opened his mouth to respond but Braasch barged in, her face contorted in tempered annoyance, and barked. "Sharp. We have to go. Thank you for your time, Minister."

The minister tilted his head to one side, confused. "What has happened? We barely discussed anything."

"Something's come up that we—I—have to deal with."

"Please, tell me," he begged, "if it's a matter concerning the ministry then I should know."

Braasch hesitated, her jaw fidgeting for control, then relented. "A suspect was apprehended last night, relating to the bombing."

"Oh, that's good."

Disappointment capped her words. "He's been found in his cell—dead."

The Minister gasped. "How is that possible?"

"That's what I need to find out," she remarked. "Come on, Sharp."

"Please. Were they able to get anything from him?"

She shook her head. "Died before the interrogation could begin. All we've got is a name, and some other basic details: he was 27, a poor farmer, and lived in Pernambuco."

"Pernambuco? Really?" The minister marveled. "Things haven't been going well there for the last few weeks."

"Like what?" Braasch inquired.

"Just the largest occupation in Brazilian history."

"Really?" She stepped to her chair, stunned, and perched her hands on the backrest. "I haven't heard anything about that."

"I can understand why." His chair squeaked as he wheeled around to inspect the outside, though all that could be viewed through the window was the identical ministry building on the other side of the street. "Brasília's undergoing its own uproar right now, can't be bothered with events unfolding in the North." The minister paused, then spun back around. "And not a situation I'd want to get my ministry involved in just yet."

"Why?" Sharp asked.

"Because they're occupying the land of the Bezerra family, the second most powerful agricultural family in the Northeast. But can you guess who's supporting this occupation?" He waited for the Americans to shake their heads before answering. "The first most powerful family." He couldn't help but scoff at the irony.

Sharp pressed forward at the sound of a howl. "And who is the first most powerful family?"

"Why it's the Balthazars, led by Alexander Balthazar," the Minister replied as if the answer were common knowledge. "He's the undisputed leader in sugar production. His headquarters is located in Limoeiro,

Pernambuco at his main *usina* called *Santidade através do trabalho celeste,* Holiness through Heavenly Labor—" Sharp's lower lip quivered "—he's been very active in the fight for equality. He's donated millions to help improve the lives of his workers, who've started to view him as something of a savior. Even started calling him the 'Pope of Sugar.'"

Sharp expelling a muffled gasp. The minister heard this and eyed him. His brows knitted together, but whether out of suspicion or concern Sharp couldn't tell.

Sharp hurried to cover his excitement, "Did Quadros have any intention of visiting the occupation?"

The Minister shrugged. "If he did, we'll never know. The occupation began while he was on his trip. But I don't doubt that it was on his mind once he learned of it. Developments like this tend to hurt political negotiations rather than help."

"And what of Stedile?" Sharp asked. "Was he active in this occupation?"

"Of course. He took it upon himself to negotiate a peace between the Bezerras and the MST. How far that went, or what's become of it, I can't say though. But I'm sure his death is going to make finding peace a lot harder."

"I'm sure it will," Sharp muttered.

"We'll have to take a look into this," Braasch offered. "But for now it's time we headed out." She turned to Sharp and gestured to get up with a bob of her brows. He rose from the chair.

The Minister followed in kind and walked them to the door. "It was a pleasure. I hope you get to the bottom of this right away. I'd hate for any further tension between our two countries." He held the door open for them as they left.

"Me too." Braasch and the Minister shook hands.

"Same here," Sharp said when it was his turn to shake hands. And in that moment, something Braasch said the other day popped into his head: 'Once you eliminate the impossible, whatever remains, no matter how improbable, must be the truth.' His brief time with the Minister had revealed that improbable truth. Sharp smiled wide at the thought, and looked the Minister right in the eye and said, "you've given us a lot to think about."

When the elevator doors closed, Sharp spoke up, "I want to investigate this occupation more. I want to go to Pernambuco."

"We should wait till the subdivisions have issued their reports," Braasch countered matter-of-factly. "We can't be jumping at the first thing that grabs our attention."

"But I think this could be it."

"Why?"

Sharp bit his tongue, he couldn't disclose what he knew, not yet. The wolf inside him refused to submit just yet.

"I don't know," Sharp bent the truth a little. "But surely Quadros would have overseen the occupation himself if he had lived, perhaps that's why someone didn't want him returning home. And you heard the minister. Stedile was involved as well. The Bezerra Occupation might be what connects everything together."

"But this is a Brazilian matter—this has nothing to do with the United States."

It was becoming too easy to predict where Braasch's mind went. Sharp pounced. "If President Rousseff managed to broker a deal at the eleventh hour, that would surely garner great support from the MST and bolster her standing against the United States."

Braasch mulled over his analysis for the rest of the elevator ride. Before the doors pinged open, she submitted, "it's the best lead we have so far." She walked out, leaving a gleeful Sharp in her wake.

They passed through the jam-packed lobby, the mob still as rowdy as ever, and emerged onto the street. As they walked away from the commotion, Sharp kept his eyes on Braasch, waiting in anticipation to hear what he so desperately wanted to hear. Internally, he whimpered like a wolf salivating impatiently for his share of scraps.

Finally Braasch spoke, "Alright. I'll make a few phone calls. We leave for Pernambuco as soon as possible."

PART 2

PERNAMBUCO

Arms raised we dictate our history
with suffocating force. The oppressors
let us fly the colorful flag
to wake up this sleeping nation.
Tomorrow belongs to us workers!
Come, let us fight fist raised!
Our Strength leads us to build,
Our country free and strong.
Built by people power!

- MST ANTHEM

BEZERRA OCCUPATION

Home to roughly 8.8 million Brazilians, Pernambuco is the undisputed leader of the Northeast. Its capital city, Recife, is the most important industrial and commercial center in the region. Unique to Pernambuco is the narrow coastal plain of the Atlantic Ocean known as the *Zona de Mata*—a tropical climate with rich and nutritious soil highly favorable for sugar cultivation. Tucked away within this zone was the city of Limoeiro which produced millions of pounds of sugar a year and was home to the undisputed sugar tycoon of the Northeast, Alexander Balthazar.

Miles away, on the outskirts of the Bezerra property, Sharp stepped out of the vehicle, the souls of his shoes crunching the dry and dusty dirt road flat. No matter which way he looked he saw nothing for miles except a wide empty expanse of brown earth and unkempt grass. A barbed wire fence ran the length of the road alongside a line of parked cars.

"That must be it over here," he gestured with a nod of his head towards the noisy commotion of camp life emanating from the black polythene tents clustered on the other side of the fence. From afar, it resembled the thoroughfare of a county fair or a circus just came to town.

Braasch popped up from the driver's side of the car, little droplets of sweat already forming on her forehead. "Let's get this over with," she rasped out, unable to hide her discomfort from the heat.

Following the fence, they came across a section where someone had cut away the barbed wire. They passed through and entered an occupation abuzz with activity. Most prominent was the large gathering of occupiers huddled together in what could roughly be called a central square of a haphazard village. At the very front a man dressed in an all-white suit and white fedora stood before the crowd gesticulating wildly, his speech reminiscent of a pastor's Sunday sermon. Behind him stood a twelve-foot-tall cross flanked on both sides by the MST's red flags.

Braasch and Sharp fell in with the onlookers and watched the show already in progress. Scanning the crowd, Sharp spotted several red shirts and ball caps emblazoned with the MST logo. A cheer rose from the gathering at what the gentlemen in white had said. He held his hands out to quiet them—a cigar protruding from his fingers in his right hand. A beaming smile split his face as he basked in their adoration and good humor. When they finally calmed some he continued his sermon.

Though he spoke in Portuguese, his gestures and tone of voice conveyed to Sharp what he was saying, and the cheers confirmed the impact of his words. Sharp leaned to his left and whispered to Braasch, "How long do you think this'll last?"

"Who knows," the person on his right replied, "he's a bit of a talker."

Sharp fixed his gaze on the fellow who came up to his chest. "Pardon me?"

A flash of embarrassment crossed his face and he whimpered apologetically in a nasally voice, "Oh, I'm sorry. I thought you were talking to me. Please don't mind me."

"Nothing taken by it, seriously." Sharp soothed. The man fidgeted so nervously that Sharp worried he'd spontaneously combust right then and there. "You just caught me by surprise."

"I didn't mean to, sorry," the man groveled. Taking a large sidestep, he inhaled deeply then focused his attention on the presentation. His jaw remained clenched and his posture ramrod straight.

Sharp, bemused by his antics, inspected the funny little anxious man a little longer. He wore a suit that appeared a few sizes too large for him and his haircut suggested he visited a nearsighted barber long past his prime. He was an odd looking man. Letting him go, Sharp turned his attention once more to the man in white.

The man in white flung out a hand and announced proudly, "*...hoje também temos o prefeito Brizola aqui, que está aqui para...*"

The crowd turned around completely and stared in Sharp's direction. The hairs on the back of his neck instantly stood on end. *What's happening?* Then everyone burst into applause. Sharp's breath stopped short as the man next to him raised a hand and waved it sheepishly.

Sharp sensed Braasch physically stiffen next to him.

Concerned, he asked, "What is it?"

Braasch replied under her breath. "That's Mayor Brizola. The mayor of Limoeiro."

"What?" He asked awash in disbelief. He nearly laughed out loud, surely this had to be a joke. Mayor Brizola didn't exactly exude the dignified poise Sharp expected of a politician. He was a timidly lanky person with a long face and thin nose. His brows curved permanently in worry and his eyes contained deep blue wells of longing.

Sharp struggled to accept the truth. Yet, doing his best to cast aside his bewilderment, he turned to the little man and greeted, "Mayor Brizola. I had no idea who I was standing next to. I'm Ian Sharp. It's a pleasure to meet you." He offered his hand.

The Mayor replied timidly, "Pleasure to meet you, too." He pressed his hand into Sharp's and performed the limpest handshake Sharp had ever experienced; it was like grasping onto a fistful of boiled noodles.

"I've heard an awful lot about this occupation. Had to come see it myself. The Bezerras must be fuming right now."

Mayor Brizola shrugged. "Perhaps. It's the largest occupation Pernambuco has ever seen. Nearly five thousand families are here right now." He spoke like a toddler being forced to perform a song in front of a family gathering.

Sharp studied him, wondering whether he was shy, socially awkward, or something else. "Five thousand? It doesn't look like that many people."

"Oh no, you're right," Mayor Brizola relented. "But trust me, five thousand families are here. Wouldn't have been possible without Alexander Balthazar." He gestured towards the man in white.

"Wait, that's Balthazar?" Sharp exclaimed. "The man in white is Alexander Balthazar." He squinted his eyes for a better view of the man, but from this distance Balthazar looked nothing more than a tall pillar of sugar in his white suit.

Mayor Brizola nodded his head. "Yup, the Pope of Sugar."

Braasch cleared her throat.

"Oh, I'm so sorry," he sputtered, realizing he'd forgotten Braasch was there. "Mayor Brizola, this is Heather Braasch."

"Hello Mayor. It's a surprise seeing you here." They shook hands.

"I came here to show my support," he didn't look them in the eyes, his pupils were constantly darting elsewhere.

"Then if it isn't too much trouble, we'd like to ask you a few questions while you're here, is that alright with you?" Braasch suggested.

"Sure," The Mayor agreed, then added as an afterthought. "Why?"

"We're part of the foreign press," Braasch explained, playing the cover agreed upon before they arrived. "We've been assigned to write a story about the occupation."

The Mayor's eyes light up. "Oh wonderful. Then yes, surely, I'd love to answer some questions."

"Perfect." Braasch fished into her pocket, produced a small recorder, and pressed a button.

Sharp served the first question. "Who are all these people? Why are they here?"

"They are landless, and they are here because they have nothing left to lose." He began, his tone grew strong and sturdy as he spoke. "These are people from across the state who've had enough living in *favelas*. They've seen where their hard work has led them while those living in the fancy *haciendas* live easy, barely having to lift a finger. And they've had enough." His eyes locked onto Sharp, laser focused. "It's time they were finally given their fair share. These people are here to fight for a better future. This occupation gives them that opportunity, and that's what keeps them going."

Sharp followed up. "And how has the MST been able to achieve this?"

"Through something called *mística,* a feeling of connectedness—a sense of belonging, if you will. As you can see among the crowd, the people have gathered for a reason and they express it through flags, t-shirts, slogans, and even through an occupation. But that's not all; *mística* can also be channeled through music, dance, feasts, skits, poetry, soccer games and what have you. Essentially it makes camp life less burdensome by providing an outlet for members to express how they're feeling, and cultivating a stronger sense of community."

Sharp looked out at the crowd, an army ready to fight when given the word. "And have the Bezerras taken any precautions against this occupation?"

"Of course," The Mayor scoffed. "Should they command the gunmen standing watch to evict, then they'll evict without hesitation… and violently."

Sharp whipped his head around. "Gunmen? I don't see any gunmen here."

Mayor Brizola snorted. "The ones standing by the trucks." Raising a thin finger, he pointed off in the distance where a line of pick-up trucks outlined the outermost boundary of the occupation. Several sun-beaten men huddled near them, conversing and occasionally glancing over at the occupation. "Bezerra practically bought out all the contracts of any gunmen in the area. But, from what I could tell, there are still a lot more occupiers than gunmen. If they even tried to evict them, they wouldn't stand a chance. So I don't see that happening anytime soon."

"Yeah, that doesn't sound good," observed Sharp, staring at the line of trucks and hired hands. They stood aloof, disinterested in what was happening, but every time they stole a peak this way he noticed the itchy trigger finger they wished to scratch.

An outburst of applause caught his attention. Alexander Balthazar paced from side to side, waving his hands in the air. Stepping forward, he lowered his arms level to the ground and a cluster of hands sprung out to greet him. They grasped him eagerly, enfolding around him as he passed through the crowd. The roar of applause soon gave way to fervent chanting: "*Reforma Agrária: Pela Lei ou pela Força,*" and "*Ocupar, Resistir, Produzir.*"

"They really love Balthazar," Sharp remarked, "Why is that?"

The Mayor replied, lowering his head, his voice becoming something of a muffled whimper again. "He's become somewhat of a messianic figure within the MST."

"Seems a little strange, don't you think?"

Mayor Brizola snorted again, "No, the MST is riddled with such figures like Zumbi or Antônio Conselheiro." He exhaled a heavy sigh. "His charity has made Balthazar the latest of these. He wants Brazil to live in harmony, and so does everyone here."

And how far would he go to achieve that? The thought popped into Sharp's head.

"This might take a while," Mayor Brizola said, pointing out how slowly Balthazar maneuvered through the occupiers. "Why don't you come with me? I can show you around. There's someone I'd like you to meet."

"Would that be alright?" Sharp turned to Braasch.

She stopped the recording. "Sure, I'll stay here and see if I can get a word in edgewise with Balthazar."

Leading the way, Mayor Brizola guided Sharp through the narrow labyrinthine path between the hastily assembled pavilion of polythene tents. A stench of plastic chemicals, earth, and human musk floated through the air. Every now and then the Mayor stopped at a tent and inquired how well the residents were holding up. Their responses were all friendly and kind. Sharp observed how Mayor Brizola cultivated a relationship with the occupation's residents; perhaps he was a politician after all.

Up ahead someone crossed into their sightline and Mayor Brizola kicked into a trot, practically skipping towards them. Sharp double timed it to keep up.

"Luís," the Mayor yelled, approaching him. "Just who I was looking for. Mr. Sharp, this is Luís Alves de Lima e Silva—the leader of this occupation."

"Oh hello there," Silva greeted, shaking off his initial surprise. Alert brown eyes examined Sharp's slightly taller stance. Assessing no immediate threat, he softened and offered a calloused hand. "Hello, Mr. Sharp."

Sharp shook hands. "Hello."

"He's with the foreign press." Mayor Brizola burst out. "Going to write up a story about the occupation."

"Are you now?" Silva asked. Though his hair was ghost white, the tautness of his skin placed him in his early-to-mid-30s. "Didn't think anyone was watching."

"No, we are," Sharp countered. "Not everyone can cover the standoff, you know. And once I heard about this, I had to come check it out for myself."

The Mayor piped up, "Yes, and that's why I wanted him to meet you. Thought maybe you'd like to offer a little background on what's going on here."

"Splendid idea," Silva pronounced. "What would you like to know?"

Sharp thought for a second. "I guess to start off: Why are you here? What made you join the MST?"

"Well, I've always lived in Pernambuco," he began, "in the *agreste,* where it can get really dry. And one year my family got the worst of it. My parents struggled hard to make anything grow, but ended up having to give up and take up work on a sugar plantation. Two years after that, the plantation got all this new machinery and we found ourselves out of work. So I left to find a job elsewhere. I traveled south to São Paulo where I got a job in an auto-factory for a while. I saved up as much as I could, and sent money home to Mom and my two brothers. Yet, it still wasn't enough. My life had been in the field, in agriculture, and that's what I wanted to do with my life. But I knew it wouldn't be possible as long as these large plantations continued to exist. That's when I learned about the MST, and what they do, and I jumped at the first chance to be a part of an occupation. From there I became a *militante,* and that's what I've been doing ever since."

"*Militante*?" Sharp queried.

Mayor Brizola answered, "*Militantes* are mostly youths who are given special practical and political training by the MST—grooming them for future leadership roles. Mostly they're in charge of organizing, establishing, and maintaining occupations"

Silva nodded. "Exactly. Once I finished my training they sent me home to Pernambuco where I led my first occupation."

Sharp asked eagerly, "How did this occupation start?"

Silva smiled. "An occupation of this magnitude is not something that we could just jump into. It took a lot of planning and time to get everything ready. We had to first make sure we had enough polythene tents and enough people coming to ensure its success. I spent about six months traveling through Pernambuco, going from one *favela* to the next and persuading people to come. Then we arranged for transportation so that they would be in Limoeiro when we officially cut the wire."

"Cut the wire?"

"Yes, it's a little saying of ours. Whenever we begin an occupation we call it 'cutting the wire' because to get onto the property we first have to cut through the fence." He chuckled. "Anyway, once we had everyone ready to go, we waited until nightfall and loaded up buses with families and brought them here. It sounds easier than it actually was. See, the Bezerras had been tipped off earlier that the MST was up to something, so they sent out their hired gunmen to prevent it." He leaned in closer to Sharp, and recounted proudly. "They thought that our land invasion was going to begin at this one *favela* called Alto do Céu. That we were gathering people there before we headed off as one big group. So they spent the day cruising around the place and distributing leaflets warning violence and offering hollow promises of land grants. When our bus showed up, the gunmen surrounded it and threatened the driver to leave, and to take back whoever didn't belong in Alto do Céu. Which the driver did, taking a busload of people with him. The gunmen were so pleased with themselves, but what they didn't know was that the bus wasn't bringing people in, it was taking people out. Fools." Silva laughed triumphant.

"Then what happened?"

Silva calmed down and continued his story. "Well, we cut the wire without incident and set about making the camp. We had less than twenty-four hours to get ourselves ready before news spread that we were here. Sometimes all this can be dashed instantly by the police or a private army, but fortunately that didn't happen here. This occupation on the first day had so many people that we overwhelmed the gunmen and police before they could even think of evicting us. And thanks to Balthazar, we're doing a lot better than we were sixteen days ago. I'd say the Bezerras will give in to our demands in about another month or two."

"He certainly is keeping morale pretty high, it would appear." Sharp glanced behind him in the direction of where the central square was, but all he saw was a scattering of tents and occupiers getting along with their day. Returning to Silva, he asked, "How have the Bezerras reacted so far?"

"They're lying low for a time. Waiting for the right moment to strike. You know how it is. Can't let another Eldorado happen."

"Eldorado? The city of gold?"

Silva laughed. "No. It's a long story, but if you have time I could tell it to you?"

"Oh, I don't know…" Sharp glanced at his watch. "…My partner's waiting for…"

As if the very thought had summoned her, Braasch emerged from the tents and stepped up to the three men. Her lips pursed tightly together. "I wasn't able to talk to Balthazar. Once he finished he got right into his limo and drove off."

"What?" The color from Mayor Brizola's face drained away.

"Yeah, he seemed to be in a hurry for something," Braasch deduced.

The Mayor glanced away absently at the row of cars across the fence. He muttered to himself, "Probably distracted by the *Safra* dinner. That's probably it. The *Safra* dinner."

"What's that, Mayor?" Sharp couldn't help but notice his sudden discomfort.

Snapping out of it, the Mayor steadied himself and explained, "the *Safra* dinner, a celebration of the coming harvest season. It's scheduled for tonight, next to the *usina*." He dismissed the digression with a wave of his hands. "But that's not important here. Silva was talking about Eldorado."

"Yes, please stay," Silva insisted. "I think it is a story you should hear. Something to captivate your readers."

Braasch hesitated, "I'm sorry, Mr…?"

"Silva."

"Mr. Silva," Braasch repeated. "But we should really be going right—"

"It is a good story," Silva pleaded. "Give you some good perspective on what we are up against."

"Braasch, I think we should hear this." Sharp seconded, "if there is to be another Eldorado, I'd like to know what's to be expected first."

Rolling her eyes, Braasch relented, "Fine."

Silva clapped his hands together. "Wonderful. If you'll follow me."

Leading them deeper into the labyrinth of black tents, Silva brought them to a small community space where several benches and chairs wrapped around a campfire. Once all were properly situated, Silva began:

"Eldorado for us is not a city of gold, but a city of blood…"

ELDORADO DE CARAJÁS

"...West of here is the state of Pará, located in the Amazon," Silva recited. "You see it's a remote area, barely accessible, which makes it practically impossible for Brasília to provide any real oversight or enforcement. Pará, in essence, is a fiefdom dominated by the local powerful landowners: state officials swim deep in their pockets, the police obey their every command, and the hired gunmen resolve complaints without it ever reaching the newspapers."

"Violence is so baked into their culture," the Mayor chimed in, "that it's nurtured a groundswell of new words for a hired gunman—" He counted them on his fingers "—*jagunço, cabra, cabra-de-peia, cacundeiro, curimbaba, guarda-costas, mumbava, peito-largo, pistoleiro, quarto-paus, sombra, satelite.*"

"Yet that didn't stop the MST from pursuing their own usual brand of resistance there." Turning his head, Silva looked over his right shoulder. Sharp followed his gaze and saw several women preparing food in a makeshift open-air kitchen underneath an awning made of garbage bags. "I thought I smelt lunch," He said, distracted. "Hope you're in the mood for some *feijoada.*"

A pleasant aroma of smoked meat wafted across Sharp's nostrils. A dull pang turned his stomach.

"Anyway, as I was saying," Silva continued. "The MST set their sights on Pará as a means of testing their growing strength against a formidable oligarchy."

"With an occupation," Sharp deduced.

Silva nodded his head. "Exactly. They launched an encampment right outside the INCRA office in Marabá, a municipality of Pará. Five months later INCRA capitulated and bought a large area of land for the MST—granting them fertile ground where they could finally sow agrarian justice in a hostile Pará.

"But in a year's time talks between the MST, landowners, and INCRA broke down completely. In frustration, 1,500 families united to march on the capital of the state. Taking a route that would lead them right through Eldorado de Carajás, a sad ugly frontier town vastly underdeveloped; like an old ghost town you'd see in one of your American Western films. Rundown and desolate.

"The families walked for hours, covering nearly three kilometers—or two miles—till they reached Eldorado. By then, their food supply had run out, and now they had a difficult choice before them: turn back or push forward. But they were not to be deterred. Together, they decided the cause was too important to abandon, and so they formed a roadblock on the highway going from Parauapebas to Marabá, demanding the state government deliver them ten tonnes of food and fifty coaches to carry them to Belém, the capital of Pará."

Sharp's stomach growled, the smell of food was intoxicating. Glancing at Braasch, she looked like a stone statue. *She's been oddly quiet today.* His concentration slipped and his mind wondered. *Doesn't seem like she wants to be here. Why'd she come?* He forced his attention back to Silva.

"A few weeks later Major Oliveira and a small army of military police arrived at Eldorado de Carajás. He first offered diplomacy to clear the roadblock, promising them the fifty coaches in exchange for abandoning the road. None the wiser the families accepted the terms happily. They stepped off the highway, set up a camp, and waited. They were told the coaches would arrive by eleven o'clock the next morning.

"Well, the next day, nine o'clock passes, then ten o'clock, and nothing. But that's okay, it's early. Eleven o'clock goes by and still no sign of the coaches. The protesters grow antsy but decide to wait a little longer—it takes a long time to organize fifty coaches, after all. Well twelve o'clock goes by, then one o'clock, and that's when the protesters became ever more anxious and realized that Major Oliveira had no intention of keeping his promise. So they reoccupied the highway.

"The landowners would have none of it, they demanded that more forceful measures be taken. And the commander-in-chief of the military police in Pará was more than willing to oblige. He dispatched Colonel Pantoja to end the protest once and for all."

Mayor Brizola lowered his head, shame weighed heavy on his shoulders. Sullen, he stated, "No doubt violence was premeditated. They intended to teach the MST a lesson they would never forget."

"On one side of the highway," Silva recounted, "Colonel Pantoja readied himself with eighty seven military policemen. They parked a row of lorries across one length of highway for cover. Then began throwing tear-gas, and firing their weapons into the air. Unintimidated, the MST marched bravely towards the military police." Rising from his seat, Silva looked off into the distance as if narrating events unfolding before his eyes. "As they grew closer, the police panicked and opened fire directly into the crowd with their machine guns. A few protesters scattered but Amâncio Rodrigues dos Santos, a deaf mute, kept going, waving the MST flag high above him, unable to hear the guns going off. He reached the barricade before several police officers grabbed him, threw him on the ground, beat him, and shot him dead. The first to die that horrible day."

Water welled around his eyes. Silva charged on attracting the attention of passing occupiers.

"Shaken, the MST fell back, fleeing from the gunfire. But as they retreated Major Oliveira suddenly appeared behind them on the other side of the highway with sixty eight military policemen. The protesters were surrounded!

"From both sides bullets and tear gas flew. And their only hope of surviving this slaughter was by escaping the roadway and taking refuge in the foliage. Chaos ensued."

An extended audience began to congregate around the campfire, murmuring their anger and sorrow. Sharp felt a shift in the air. This wasn't just a story for these people.

"Jurandir Gomes do Santo, shot in the foot, staggered off the road and into some undergrowth. A bullet sailed just centimeters above him. An older gentleman came up to him and yelled 'if you stay here, you'll get killed.' He helped Santo up and carried him further away from the firefight, safe behind a tree. The old man ran off never to be seen again. Santo scrambled further on into a rice field and laid low until it was over. He still wakes up at night hearing the screams and gunfire of that day. He survived, but the lucky ones are those who didn't.

"Bullets ripped through many that day: exposing bone, knocking out teeth, shattering jaws. It was a bloodbath. Blood everywhere with the dead and wounded splayed across the highway. And the police. Enjoyed. Every. Minute. Of. It." He bit into each word as if chewing on a hard piece of gristle. A hiss slithered through the audience.

Silva stared down at the dirt, forlorn, "Oziel Alves Pereira," he pronounced solemnly, "hoped to appeal to the murderers' good senses. So he abandoned the hut where he had been hiding with several women and children. They begged Oziel not to leave. They cried, 'Don't go, Oziel. They'll kill you.' But he refused to listen." Silva collapsed into his seat, his grief overcoming him, and wiped a hand across his creased brow. "Once he reached the road, the police seized him. Put him in handcuffs. Beat him senseless. Ordered him to shout: 'Long live the MST! Long live the MST!' They kicked him and punched him every time he said the words. And with every 'Long live the MST!' he grew weaker and weaker, till finally he could no longer muster the breath to say it. He died with the MST on his lips." Silva sniffed a tear away.

Out of the corner of his eye Sharp noticed someone remove their red ball cap and place it against their chest, their head bowed.

"Altamiro Ricardo da Silva was shot in the head in front of his little girl. Inácio Pereira survived only by pretending to be dead as they dragged him by the hair to a lorry full of corpses. Not till he reached the morgue did he reveal himself to be alive. His son Raimundo Lopes Pereira was not so lucky."

Silva spat on the dirt ground and shuffled dirt over it with his shoe. "Major Oliveira informed his superiors that there were 'six dead men and a lot of wounded' when the guns finally stopped. Yet when the official report came out that number changed to nineteen dead and no wounded. Odd, don't you think?"

A tempered muttering rumbled across those gathered.

Silva jumped out of his seat and addressed all who listened, shouting, "These men killed the rest in cold blood. And thirteen of them were local MST leaders, specifically targeted." He locked eyes with one person and approached them, leveling his volume to a near whisper. "The soldiers returned to their vehicles and cheered their success—as if returning home after a hard day's fight with an enemy country." Spinning around, he stated with measured calm, "the war might have been over for them that day, but for the MST the highway was just the beginning.

"The police drove to the hospital in Curionópolis, they sauntered right into the waiting room, approached one gentleman there, and shot him just like that. For the rest of the day they scoured every nearby hospital for those wounded in the massacre.

"The landowners believed this to be the end of the MST; that we had been taught a violent and bloody lesson." Silva, now fully revved up, paced around the campfire. "And we did learn a lesson that day. No matter how violent they get, we will not be intimidated. Relatives refused to let their deaths be in vain. They refused to be bullied into submission. No, they would fight on, more determined than ever to win. And, fifteen years later, we're still fighting. Here we follow in their footsteps willing to endure whatever they throw at us. They can send in the police to evict us, but we will refuse to give up. That I can promise you!"

The audience burst into wild applause and cheering. The *mística* on full display.

"And with Alexander Balthazar on our side we can finally achieve something here in the Northeast. For too long the sugar tycoons have dominated this area, exploiting our labor and drowning us in poverty for nearly four hundred years. And we're finally standing up and shouting 'Enough.' And with the Pope of Sugar on our side, nothing will stop us! Once we're finished here then we'll occupy the Barbalho's then the Afonso's. We'll reclaim the land for those who've tilled and toiled their whole lives on these plantations. So that we may one day be given the fair reward of a hard day's work!"

Silva pumped a fist into the air punctuating the finality of his impromptu speech and those gathered celebrated with a chorus of "*Ocupar, Resistir, Produzir.*" Silva waved to those shouting his name and offered words of humble thanks in reply. Then gently told them to return to whatever they were doing, to get on with their day.

Cheeks red, Silva turned to the Americans. "Sorry, got carried away there," he said bashfully.

"Don't be, it was a marvelous performance," the Mayor complimented. "It's better than any speech I've ever given." He clapped Silva on the shoulder, then jerked it back as if suddenly remembering the importance of boundaries.

"Yeah, yeah," he dismissed with a wave of his hand. He peered over at the kitchen. "It looks like lunch is ready. Why don't we eat?"

Sharp's stomach growled softly in reply.

The women dished out several plastic bowls full of *feijoada* and distributed them to all who came. The four collected their portion and returned to their seats around the campfire. The bowl contained a thick black bean stew with smoked beef, sautéed greens, and rice. Sharp dug his spoon into the stew, scooped up a healthy dose, and shoved it into his mouth. The combination of exotic tastes melted on his tongue, it was exquisite.

"What do you think?" asked Silva.

"Delicious," Sharp replied, swallowing down another spoonful. "The food here just keeps getting better and better."

Silva smiled. "Nothing can beat a good Brazilian dish, though others have tried."

"Oh, I'm sure." He looked at Braasch, who ate her *feijoada* in silence. *What is she doing?*

"But getting back to what we were talking about," Sharp refocused the conversation as they ate. "You seem to put a lot of faith in Balthazar to protect you."

Silva talked and chewed at the same time. "He's our armor. You see, Sharp, those with power never attack those with power. It's foolish, and stupid. If the Bezerras laid a finger on us Balthazar would react and raise holy hell against them. And they don't want that happening, so they leave us alone."

"Wow," Sharp marveled. "I'd love to meet him, if possible."

"Why not come to the *safra* banquet tonight?" The Mayor offered. "I can introduce you to him."

Braasch spoke for the first time, "Oh no, we don't want to—"

"Please." He pleaded. "It wouldn't be a problem. And it'll be great for your story. Might even attract more readers if you got an exclusive interview with Balthazar. Please."

Braasch wavered, caught between a rock and a hard place. Finally she sighed, "Alright. We'll come to the banquet."

The Mayor perked up. "Splendid."

"Which means we should probably go get ready for tonight." She stood up prompting Sharp to follow in kind. They set the empty bowls down on their seats. "Thank you for the meal. It truly was delicious. And for the story."

Silva opened his mouth to say something but Mayor Brizola stopped him, blurting out. "Before you go, can you do me a favor?"

"What is it, Mayor?"

"Can I get a ride back to city hall?" An awkward silence lingered between the four of them, all eyes on the Mayor. He explained himself, "Well, it's just that Balthazar was my ride here, and surely he's got a lot of preparations to do for tonight, and must have forgotten me. Since you're already here, would it be alright?"

Braasch and Sharp glanced at each other. Braasch answered, "Sure. We'll get you to city hall. Should be on the way to the hotel."

Like a dog hearing the jiggle of his leash, the Mayor shot out of his seat. "Thank you. I greatly appreciate it."

THE *SAFRA* BANQUET

"How long have you been mayor?" Sharp asked Mayor Brizola once they were settled in the car and on their way back to town. Sharp had his neck craned around the passenger seat so he could fully see the Mayor's expressions behind him.

Mayor Brizola was looking down at the floor when the question caught him by surprise. He whipped his head up and flashed deer-in-the-headlight eyes. "Oh," he sputtered. "Why, since 2008." A bit of color lit up his cheeks, he seemed embarrassed.

"So then that must mean you've been working with Balthazar for a while now, huh?" Sharp prodded.

"Yes," he replied flatly. "We've collaborated on several of the development projects he's funded. Without him, none of it would have been possible."

"And how do the citizens of Limoeiro feel about him?"

Mayor Brizola lowered his gaze back to the floor. "They love him... for what he's done."

Sharp caught a trace of resentment in his voice. He couldn't put his finger on it just yet but he sensed something was amiss between the Mayor and Balthazar. He decided to prod a little further to see how the Mayor would react:

"What are your thoughts on Alexander Balthazar?"

"Alex is a good man," he said lamely. "Limoeiro has improved greatly since he became the Pope of Sugar. Everyone is treated like a human being and paid adequate living wages. His work with the MST is unprecedented." It sounded perfunctory, devoid of heart. Nothing like the Mayor Sharp had heard at the occupation who fully advocated for the cause of the occupiers and the MST.

"It's a good thing you two are able to work so well together."

"Yes," he nodded. "He was one of my largest supporters during the election."

"Really?"

"Yeah, he urged me to run. Even funded my whole campaign, and staffed it as well. He's done a lot for me."

"Interesting." Sharp turned away facing front again. His interest piqued, Sharp filed this away for a later date when he could adequately tug at this loose thread. Might unravel something worth discovering. Alone.

Somewhere deep in his subconscious a wolf howled encouragement.

That evening, Braasch and Sharp arrived at the *Safra* banquet already underway. Sharp had changed into a navy blue suit with a white button down and black tie. His Oxford shoes, recently polished, shined in the effervescent lamplight.

As for Braasch, she stepped from the car wearing a black dress purchased earlier from a local shop in Limoeiro. Just like her uniform, it accentuated the curves of her body but left open a window exposing a slight peek of her cleavage and bare shoulders. Due to the last-minute nature of this event, she managed to apply only a layer of makeup on her cheeks while leaving her hair untouched. Walking across the asphalt, she strode confidently, back straight head high. Sharp snuck a peak at her.

Before them stood two massive structures: a giant white canopy tent erected for the banquet and the gunmetal gray *usina* lit up by a series of overhead lights. One light shone directly at the plantation's insignia plastered on the *usina*'s grated side. It depicted a wasteland of charred earth and burnt sugarcane, ash wafted like snowflakes through the blackened remains. Yet in the middle of the desolation stood a single solitary golden stock of sugar, long verdant leaves jutted out from its crown. Amongst the leaves perched a blazing red Phoenix with outstretched wings ready for flight. Its beak was wide open, cawing out to the heavens. At the bottom, painted in a curvy scrawl, was the *usina*'s name, *Santidade através do trabalho celeste.*

Santidade. Sharp fixated on the word as he soaked in the insignia.

Entering the giant canopy, Braasch and Sharp were greeted with a din of festive cheer and good humor. Music pounded through the speaker overpowering the causal chatter of the partiers. Little kids raced around the scattering of circular tables, giggling and shouting as they did, while the bigger kids filled the dance floor gyrating to the beat of the music. An assembly line of caterers scurried in and out from a split in the tent as they carried large metal containers to the buffet table. In the corner a DJ stared down at his console, arranging his playlist and manipulating the lights. At the very front was a long dais where the company bigwigs sat. Behind them hung the *usina*'s insignia: the Phoenix.

Before they could even step into the space, they heard someone shout at them. "Good, you made it!"

Mayor Brizola charged at them with a delighted grin. An earth green suit and muted red tie covered his frame. Shaking their hands, he welcomed, "Thank you again for earlier. I don't know what I would have done without you."

Sharp smiled graciously. "Thank you for inviting us. Would it be possible to have a word with Balthazar?"

"Actually, he's not here yet," the Mayor corrected, the grin slipped some. "He'll be here in a few minutes, that's when we officially begin the banquet. For now we're just waiting for everyone to show up and settle in." A person crossed into his peripheral. He latched onto the forearm of the person, halting their motion. "Here's someone I'd like you to meet."

The gentlemen whipped his head to the side, his eyes fierce lasers till recognition softened them. "Mayor Brizola," he said with a German accent. "What can I do for you?"

"Senhor Scharnhorst," the Mayor introduced, "I'd like you to meet Mr. Ian Sharp and Miss Heather Braasch. This is Senhor Gerhard Scharnhorst, the *gerente de usina de açúcar,* mill manager, for Senhor Balthazar."

"*Olá,*" Scharnhorst greeted mechanically. Standing a good four inches taller than Sharp's six-foot frame, he wore an all-black suit with a white bowtie. A perfect right triangle of a nose hovered above a humorless smile.

"They're journalists writing a story about the Bezerra Occupation."

"Really?" His eyes scanned the Americans. "How is that going?"

"We've only just started," Braasch replied. "Still only gathering information right now."

"I see. And what paper do you work for?"

Braasch opened her mouth to speak but nothing came out. She retreated somewhat into herself, folding her arms across her chest as if only realizing how exposed she was in front of a bunch of strangers. Sharp noticed, and blurted out the first thing that came to his mind.

"The New Yorker."

The three flashed a glance at him and Sharp did his best to appear calm. But the scrutinizing gaze of Scharnhorst left him slightly unsettled.

The Mayor explained cheerfully, "I invited them so that they can have a chat with Balthazar. An interview with him would do well to boost coverage of the occupation."

"Yes, it would." Scharnhorst agreed flatly without taking his eyes off of Sharp. "If you'll excuse me. I've got some matters to attend to." He bowed his head and stalked off.

Once released from the German's gaze, Sharp exhaled and remarked, "He's quite intense."

Mayor Brizola nodded. "Yes, but tonight is a big event. He's in charge of making sure everything goes right. He's got no time to stay in any one spot for too long." He then changed the subject. "I'd like to introduce you to some others if you'd please. Just follow me."

Braasch piped up, "If it would be alright, I'd like to find a place to sit, actually."

"Yes, yes." Mayor Brizola stammered and stepped aside. "Please find a seat anywhere. And please take advantage of the bar while you're here. It's complimentary." He set his sights on Sharp. "How about you?"

"Oh, I thought—" He was caught off guard, having believed that Braasch's polite disengagement included him as well. "Ummm." He glanced at Braasch hoping for a rescue, but she had already begun walking through the tables without looking back. "Sure," he relented.

The two waded through the collection of white clothed tables scattered across the canopy's wide grassy expanse. Little plastic sugarcane centerpieces rested on top of them. At the dais, the Mayor worked his way down the table of VIP guests introducing Sharp to each member one by one, trading names, shaking hands, and offering a bit of broken conversation.

"...Vice President, Agriculture..."

"Hello."

"*Olá.*"

"...*Ele está escrevendo um artigo sobre a ocupação*..."

"...He's in charge of finances..."

"Hello."

"*Olá.*"

"...*Ele é um americano que veio escrever sobre nós*..."

"...Administration..."

"Hello."

"*Olá.*"

"...*Ele estava na ocupação*..."

So it went with the twelve people sitting at the dais, with Sharp unable to speak a lick of Portuguese. After the first interaction, Sharp immediately realized what he had gotten himself into and resigned himself to playing the role Mayor Brizola wished of him. If anything, it seemed to bring great joy to the Mayor who was brimming at the prospect of showing off his American guest. When all was said and done, they left the dais with one last wave and maneuvered through the tables in search of Braasch.

"Now wasn't that grand?" Mayor Brizola beamed. "Alex might be the brains of this company, but they are the arms, feet, and chest of the operation. Without them, we wouldn't be celebrating as we are now. We were struggling for a time in the early 2000s, but this team Alex assembled, along with his vision, helped bring us back to prominence as the leader in sugar production."

"It is quite an impressive team," Sharp offered.

"I know. They were skeptical of me at first when Alex brought me on, but I think I've sowed some goodwill amongst them. Just got to keep at it, you know, keep tilling that soil."

Sharp spotted Braasch. "I know exactly what you mean."

Sharp bade Mayor Brizola a gentle farewell before they split apart and advanced in opposite directions. He sat down next to Braasch.

"What did he want with you?" She asked.

"Just wanted to introduce me to the big guys up there. Nothing special." He dismissed it with a wave of his hand.

Getting a chance to fully enjoy the celebrations, a sense of ease and liveliness enveloped him. "It's not every day I get to go to one of these things. We should at least get one dance in before the night is through, don't you think?"

Braasch shook her head. "I'd prefer not to. I don't like to dance."

Sharp brushed her refusal aside and scooted his chair closer to hers. "Aren't you ever off the clock? We're at a celebration. Celebrate."

"This isn't the kind of job that allows for celebrations, Sharp. We're here on business."

Sharp rolled his eyes. "Fine… I've noticed you've been awfully silent today. Thought I was the one who had to keep quiet, not you."

"You seem to know what you're looking for," she observed. "You came here with a purpose. I'm merely here to keep an eye on you."

"But why you? Wouldn't you be needed at Headquarters? Why not have Estrella babysit me?"

"He declined, preferring to stay in Brasília."

"Why?"

She shrugged. "Didn't say, but he was determined. Besides, Sir tasked me with watching over you. And I mean to do as he commands."

"Alright," Sharp allowed. "Then tell me what you think so far."

Braasch licked her teeth with her tongue. "Too early to tell. But I haven't been convinced yet. I'm not seeing how this relates to Quadros's assassination, or how it ties into the standoff. For all we know this could very well end up as a waste of time."

Sharp listened internally giggling at her words. She was completely oblivious, just how Sharp wanted it to be.

"I say we still talk to Balthazar at least and if we don't find anything, then we'll go back to Brasília." He countered. "That way we won't waste too much time if this turns out to be a wild goose chase."

She turned her focus away from Sharp and stared at the table. Longing filled her eyes. Softly, she breathed out to herself, "Yeah… Just when I thought this was my chance."

Sharp caught a whiff of what she said. "A chance at what?"

"When Sir recruited me," she began. "I thought this could be my chance to make something of myself. I came from a small town in Oklahoma and had these big dreams when I left. That's probably how it goes: the smaller the town the bigger the dreams. I thought I'd make them here at Sector Seven. So I gave everything to the Agency. Even uprooted my whole life when I volunteered to come to Brazil and help establish a Branch. I put my blood, sweat, and tears into this department. I became the youngest Branch Commander in Sector Seven. But no one seemed to have noticed."

"Sure they have," Sharp encouraged, though a little surprised at the sudden flash of vulnerability. "Sir certainly has, or else he wouldn't have made you Branch Commander, right?"

Braasch waved her head from side to side unbelieving. "He had no choice, I was the only one who knew how to manage it. Last time he took an interest in me was when he first recruited me, when I saved my partner from drowning."

Sharp tilted his head, intrigued. "Oh, what happened?"

Braasch eyed him. Relaxing, she said, "Perhaps a drink first. Then, maybe, I'll tell you."

"Sounds good," he replied, rising from the table. Together, they went over to the bar and ordered their drinks from the bartender. Sharp selected a Brazilian brewed beer called *Itaipava*, while Braasch went with a classic rum and coke. Returning to their seats, they sipped from their drinks and Braasch recounted her story:

"I was in Hawaii, doing some research." Her focus fully locked on to the sugarcane centerpiece.

"What kind of research?" He asked.

"Studying underwater flora and fauna."

"Oh, so you wanted to be a scientist."

"I am a scientist," she corrected him proudly. Taking a swig of her rum and coke, she swished the biting liquor around her teeth, then swallowed. "Anyways, my partner and I were collecting underwater specimens that day. When it was time to resurface, I turned to look at him so I could gesture for him to follow me. I didn't know immediately that something was wrong, but I sensed something. He was sinking. At first I thought it was because he spotted something below he had to examine. But his arms and legs dangled at his side lifelessly. He simply floated to the ocean floor.

"I swam to him thinking that he was just having some fun with me, but the closer I got I soon realized his eyes were closed. And a trickle of blood oozed out of his nose. He had fallen unconscious. I didn't know what to do. Time froze still at that moment." Her breathing quickened as she recounted that moment. "Thinking quickly, I hoisted him onto my shoulder and pushed off the ocean floor, but an underwater plant snagged onto his tank and reeled us back like a bungee cord. I tugged at the plant but it wouldn't release him, it held firm. I ended up unhooking his scuba tank, slipping it off his shoulders, and wedging my mouthpiece between his lips. We shot up through the water."

She paused, taking a long swig of her drink. The muscles in her neck were tense. Sharp listened silently, his body bent forward close to her, enthralled in her story.

"We were a long way down and, about half way, my lungs began to cry out for air. A fire consumed my chest. But I kept paddling my flippers as I held on tightly to my partner. I willed myself to keep going. I saw the sun's reflection on the ocean surface and I paddled harder, ignoring the feeling that my chest was about to explode. I kept going. I was nearly there. I grew exhausted, my grip began to go lax and my legs couldn't bear it much longer. I almost let him go just to save myself. But I held on, determined to reach the research boat. A pain ripped through my sides by then. My heartbeats slackened into dull thuds. I thought I was going to die right there, but I refused to give up. I could feel the heat of the sun. My vision blurred and my throat nearly collapsed. I kept swimming, and swimming. I was about to lose consciousness. But before I officially gave out, a hand broke through the surface, latched onto me, and hauled me out of the water. I flopped onto the deck gasping for air as the rest of the team went into survival mode. They rushed us to a hospital. If I hadn't been there my partner would have died that day. I saved his life." She sighed. "Soon afterwards Sir showed up, and the rest is history."

"Wow," Sharp exclaimed. "You're a hero."

She waved the idea away. "That was a long time ago."

"No, you are," he implored. "You risked your life to save him. That takes guts. My adventure was nowhere near as harrowing as yours. I just talked a guy down from jumping off the flight deck of a carrier. At no time was my life threatened."

"But you were there for him, he's still alive because of you. And that was enough to get Sir's attention." She swung her eyes from the table and peered into Sharp's. "I'd like to hear more."

Sharp shook his head embarrassed, but the pleading in Braasch's eyes overpowered him. He took a sip of his drink. "We just talked," he began hesitantly, "that's about it. We were three months into our year-long tour aboard the *USS William Jefferson Clinton*. And this one sailor was not taking it well, he'd become very homesick. Mix that in with a little cabin fever and you've got yourself a dangerous concoction. Well at one point he started stepping up really close to the edge of the carrier and looking down at the breaking waves below—a good breeze could have knocked him right over. He did this for a few days, probably trying to gather the courage to jump, and wimping out every time. Well one of his fellow seamen noticed this and grew concerned, so he came to me."

"Why you?"

"Proximity, I'm assuming," He suggested. "So the next day I went atop the flight deck and waited for the homesick sailor to step up to the edge, then I joined him. Spooked him at first, but once we struck up a conversation we ended up having a nice chat. Together we watched the sun go down over the ocean. It was a beautiful view."

"And what did you two talk about?"

"The usual things: home, life, relationships, the future. He did most of the talking; just needed someone to talk to. Sometimes you forget how much we need that feeling of comradery, and I was happy to listen." He downed the last of his beer and set it aside on the table. A server snatched it up almost immediately.

Slouching a little in his chair he crossed his arms. "From there things snowballed unexpectedly. Word got out that I had stopped a jumping, though I was just doing what I know how to do best: talk. I just wanted to make him feel less alone so that he'll stop getting dangerously close to falling overboard. And it worked. But that's when everyone started coming to me to have a conversation with. They'd come to my quarters, sit on the bunk, and just unload. It surprised me at first, but they seemed to really trust me—and I couldn't throw them out. So I listened. For the rest of the tour people would come to my quarters from time to time and chat."

"Must have thought you were a shrink," Braasch mused.

"If only I were paid like one," he joked. "Still, I didn't think of it much at the time, until my Commanding Officer brought it up near the end of the tour. He mentioned how good I was for morale. That the men were happier and working harder because of me. And it's all because I reached out to this one kid who was feeling a little homesick. That's how it happened. See, not as exciting as yours."

"No, it's not," she agreed. "But what you have is a valuable skill. I've now had a chance to see it on full display today and, I have to admit, it showed promise."

Surprised, Sharp straightened in his seat. A feeling of pride washed over him.

Her tone turned hesitant. "Listen, I know this is your first time out, and I probably shouldn't have been so…" she struggled to form the word, "…dismissive of you. But I want you to understand where I'm coming from."

Sharp opened his mouth to speak, but she barreled on. "I've been in Brazil for about three years now and, as you can tell, a case like this doesn't happen very often. This is my chance to impress Sir. Then he assigned you to assist me even though I never asked for it, or wanted it." She took in a breath, her face strained as she opened up. "But you've been helpful so far, and maybe one day you'll be a good agent. But this is my case." She emphasized. "This is an opportunity I can't afford to lose, is that clear?"

"Crystal, ma'am," Sharp replied, suddenly aware how similar their personal objectives were. And yet, here was Sharp withholding valuable information that might solve the case. He rubbed his chest with the palm of his hand, feeling the clump of guilt lodged in his heart.

Refusing to acknowledge it, he reached out for Braasch's hand, tugged, and declared jovially, "Now then, why don't we have our dance?"

Braasch resisted. "No, that's ok. I don't dance."

"Come on, it'll be fun." He persisted, pulling her from the chair.

Braasch reluctantly allowed herself to be dragged to the dance floor. Her black dress glistened in the shifting lights. Taking up a position in the corner away from the mass of teenagers, Sharp faced her and extended his hands. She stepped into his embrace and placed her hands on Sharp's side and shoulder. A good chasm lay between them.

Though the music was typical of a dance setting with its heavy bass and rapid pace, the two of them simply swayed from side to side as they twirled. Stiff on her feet, Braasch moved like a clock's pendulum. Sharp stepped into the chasm and teased, "Lighten up a bit. Bend your knees. Look like you're having fun."

She stretched out her lips in a wide mocking grin, her resentment plain in her eyes.

"That's more like it," he laughed.

They swayed on like an awkward couple at prom. Eventually the chasm disappeared and their bodies pressed against each other. He thought of Katelyn and how she felt in his arms. He hadn't had the chance to hold her like this in a long time.

When the song ended Braasch detached herself from him and announced, "I'm going to get something to drink, see you back at the table."

"See you there."

Separating, Sharp ventured through the tables and sat down. His heart felt lighter, the lump gone, and, in that moment as he watched the merry festivities around him, he truly enjoyed life.

The music cut out, the light dimmed, and the chatter faded. A German accent blasted through the speakers: "Ladies and gentlemen, please welcome our host for the evening. Our Pope of Sugar, Alexander Balthazar!"

Alexander Balthazar strode in through the entrance, and everyone burst into wild applause.

THE *SAFRA* CELEBRATIONS

Everyone was on their feet, cheering and clapping and whistling, as Alexander Balthazar passed through the tables basking in the love and adoration thrown his way. Nearby workers let out their hands, and Balthazar grasped them as he went by. They shouted in Portuguese, and he shouted right back with the same level of exuberance. The dance floor parted like the Red Sea presenting Balthazar easy access to the dais. There he traveled down the table, shaking hands with those privileged enough to sit there, till he claimed his spot next to the podium. The proud Phoenix observing all.

Shouting over the applause, Scharnhorst spoke directly into the microphone:

"Ladies and Gentlemen, now that our Pope of Sugar has made his gracious entrance, let us dine."

The lights flashed to life as the applause faded. A growing line snaked from the buffet table and wrapped around the outer rim of the tables. Sharp, however, remained where he was, deciding instead to wait till the line died down; let the employees eat first.

As he waited, Sharp watched the workers shuffle about the grand expanse and, as he did, his observations noted the stark visual disparity between the laborers. Though all would have benefited from Balthazar's patronage, those tasked to work in the fields displayed rough leathery skin and deep sunken eyes. Their faces were wrinkled like a raisin after so long left exposed in the hot harvest sun. Dry cracked calluses covered their hands. When they smiled they bared teeth that had been reduced to nothing more than black nubs after decades of munching raw sugarcane while they worked.

Then there were the mill workers. Protected from the sun, their complexion remained healthy with few creases marking their faces. A majority of teeth filled in their smiles. And their hands, though worn, were not as desiccated as their counterparts out in the field. For Sharp they appeared no different than the Brazilians he'd seen walking down the main streets of Brasília. Despite Balthazar's efforts, there were some inequalities that money simply couldn't rectify.

Braasch appeared and planted herself next to him.

"So, that's Balthazar," she said inspecting the man. His white button down shirt held taut against the noticeable girth hidden within while an unlit cigar hung lazily from his lips as he talked. An outline of black facial hair wrapped around his jawline and thick brows hung over brown eyes. "Really going all in with this pope thing, isn't he? But, let the billionaire have his flight of fancy. I'm hungry, let's get something to eat."

At the buffet table, Sharp loaded his plate full of *Picanha,* picked up another *Itaipava,* and returned to his table to eat.

Picanha was a Brazilian specialty where the top sirloin cap was roasted over an open grill usually with the fat left intact, that way when the fat drips onto the coals the flames will flare up, charring the meat to perfection. Sharp forked his first piece into his mouth and a wave of juices flooded his tongue. A sensation of flavors set him back to his younger days when his mom would grill steaks for dinner. Sharp chewed on, savoring every bite. Brazil once again had outdone itself.

As everyone scarfed down the last bits off their plates, Gerhard Scharnhorst rose from his chair at the dais and approached the podium. He lifted a hand and called out, "Can I have your attention, please? Please, settle down." The chatter diminished as they turned their attention to him. A few stragglers hurriedly filled their plates with seconds. Mothers quieted their little rambunctious children next to them.

"Thank you for coming," began Scharnhorst. "I hope everyone enjoyed our lovely meal." The crowd offered a satisfied and satiated applause. "Tonight we celebrate a bountiful harvest, which would not have been possible if it wasn't for the constant devotion and unyielding perseverance of everyone in this room. I am humbly thankful for all your hard work this year. And I have no doubts that we'll reap in a larger yield this season than we did last season. Thus, allowing for our ever benevolent manager to continue on his crusade for the betterment of Limoeiro." He gestured towards Balthazar and a loud round of applause exploded from the crowd. Balthazar gushed with flattered embarrassment. Scharnhorst continued as the cheering faded. "So tonight let us kick-off the harvest season with a blessing."

Like a magic word spoken aloud, any extra ambient sound fell into silence as everyone lowered their heads in prayer. Alexander Balthazar switched spots with Scharnhorst. He removed his fedora and eyed his congregation. A wave of black hair flowed across his head. When he was ready, Balthazar delivered his blessing:

"Lord, we have asked so much of you and you have given us so much already," he spoke in a booming bass, "We are eternally thankful. But, still tonight, I must ask more of you. Please, Lord, give us the strength to not act out in malice toward our fellow brothers and sisters. Guide our hands not in violence, but in cooperation. Please help us build upon what others have destroyed—what others have hoarded for themselves—so that we can learn to grow closer together and become one with you. Teach us the ways of love and kindness, so that we may better all of mankind—to take those in the dark and bring them to the light. This is all we ask of you. And in return we offer thanks for everything you have graciously supplied us with so far.

"Thank you, Lord, for the food we ate tonight and showing us that, through hard work and determination, we as a community can truly create wonderful things. We would never have been able to build our new hospital without your guidance, Lord. And for that we are thankful. And we hope to receive more of these treasures from you in the future. But tonight, we call on you for a different reason.

"Lord, hear our pleas for a plentiful harvest and, with all your heart, make it come true for the sake of your children. Make the hands of our harvesters hard as a rock and strong as an ox so that they can cut down that resilient sugarcane. Yet still soft enough to hold every shoot of sugar in their arms like a newborn baby. Please have the sun send rays of refreshing light onto our fields so we can bask in your glory, but let it not be so hot that it burns our souls as we collect this gift of sugar you have given us. Keep sickness at bay so that no man or woman shall lie confined to a bed this season while their brethren work twice as hard. Please Lord, allow no accidents to occur in the sugar mills, let every limb finish the season without harm and have every miller return home to see their family every night. For all you have given us, we put our lives into your hands for safekeeping and will do anything you ask of us without question. Please watch over us and protect us and we will never lose faith. Amen."

In one solemn voice the whole congregation muttered, "Amen."

Balthazar repositioned his fedora on his head and made way for Scharnhorst to take up the podium again.

"Thank you, Pope Balthazar. That was truly a lovely prayer, one that surely touched upon the attentive ear of our Lord." A muffled chorus of amens seconded him. "Now, on with the festivities. Please bring out the *chimarrão.*"

A classical church hymnal sounded through the speakers as a young boy dressed in a white collared shirt and black pants appeared from an opening in the canvas of the canopy. Walking to the dais, he carried a large decorated gourd, known as a *chimarrão,* in both hands. He passed from person to person offering the *chimarrão,* and each person graciously took it in their hands, drank from it, and returned it to the boy.

The passing of the *chimarrão* originated from the indigenous Tupí tribe of southern Brazil. When a person drank from the gourd it confirmed their promise to conduct themselves cordially in a public setting, as well as fulfill their obligation of spirited participation. In time the *chimarrão* became a distinguished talisman throughout Brazil, with many southern companies using it as their logo, and families displaying it proudly in their homes like a holy statue. The MST also incorporated the *chimarrão* as a part of their blossoming *mística.*

Once the boy had reached the end of the dais, he stepped onto the dance floor. Then three other boys appeared, dressed the same as the first, and positioned themselves equidistant apart at the lip of the floor, each carrying a gourd. The congregation abandoned their tables and formed four lines in front of them. One by one, the patrons accepted the offering of the *chimarrão.*

Joining in, Sharp waited his turn alongside Braasch for a taste of what was in the gourd. When it touched his tongue a scolding caffeine-rich liquid burned him. He hadn't been expecting it to be hot. Hurrying inconspicuously to his table, he gulped down the rest of his beer.

Another ten minutes went by before the tradition of passing the *chimarrão* was completed. The boys disappeared through the canvas opening, and Scharnhorst took up the podium again:

"Thank you, that was marvelous. Now, please put your hands together for a number specially choreographed for tonight's celebration. I welcome to the stage Limoeiro High School's all-girl dance troupe."

Boisterous cheering accompanied the rush of roughly twenty girls filing onto the dance floor. Each one a carbon copy of each other: tight black dance attire covering their slender frame, hair pulled back into a mathematically perfect spherical bun, and makeup painstakingly applied to highlight their rosy lips and smokey eyes. With heads bowed down, the music brought them to life and they wowed the audience with their performance.

Sharp watched their routine for a time till he absentmindedly muttered to himself, “That’ll be my daughters one day.” Fatherly pride washed over him.

Overhearing Braasch eyed him. “Daughters? You have daughters?”

“No,” Sharp blurted out, covering his slip. “I’ve always wanted daughters. They always seemed so much easier to raise than boys—my brother and I were such a hassle for my mom. I thought it would be nice to have girls instead. Be a whole new experience, you know? Helping them with their hair; having a tea party and voicing all the stuffed animals; dropping them off at dance practice. Encourage them to be whatever they wish to be, even if one of them wants to grow up to become Captain Princess, a daring superhero who can speak to animals and uses the power of love to create force fields. Then after we’ve had our fun, I tuck them into bed for the night and read them a bedtime story, or, if they’re particularly energetic, dance with them.” Realizing he’d been rambling, he tore his gaze away from the hypnotic twirling of the girls and demurred, “Of course, that won’t be for a while. But sometime down the line hopefully.”

“Sounds like you’ve given it a lot of thought already. That’s good. I never really got to know my father…bad alcoholic…but, from what I understand, being a parent is just about being there for them.”

Sharp bit his lip, suddenly unsettled. Her words struck him directly where the clump of guilt lay in his heart. Then a wave of homesickness consumed him.

As Sharp brooded, the dance number ended to loud applause and Scharnhorst returned to the podium. “Wasn’t that great? Now, please welcome to the podium a man we are lucky to have join us tonight, Mayor João Brizola.”

Mayor João Brizola walked up and took the podium. He appeared awkward at first, his voice cracked as he started his speech, but as he talked his stage fright gave way and the tension in his stance dissipated. He settled at ease behind the microphone.

Braasch noticed Sharp's withdrawn demeanor and asked, "Are you feeling okay?"

He snapped out of his inner world and replied, "Yeah, yeah, I was just thinking."

"What were you thinking about?"

"Nothing, it's not important," he dismissed. He refocused his attention onto the Mayor, but his words failed to break through the muddle in his brain.

When Mayor Brizola finished, he stepped away from the podium. Scharnhorst addressed the congregation:

"We are now coming to the end of the formal portion of our evening, and I want to thank you all once again for coming out tonight to celebrate. This harvest season would not be possible without you. But before we finish, there is one more thing left to do." He shifted his body completely towards Balthazar. "Pope Balthazar, in honor of everything you have done for this community, we have a small gift for you."

Balthazar tilted his head, cautious curiosity furrowed his brows.

"Because of you Limoeiro is experiencing a revival. Because of you our children are no longer receiving a third-rate education in dilapidated classrooms. Because of you we have one of the most modern hospitals in all of Brazil. The people needed a miracle and you provided it. And for that everyone is truly in your debt. Though it is impossible to ever repay you for what you have given us, the children of Limoeiro have worked hard on something to say thank you. However, I must warn you that you'll only have tonight to enjoy it." Scharnhorst gestured toward the opening in the canvas and shouted into the microphone, "Bring it in!"

All heads turned to see two boys pushing a cart with a life sized statue of Balthazar. A collective gasp pervaded the congregation. The real Balthazar at the dais covered his mouth with his hand in shock and awe, his eyes bugging out of their sockets. As the statue wheeled past Sharp and onto the dance floor, he was surprised to discover that it was made out of sugar.

The boys pushed the subtlety, as this sugar statue was called, to the middle of the dance floor as Balthazar jumped out of his seat and maneuvered his way to his manufactured likeness. It matched his white suit, café colored skin, and black licorice hair perfectly. Water welled in his eyes as he marveled at the children's creation. He opened his mouth to speak, but failed to find the right words—a round of encouraging applause championed him on. Finally, he whimpered, "From the bottom of my heart, I thank you. This is too much."

He circled around the subtlety inspecting every aspect of it and mumbling out his praise. His shock never abated. After several minutes Balthazar glanced at the cadre of children newly gathered at the lip of the dance floor and thanked them all, hugging each one fondly. Then he addressed the rest of the congregation, his voice choked up. "This is the greatest surprise of my life, and I'm so greatly touched." He struggled to find his next words. "All I can think to say is, let's have dessert!" He reached out a hand, snapped a finger off the statue, and threw it into his mouth. Balthazar grinned delightfully as he chewed.

The congregation hooted and hollered joyously before rushing the statue and disassembling it piece by piece.

As Sharp and Braasch watched the festivities unfold Mayor Brizola slinked up behind them and blurted out:

"Hope you're having fun."

Braasch jumped in her seat startled while Sharp snapped his head around so hard he nearly gave himself whiplash.

Settling some when he realized who it was, Sharp complimented, "Yes, the food was delicious."

"Good, that's great to hear," He smiled relieved. "Say, now would probably be a good time for me to introduce you to Alex, what do you say?"

"Yes, please," Braasch replied.

Following Mayor Brizola, they approached the man himself who stood in the corner of the dance floor enjoying himself as he watched his laborers dismantle his visage.

"Pope Balthazar," Mayor Brizola greeted.

Balthazar turned to the Mayor and his face fell flat. "Mayor, how may I help you?"

"I wanted to introduce you to these two." He gestured toward the Americans. "This is Miss Heather Braasch and Mr. Ian Sharp. They're journalists from America. Doing a story on the occupation."

"Is that so?" He asked, regaining his joyous composure. "Glad to see we're getting attention."

"Yes," the Mayor went on, "and I was hoping to arrange an interview with you." Balthazar shot him a look. "Since you're our biggest supporter, I thought more people might actually read the article if they got an exclusive with you. What do you think?"

"Of course, that's a brilliant idea." He turned to the Americans. "How long will you be covering this story?"

"Just a few more days," Braasch answered. "Once we get everything we need."

"I'm pretty busy these coming weeks, what with the harvest and all," He thought aloud. "Best fit you in as soon as possible. How does tomorrow sound?"

Sharp jumped at the opportunity, "Of course, yes. That'll be perfect."

"Good. I'll be at the *usina* tomorrow overseeing final preparations. Why don't we meet there? We can discuss the occupation in Scharnhorst's office. How does that sound?"

"Yes, we'd love to. Thank you for giving us some of your time."

Balthazar returned his attention to his statue, half of it now digesting in his employee's stomachs. "Anything for the press. Otherwise how would anyone outside of Brazil hear about the plight of the landless here in—"

A loud roaring overpowered the celebrations. The four whipped their heads in the direction of where it came from; each with the same curious look on their faces. The roaring grew louder and soon the congregation as a whole fell into a hushed whisper.

"What is that?" Balthazar asked no one in particular. He started towards the canopy's entrance with Sharp, Braasch, and Mayor Brizola following in tow.

Crossing through the threshold of the canvas, they found several pickup trucks pulling up to the entrance, their engines a cacophony of blaring whines and screeches. They stopped and rough looking men piled out of the truck beds. Falling into formation several feet away from where Balthazar and the rest stood, the men eyed them with daring in their eyes. Pistols hung from hip holsters for all to see.

Sharp felt a change in the air.

SINKING

Balthazar approached the line of men and shouted, "What is the meaning of this?"

One gunman separated from the staggered line. Draped in a green jacket and blue jeans, he rested his hand casually on the butt of his holstered pistol. An air of arrogance screwed up his face as he talked. "We've come to join the party, *falou*. We hear you have some good food."

He stopped within a foot of Balthazar and bared his teeth, a plagued smile. Balthazar stood his ground, unflinching.

"You were not invited," he declared sternly.

"And imagine how upset we were when we heard that." The gunman swung around and gestured to the rest of the men lined up behind him. "Figured it must have been a mistake—invite got lost in the mail. So we came."

"You are still not invited," Balthazar repeated, his jaw tightly clenched. "Please leave this property before anything unwanted happens."

The gunman scoffed.

Near the entrance of the canopy Sharp, Braasch, Mayor Brizola, and an ever increasing number of laborers watched the confrontation unfold. Then, just in sight of Sharp's peripherals, he spotted a figure slip beside Mayor Brizola and leaned close to his ear. Scharnhorst whispered a few words of Portuguese and the Mayor replied with a nod of his head. And, as quickly as he appeared, Scharnhorst was gone.

Spurred to action, Mayor Brizola spun around, raised his hands in the air, and addressed the gathered workers in Portuguese. Following his words, they started shuffling slowly towards the *usina*.

Sharp asked, "What did he tell them?"

Braasch filled him in. "He's getting them into the *usina*. It'll be safer there. We should help." Taking up the Mayor's lead, she began shouting in Portuguese and guiding everyone to the *usina* with a wave of her arms. Sharp followed the best he could while keeping one ear attuned to Balthazar.

"You have no right to be here," Balthazar exclaimed. "This is private property. Leave now."

"Please, *Pope* Balthazar," the gunman emphasized sardonically, "it would be better if you spoke less and listened more."

Balthazar reeled back, insulted. "You think you have the right to tell me—"

A fist across the jaw silenced him. Balthazar stumbled, before he could recover he felt the barrel of a pistol jab his stomach. Securing his footing he glowered at the gunman.

"You ready to listen now?"

Balthazar didn't respond.

The gunman continued in a sickly sweet tone. "The Bezerras simply wanted us to send you their regards for a bountiful harvest. And they will pray nothing goes wrong a day from now."

"If they do anything—"

"All they say—" he bulldozed over Balthazar, "—is that your *tradition* is quite hazardous. Setting fire to a hectare of sugarcane? That is risky. A simple change in the wind could ruin your whole harvest if you are not careful."

"We have taken every precaut—"

"AND! this year is scheduled to be very windy, I hear."

"If you think this intim—"

"SO! it'll be best if you keep your head down and focus on your own land for a change."

A stampede of pickup trucks clipped the spokesman's warning—Balthazar's security detail had finally arrived. They swerved through the maze of cars parked in the lot and formed a barricade separating the gunmen from the canopy, right behind Balthazar. Men flooded out and fell into formation.

Mayor Brizola shouted louder, a newfound urgency in his voice, as the laborers quickened their pace through the small personal entrance of the *usina* next to the giant sliding factory doors. Ghost lights shone pools of light down upon them. Once everyone was in, Mayor Brizola stationed himself at the doorway, acting as guard. Braasch and Sharp stood beside him. Soft muttering pervaded the dark expanse of the factory floor.

Scharnhorst emerged from a gap in the newly formed line of trucks. He called out, "I'd suggest you remove your pistol from senhor Balthazar immediately."

The gunman in green lifted his gun to his shoulder submissively, playing friendly. Stepping back, he cooed, "Easy there. No need to go crazy. Message has been delivered. And, I'm sure, message has been received. Am I right?" He flashed a smirk Balthazar's way.

The gunman turned to the rest of his men, swirled a hand in the air, and they all retreated back to their trucks. Several heaved themselves into the truck bed while others positioned themselves into the driver's seat. Engines revved to life and, one by one, they pulled away.

The workers expelled a silent collective sigh. Yet for Sharp a tension remained. As he watched Balthazar nurse his jaw with the palm of his hand, a mist of doubt spread across the back of his mind.

Balthazar locked eyes with Scharnhorst and shouted a command in Portuguese. Scharnhorst replied promptly and turned to his security team. They scrambled once given their orders. Balthazar made a beeline straight to the *usina*.

A bombardment of questions and outcries greeted him when he entered, but he ignored them all. Passing through the gathered throng, his eyes stared only at the ground before him. Balthazar ascended the stairs leading up to the *usina* overseer's office. He stopped halfway, turned to his workers, and let out a hand silencing everyone.

"Can we get the lights up here, please?" He began. Someone did as he commanded and the factory fluorescents flashed to life, revealing the mechanical beasts used to refine sugar. "It seems we must cut our festivities short, I'm afraid." Balthazar declared, downhearted. "These brutes came tonight to send me a warning, a very brazen one at that. If I don't give up my support of the Bezerra Occupation then, I fear, I'll put this whole harvest season in danger. And with how easily they slipped by our security detail and spoiled tonight they might actually succeed in their threat. I can't risk putting you all through that. Who knows the untold damage it will cause—especially to all of you."

The air grew sullen as Balthazar's words sunk in. Heads bowed low mournfully.

Sharp looked around, and felt the heaviness of their grief.

Cutting through the silence, someone in the back shouted, "To hell with them! We stand with you!"

A groundswell of approval rang through the *usina,* but Balthazar nipped it as quickly as he could. "No," he tempered, "The occupation will survive without me. The Bezerras are powerless to evict them."

"You can't give up!" A laborer encouraged. "If they silence you then they silence us all."

"I must choose my battles carefully," he pleaded, "And losing an entire harvest—your livelihoods—is not worth the risk. You have christened me Pope, for which I am eternally grateful. But it is more than just some term of endearment for me; it is a title of responsibility. I am responsible for protecting my flock. And right now the wolves are at the gate."

"Then we will fight them with you!" A cry rang out.

"They can't take on all of us." Someone seconded.

"Nor will we be intimidated." A third broke the dam, and an outpouring of unity flooded the congregation. Their voices sang as one, reverberating hard against the corrugated walls.

Balthazar attempted to settle them down, but the laborers' revelry took on a life of its own. Sensing the futility of his resistance, he leaned against the railing of the stairs and observed their spontaneous rallying.

Sharp's heartbeat quickened and his shoulders slackened. He suddenly felt lightheaded, the rising mist clouded his judgment.

When the revelry reached a natural ebb, Balthazar announced, rejuvenated. "The Lord gives us courage in these trying times, I see that now in every one of you. You have all shown me such resolve in my moment of weakness. We cannot give in to fear. We cannot let them scare us into submission. We must show them that we are stronger than their threats. And to do that, I think, the *Safra* must go on!"

The congregation hooted and hollered joyously as Balthazar sailed down the stairs and led the march out of the factory. "Yes, let the Bezerras do whatever they want! They will not stop us!" Funneling out of the factory, they paraded their way back into the canopy.

Braasch put a hand on Sharp's arm, jolting him out of his discomfort. "I think it's time we left," she said.

"Yeah," he replied passively. Together they broke away from the parade and drifted through the parking lot towards their car.

Once on the road heading back to their hotel, Braasch pondered aloud, "This whole idea of a businessman being pope is crazy, but he's really taking the part seriously."

"Yeah," Sharp responded distantly.

"Did you see his employees? They love him. I think he's the real deal."

"Yeah." Her words drifted through one ear and dissipated into nothingness.

"So whatever you're thinking, we might have to consider this a dead end."

Sharp stared out the window. "You might be right," he relented without a struggle—he'd lost sight of any firm mooring he might have had here in Pernambuco; now he stood adrift in the ever deepening mist.

Braasch went on, "I know earlier that I said I wasn't ready to have an opinion on this, but I feel like now's an important time to have one. We don't have much time, Sharp, and after what just happened, I'm wondering if we should pursue this any further. I just don't see any connection between Minister Quadros's death and the Bezerra Occupation. And if you were even suspecting the Bezerras, or even Balthazar, for whatever reason, I think it's best you let it go."

Sharp knew she was wrong, but how could he be so sure he was right? He had nothing to say.

"I think we should return to Brasília," Braasch submitted.

"No," Sharp blurted out, grasping for a lifeline. "There's got to be something here. Something with the *Sati*—" He silenced himself. Just then a howl guided him through the mist to firmer ground. Clearing his throat, he started over, "We've still got the interview with Balthazar tomorrow. Maybe he'll give us something."

Braasch sighed. "I don't see how. But I did promise you that at least. Okay, tomorrow we meet with Balthazar." Then added under her breath, "Not sure how Sir's going to take this; probably going to call for my resignation."

Silence carried them the rest of the way to the hotel. A nondescript structure typical of roadside travel. Devoid of life at this time of night, a cascade of low orange lighting cast lingering shadows across the drab façade. It looked like how Sharp felt as they pulled into the lot.

His wading in the mist had carried him over to a small island Sharp typically wished to avoid, but oftentimes it lay right in his path. It was a drab and gloomy place he'd often visit alone in his more melancholic states; a place he'd like to keep secret. Despite how much he yearned to be anywhere else at this moment, he knew he was stuck there until the mist dissipated, which would not be until the morning.

Slipping the keycard into the reader, Sharp entered his room. He flipped on the light switch revealing a small single occupancy space dominated by the queen size bed. A brown wooden dresser stood before her with a flat screen resting atop it, while Sharp's duffle bag nuzzled cozily at the foot of the bed. Crammed in a corner was a small circular table flanked on either side by two wooden chairs.

Sullenly, he fell onto the bed and stared up into the blank ceiling above. His energy was long drained. He lay there upon the island's beachhead for a few minutes before willing himself up into a sitting position—that was as far as his motivation took him. He failed to muster any more to change out of his suit and into his pajamas.

An exasperated sigh escaped his lips. As he scanned the room his eyes honed in on his wallet lying atop the table. Instinctively, he reached out for it. Then adjusted himself on the bed with back pressed against the headrest.

The first thing he pulled out was one of his calling cards—the generic make that Dr. Derek had given him. On it read: Ian Sharp, Consultant. Seeing the lie in boldface type only deepened his displeasure. *Is this what I am now?*

Sharp returned the card back to where it belonged and reached a finger into one of the folds of the wallet. From there he pulled out a bulky tiny square, folded multiple times over, no bigger than a fingernail. Undoing it, Sharp examined the picture he had secreted away.

A picture of his family: Katelyn standing beside a smiling Sharp adorned in his new navy blue uniform the day he graduated from OCS. Both held up a daughter in their arms: Susie with mom, Beth with dad. Still so young, they perched cozily in the nook of their parent's grasp with their hands wrapped around their necks. They stared forward with their best 'smile-for-the-camera' smiles plastered across their faces. All looking radiant in their vibrant Sunday dresses.

Sharp knew having this on his person went against protocol, but he couldn't bear parting with it. This picture depicted a time in his life when he felt his feet were planted firmly on the ground, yet his head was still wandering in the clouds.

But that's not his life anymore, it's someone else's. Someone else's wife, someone else's daughters, someone else's hopes and dreams. *What does that make me now?* Sharp wondered as he stared at the picture.

Rather than wallow any further down misery lane, Sharp banished the question from his thoughts, folded the picture into a tightly packed square, and jammed it deep into a crevice of the wallet. He threw it onto the table as he got up to change.

But before he could even slip out of his blazer the phone rang. Not his cellphone but the hotel phone stationed next to the bed on the nightstand. Its harsh buzz pierced the quiet of his room.

Sharp looked at the phone, confused.

He went over and picked up the receiver.

"Hello?" he answered cautiously.

"Is this Mr. Sharp?" a woman's voice asked. Sharp detected an accent.

"It is. Who may I say is speaking?"

"I know what you are doing here," the woman declared rapidly. "I know what you are looking for. I have the information. If you want it then come to room 415. And come alone."

She hung up leaving Sharp in a daze.

WADING THROUGH DARKNESS

Sharp stood in his hotel room with the receiver in hand, too dumbfounded to move. His mind struggled to absorb the flurry of words showered upon him so hurriedly.

As they congealed into comprehension, a swirl of questions swirled through his head: *who was this person? How did she track me down? Is this a trap? But who'd set a trap for him? And why?* Only one thing was certain: he wouldn't get the answers by just standing there.

Contemplating his next move he set down the receiver. *She said she had information,* Sharp deliberated, *she knew who I was. I should alert Braasch! But she said to come alone, does she know about Braasch?*

His heart racing, he went to the door and opened it. He looked to his left, then his right, all was silent. Stepping out he closed the door and felt the brisk night air on his face. He walked the length of the hotel, sneaking carefully past Braasch's room, and ascended the stairs two at a time till he reached the fourth floor. Even by then he still hadn't fully made up his mind what to do, he was driven more by curiosity and impulse than anything else.

He scanned his surroundings for anything, or anyone, out of the ordinary. His senses on high alert for any signs of foul play. The walkway was clear of any persons, and devoid of any crevices where someone could wait in ambush. The night sky emitted the usual dull tones of the late hour. Nothing appeared amiss. With that Sharp left the stairwell and advanced forward.

The lights in room 415 were out. Sharp stepped to the door, his heart beat nervously against his ribcage, and the hairs on the back of his neck stood on end. He inhaled deep, then exhaled. Glanced to his left, then his right. *This is the room,* Sharp hesitated, uncertainty bound his muscles still, *the one she gave me.*

"Mr. Sharp?" A voice called to him.

Sharp jumped to the side and fell into a fighting stance, his hands before him at the ready. Before him stood a woman shrouded in black: black gloves, black dress, black hat, black sunglasses. Only the tight brown skin of her exposed jaw lent her any color.

She stepped forward unfazed by his reaction. She was a good several inches shorter than him, roughly five-feet-four-inches. "Good, you came. Sorry to scare you, but I couldn't risk being trapped in there without an exit, in case you brought back up."

He whispered loudly, without dropping his guard. "Who are you?"

"Please, not here," she peered over the railing anxiously. "Let's go in."

She approached the door, produced the keycard, and slipped it into the reader. As she held the door open she glanced at Sharp. "Come on."

Against his better judgment, Sharp dropped his defensive stance and crossed the threshold into darkness.

He went for the light switch, but the woman barked out. "Don't. Leave it as it is."

She closed the door behind them, dousing them in complete darkness; except for the thin halo of streetlight pulsating around the edges of the closed window blinds. Sharp couldn't see anything, but he did feel the woman's presence shuffle around the room.

Swallowing down his apprehension, he asked, "Now tell me who you are." He heard something skid against a table top, possibly her sunglasses. "Why do you want to speak with me?"

"You're looking for who killed Luís Quadros," she stated, ignoring his question. Her voice was firm and business-like, but slightly frayed around the edges. "I know who did it."

Sharp's eyes nearly bugged out at the strange fortune at such a precipitous time. His lips failed to form words. A rush of excitement flooded his being. The mist evaporated revealing his escape from his desolate island.

The dim pulse of light shone upon a table beneath the window. Using that as his guide, Sharp motioned towards it with an outstretched hand. His fingers found a hard wooden plank floating in the darkness, and latched onto it. Easing into the chair, Sharp beckoned, "Go on."

"Before I tell you," she rasped pleadingly, "You must promise me that you'll believe me."

"That's a hard promise to make. I'd have to hear what you have to say first."

"No one else believes me," her voice broke, shaking like ice in a tumbler. Her silhouette came into focus as Sharp's eyes adjusted to the darkness. Her arms were crossed, and she appeared withered in her stance. "They just assume it's nothing more than the mad ravings of a woman in grief. But you'll believe me. Otherwise you wouldn't be here, right? In his neck of the woods."

Sharp slid his tongue against the back of his teeth as he listened to the woman's words tumble out of her. She tried her best to maintain control over herself, but her nerves were clearly shot to pieces. Any false step could send her plunging off the edge.

"Grief," he mulled the word aloud, dissecting its value in this given context till he discerned the woman's identity. "You're Anir Quadros, aren't you?" He asked pointedly.

She didn't respond immediately. Instead she fumbled for the other chair and sat down. Her jaw lifted high in the halo of streetlight. "That is correct."

"I heard you went missing. Got on a plane in the United States, but never got off in Brazil."

"Yes. It was the only way I could protect myself. I had to go into hiding. And it's been awful. I had to miss my own husband's funeral—can you imagine how hard that was? Not being able to share in his final moments as he's laid to rest six feet under? Would you be able to handle the loss of a loved one any better?"

"I'm not married," the lie came out easier than he would have liked.

Anir brushed his comment aside. "But I had to do it. Otherwise there would have been nobody to protect and carry on his vision for this country. *He* would have seen to the complete destruction of my husband's legacy. I refuse to let that happen."

"This 'he' you're talking about," Sharp ventured a stab in the dark, "is it Alexander Balthazar?"

Her silence was all the confirmation he needed—a howl reverberated through his subconscious and safe harbor seemed not too far in the offing.

Anir turned away, as if the very name were a burning brand upon her.

Sharp prodded on. "He killed your husband. And Senator Stedile too, right?"

She whipped her head forward and declared with complete conviction, "It was him! He murdered my husband. And he'd kill me too if he knew I was here. Send out that behemoth of a beast who's always with him. And he'll do it with a smile." She shuddered at the thought.

Behemoth of a Beast? Who's that? Sharp wondered. He decided to save that line of inquiry for later. Now was the time to tease out whatever information she had on Balthazar. He played skeptical. "How can you be so sure? I've only been here a day and have seen firsthand how supportive and charitable he is. He's sacrificing a lot by going up against the Bezerras. What you describe doesn't seem like something a man like him would do."

Anir exploded out of her chair and paced the room, drifting in and out of darkness, and berated Sharp in a fury. "Don't be an idiot! Don't think you can know someone after one day! I know him better than anyone else—I've seen the real side of him. His holier-than-thou persona is nothing more than a performance. Everything he's done has been expertly calculated to cultivate that image of him. The philanthropy, the religious devotion, his support of the occupation, all of it's a sham. The only person he cares about is himself. And if you believe he's got a single charitable bone in his body, then you're nothing more than a dupe. Just like all the rest!"

"But surely he cares for his workers? They worship him." Somewhere in his heart he could still feel the residual charge that surged through the congregation in the *usina*. A palpable energy that had sent Sharp adrift.

Anir stopped pacing, and stared at Sharp as if he were nothing more than a poor innocent naïve child. She scoffed. "They don't know any better. All they see is material improvement, and that's enough for them to turn a blind eye to the much more nefarious things he's done. And now he's trying to infiltrate the MST. He has to be stopped."

Sharp yearned to believe her, was ready to jump into the choir and sing alongside her, but he still found himself wading through darkness. No, this time he'd wait till he had the concrete evidence that went beyond mere coincidences to get his hopes up. He waded cautiously, "Why? And how do you know he's connected to the deaths of Quadros and Stedile?"

She stepped forward, her back ramrod straight, her eyes leering down at him. Anir spat out, "Integration."

"Integration?" Sharp repeated, his brows furrowed perplexed.

"It's been a dream for many Latin Americans ever since we declared our independence: One continent united, defending the region's autonomy and promoting our mutual interests. We achieved this somewhat with the formation of the Organization of Americans States in the mid-20th century. Twenty-one nations, including the United States, banded together to fight the spread of Communism in the Western Hemisphere. The integrationalists cheered its success, but their victory was short lived. When the Soviet Union fell, and the United States had long worn out its welcome, the integrationalists' vision soured. They began to grumble for an alternative—something truly independent from outside influences."

"That seems fair," Sharp commented, considering this desire no different than those that eventually spurred on the founding of the United Nations, or the European Union, or even NAFTA. Why would Latin America act any different?

"Not if Balthazar has his way," Anir countered. "He wants to take integration to the extreme."

"What do you mean?" Sharp inquired. "Why is he an integrationalist?"

Anir plopped into her seat, her upper body arched forward over the table as if ready to pounce upon an unsuspecting prey. She eyed Sharp. "How much do you know about Brazil's history?"

"Not much, I'm afraid," he replied sheepishly, squirming a little in his seat.

She sighed. "Well then, you're at least familiar with our military dictatorship, right?"

He nodded his head. Braasch—or was it Minister Griesel—had mentioned something about it in passing.

"Good." She eased back into her chair. "From '64 to '85 a succession of military dictators ruled over Brazil. It began when a coup overthrew the left leaning President João Goulart. And each one grew increasingly worse as they deepened their authoritarian control. They censored the media, exiled dissidents, and arrested and tortured those believed to have communist ties. It was awful. But all of that paled in comparison when Emílio Médici became president. His policies had the greatest impact on Alexander Balthazar, and helped shape his worldview.

"He was probably no more than four or five years old when it happened. When, in 1969, an armored vehicle drove up to the Balthazar Plantation, right up to their *hacienda*. It parked and several Military Police officers stormed in. No courtesy, no announcement. They simply rushed in and ransacked the place. Timothy Balthazar, his grandfather, confronted them, and demanded to know what they were doing. They said they were ordered to inspect the premises for anything subversive. Well Timothy Balthazar, angered now, yelled at them to stop, that his family had no connection to any communists. But the soldiers refused to listen and this led Timothy Balthazar to get physical.

"But it was useless. Timothy Balthazar was all bark but no bite. His temper ultimately got the better of him, and a soldier's fist laid him out flat on the ground almost instantly. Ending their search, the soldiers dragged the unconscious Timothy Balthazar to their vehicle and drove away. Alexander Balthazar watched all of this unfold.

"Days later the family finally received word of Timothy Balthazar. He had died in custody. This news shook the whole family. But that wasn't the end of it. When Timothy Balthazar's body was returned, his face was horribly disfigured, beaten badly when the police interrogated him. Seeing his grandfather's body sparked a burning rage inside Alexander Balthazar, fueling a hatred for the dictatorship, the government, and, especially, the United States."

"And what does the United States have to do with this?" Sharp asked.

She replied slowly, emphasizing each word. "They were the ones who approved the coup. They were the ones afraid that President João Goulart would bring communism to Brazil, and so they convinced the military to overthrow a democratically elected president. If they hadn't gotten involved then the Balthazar family wouldn't have suffered twenty years under dictatorial rule. Timothy Balthazar wouldn't have died. They, along with all of Brazil, might have prospered and grown in its own right as a regional superpower. If it hadn't been for the United States."

Sharp mulled this over silently in his head, *could this be a motive?* As he did his eyes screwed up reflexively in thought. However, Anir interpreted the expression as skepticism, and hurriedly blurted out to explain further:

"The United States has always been interfering in our development ever since the Monroe Doctrine. But, perhaps, the 1960s was the worst of it. Following Roosevelt's Good Neighbor Policy, it looked like the US was finally going to leave us alone in peace, develop the way we want. But then came Kennedy's Alliance for Progress which was anything but. So gung-ho on preventing another Cuba, his Alliance inadvertently propped up more dictators than ever before, and dismantled any democratic progress made up to that point. Growing up in a time like that would surely sour your view of the United States."

"So he'd want a united Latin America that could stand up against the United States," Sharp mused aloud. Anir nodded her head. Despite her confirmation, he still felt uncertainty at the new discovery, something in the logic wasn't lining up to his satisfaction. "I see why he'd be a strong integrationalist, but why go about it this way? Why kill Quadros and Stedile? Why support the Bezerra Occupation?" *Why the Santidade?* He left unsaid.

Anir deflated with a sigh. Slouching in her seat she reflected, "I don't know, but my husband knew. After he had been appointed Minister of Agrarian Development, Balthazar came to visit him. They discussed for roughly an hour in my husband's home office, and then Balthazar left in a huff. When they emerged I could tell immediately that they had been arguing. My husband came out shaking. Concerned, I asked what had happened, but he brushed it off as nothing more than a tense conversation. I should have pressed harder," she chastised herself, "If

I had made him tell me then I could have been better aware, and had prepared something. If only I had known."

"There's nothing you could have done," Sharp reasoned. "Even if you knew everything, there's no way you could have expected this."

"But I would have been alert!" She snapped, her body once again ready to attack. "I could have done something."

"Yes, you're right," Sharp submitted, noticing the fierce resolution in her eyes. This was not a fight worth having.

"So you do believe me, right?" She pleaded.

Sharp nodded. "But right now all this is still mere speculation. I need evidence, something a lot more concrete than this."

"I have something." Anir jumped up from the table and faded into the darkness that was the rest of the unlit room. Sharp heard her scrounging around a moment then reappeared holding a manila folder in her hands. "My husband had been collecting information." She plopped it onto the table before Sharp.

"Soon after that meeting with him, he started keeping a secret file on Balthazar. He thought I wouldn't notice, but I'd catch him staring intently at the morning newspaper and his eyes going big whenever an article mentioned Balthazar. He'd then hurry into his office and rip it out and put it in this folder." She fell into her chair. "Of course, I put all this together after Luís died. I'm just glad I had the foresight to have someone search his office for this file before Balthazar got to it."

Sharp reached a hand out, his heart thumping in his chest. Would this be his safe harbor? Flipping the file open, he found a treasure trove of torn out newspaper articles, official state documents, printed information from online sources, and scribblings jotted down on a single sheet of legal pad paper. All of it written in Portuguese.

Sharp stumbled and the mist threatened to consume him again.

As he sifted through the file, he expressed dejectedly, "I can't read any of this." He recognized some Spanish cognates, but not enough to gain a level of comprehension necessary for complete understanding. Perhaps in a week's time if he studied every document assiduously, but time was not on his side. Falling back in his chair Sharp sighed. "I can't use any of this."

"But it's all there!" Anir implored. "Everything I've been saying is supported by what my husband has collected here."

"I believe you," Sharp consoled, "it's just that I can't accept what you're saying at face value if I can't read the primary documents you say backs you up. You understand?"

Anir shuddered, her body contorting in a wild fit of exasperation. "Come on! Why would I lie to you? Alexander Balthazar killed my husband!"

He struggled to find the right words as his brain began shutting down for the night. It had endured enough for one day, and was now calling for sleep whether Sharp liked it or not. "Listen, I'm going to do everything I can to get to the bottom of this. Why don't you hold onto this," he motioned to the file with a nod of his head. "Keep it safe. And I'll figure out what I can do with it later. But for now I need to rest up for my meeting with Balthazar tomorrow."

"Okay," she relented. Leaning over, she started gathering up the collection of documents and returning them to the folder. "But I'm not staying here while you're off figuring out what to do," she declared disdainfully. "I have a flight tomorrow, and I'm going to be on it."

"Then how can I reach you?"

"I'll reach out to you. Hopefully it won't be too late by then." She swung the file under her armpit, then stated stoically, "Thank you for believing me."

He dismissed her platitude with a wave of his hand. "You have nothing to thank me for." Rising from his chair, he shuffled to the door. Before opening it, he glanced at the darkened outline of Anir

Quadros and said, "Thank you. I'll keep in mind what you've told me. And whatever happens, I will stop Balthazar."

"I trust you, Mr. Sharp," she whispered.

He stepped out into the walkway, closed the door behind him, and sighed. He felt horribly adrift.

THE PHOENIX

A loud cacophony of whining, revving, and screeching reverberated through the factory when Braasch and Sharp entered. Braasch looked well rested in a conservative pantsuit while Sharp appeared haggard with reddened droopy eyelids and the same suit he wore the night before—sans the tie due to the heat.

To the left of them stood a guard station where a heavyset security guard lounged about, moving only when his job required it. A puny fan directed hot air his way in a vain attempt to cleanse the perspiration dripping from his forehead. Seeing the Americans enter, he heaved forward, the chair squeaking under the pressure.

"*Olá, estamos aqui para ver Balthazar.*" Braasch had to shout in order to be heard, the large milling machines hummed a discordant tune that drowned out all other noise.

"*Deixe-me informá-lo de que você está aqui.*" The guard grabbed the phone. His armpits stained dark by sweat. When the line connected, he spoke for a moment then set down the receiver. "*Ele estará aqui em um momento.*"

"*Obrigado.*"

The Americans signed their names onto the visitation list and the guard handed them little badges marking them as visitors. Then handed them two sets of earplugs which Braasch and Sharp happily accepted. Once finished with the usual formalities, they waited for Balthazar.

Sharp undid another of his buttons, the heat was stifling despite all the open windows. How the laborers put up with it day after day, he couldn't imagine. And yet, here they were hustling large sacks of sugar around the factory and pouring its contents into the various machines. One millworker rolled a giant drum across the floor and positioned it with its brethren stationed at the ready. What it contained, Sharp had no idea.

A few minutes later the *gerente de usina de açúcar,* Gerhard Scharnhorst, approached them.

"Welcome," he shouted as he clapped the Americans on the shoulder and subtly pressed them together. Violating their personal space, he positioned his lips equidistant from their ears. "Senhor Balthazar is attending to a few things at the moment. He's asked me to show you around while you wait."

"It would be a pleasure," Sharp yelled back, unsure whether to be intimidated or not. Scharnhorst's massive build would have been cause enough, but the ease at which he physically repositioned them to his liking raised some alarm bells.

The German smiled gleefully, like a child gearing up to present his favorite toy during show and tell. Turning around, he motioned for them to follow as he explained the sugar-making process.

"Once the cane is cut," Scharnhorst began, "usually by hand, it is loaded onto trucks and transported to the *usina* to be processed. Unlike sugar beets, sugarcane can't be stored for later, it must be milled as soon as it leaves the field or else risk the loss of sucrose." He first guided them to the dock where several harvest trucks lined up in a row unused. "Of course, that won't begin for another few days. We're just getting the *usina* prepped for now."

From there he led them into a section where the machinery brought back memories of woodshop in high school. Several laborers hovered over exposed blades, sharpening them or setting them into place. "The cane is then fed into the machines here where they're shredded, crushed, and grinded to a pulp. Then transferred to that machine where imbibition occurs." He pointed to a contraption that looked like a giant industrial printing press merged with a car wash. High pressure water shot out of tiny spigots and blasted the empty rollers.

"Imbibition?" Sharp repeated, testing the word with his mouth.

The German nodded, smiling. "The water helps extract the juices from the crushed cane at a higher yield. A byproduct of this is bagasse, the residual woody fiber of the cane; used for fuel, paper products, and chemicals."

"Interesting," Sharp expressed. Sneaking a look at Braasch, her face failed to conceal her feelings on the subject: she couldn't care less.

Continuing on, Scharnhorst detailed the rest of the process as they walked the perimeter:

"These gentlemen here are clarifying the juices by straining it till they've removed any large particles. Pretty much they put the extracted juices into a centrifuge and compress it into a filtercake we call 'mud.' That can be used as an animal feed supplement, fertilizer, or sugarcane wax."

"The clarified juice is then brought here." Scharnhorst declared stopping in a room lined with giant vats—the source of the stifling heat pervading the *usina*. It was well above one hundred degrees. Scharnhorst shouted over the loud churning of the vats. "These are the evaporators." He swung an arm towards the giant vats. "The sugar is poured in through the open top of the first one and then boiled into syrup." Stairs wrapped around the largest vat and led to a small grated platform. A laborer stood atop it inspecting the swirling of the molten sugar. "Right now, that gentleman is inspecting the vats to make sure they're good to go. Safety around the evaporators is our highest priority. The majority of deaths at any sugar mill usually occur in the evaporator station. One small slip by our workers and they could get an arm sheared right off by the burning temperature of the sugar or be boiled to death."

As Scharnhorst spoke, Balthazar, dressed in his perpetually white suit, came into view. He crossed to the stairs leading up to the overseer's office and ascended them, stopping halfway. Locking eyes onto Scharnhorst, he gave a nod of his head to indicate for them to join him, then disappeared into the office.

"Looks like we'll have to cut the tour short," Scharnhorst explained. "He's ready to see you. If you'll follow me." He led them away from the evaporators, though the heat seemed to surround them no matter how far they traveled.

"Greetings, friends," Balthazar welcomed them into the tiny office with a hearty smile, an unlit cigar wedged between his teeth. They shook hands, exchanging kindly platitudes, then settled into the chairs available. In the center a metallic desk with a computer monitor on top divided the room between Braasch and Sharp on one side and Balthazar on the other. Scharnhorst stood in the middle, his back pressed against the wide rectangular window that overlooked the *usina* floor.

"Thank you for taking the time to meet with us," Braasch offered, "especially with what happened last night."

Balthazar brushed her concerns away with a wave of his hand. "They have to do better than that if they want to scare me. All they did was show how desperate they're getting. The Bezerras are losing the battle, and now they're resorting to basic intimidation. And that gives me hope."

Removing his white fedora, he set it on the desk and leaned forward, his fingers interlocked. His voice grew business-like. "Now, what may I help you with? As I understand you are journalists for the…" He glanced at Scharnhorst.

"The New Yorker," Scharnhorst said. "Here to do a story on the Bezerra Occupation."

Balthazar's brown eyes lit up and a smile creased his lips. "Wonderful. So the American's have finally taken notice of what's going on here. Or is this merely a side effect of all the attention we're receiving from our little spat with you?"

"Neither, I'm afraid," Braasch admitted. "This standoff has sucked up all the oxygen making it hard for any other story to breathe."

"Then why are you here?" He inquired. "Shouldn't you be covering the major news of the day?"

"I said it was making it hard to breathe, not impossible. There's a story here, and, if we're lucky, we might be able to give it life. The opportunity is ripe for it since the United States has its attention turned here already. Might as well take advantage of that. Don't you agree?"

"Of course!" Balthazar confirmed heartily. "I couldn't agree more. If the Bezerra Occupation were to receive international attention then that would give us greater leverage. The Bezerras would have to surrender to our demands or face global condemnation. So then..." He fell back in his chair already basking in preemptive triumph, "...where would you like to start?"

Sharp piped up as Braasch pulled out her recorder. "Well, first things first, we'd like to know a little about you. Your employees often refer to you as the Pope of Sugar, can you tell us how exactly you came to be seen as the Pope of Sugar?"

"I took over the family plantation when my father died." Balthazar put on his stately preacher-voice. *Must come naturally now,* Sharp observed sardonically, *whenever it's show time.* "This happened not too long after the dictatorship had ended and all of Brazil was still in that transition period—a rocky time when things were still uncertain. And here I am, a young naïve entrepreneur, suddenly thrusted into this role of CEO. I was not ready—a few years out of college and still struggling to find my calling in life—I had yet to gain the experience of the real world needed to run such a massive business like this. But I did what was required of me and did my best to navigate through this time of uncertainty.

"However, the dictatorship had been rough on us. For the first ten years or so we were constantly on the verge of collapse. It was the lowest point in our plantation's history. But through it all the laborers, the men and women out there in the fields and here in the mill, showed great resolve and dedication to this plantation. They refused to give up. And, because of them, sometime around 2004 or 2005, we finally turned a corner: we were exporting more sugar than ever before and our profits skyrocketed. And I saw this for what it was. God himself had stepped in and saved us. He was sending me a message. And I listened. He shined a light upon me and bathed me in his glory. I never fully believed in Him until then. But I am thankful that He is a patient shepherd."

"And what was the message?" Sharp asked, ever mindful of what Anir had told him last night. *He thinks himself a sheep…*

"A calling. A purpose. He wanted me to use my position to take care of His flock. Because it was His flock who had saved this plantation, had saved me. And so, I dedicated the rest of my life to share my wealth—the good Christian way—and improve the conditions of His flock right here in Limoeiro. And thus, they have named me the Pope of Sugar."

…so saith the wolf beneath.

"I have done much already, donated a vast amount to help rebuild and modernize Limoeiro, but money alone will never be enough." Balthazar broke eye contact and glanced down at nothing in particular, his brows arched pensively. "If we are truly going to live in a Godly world, then so much more will be required of us. We must stamp out the worst of the seven deadly sins—" he locked eyes with Sharp, "—greed." He spat out the last word with such great venom that it struck a chord somewhere in Sharp—he nearly believed.

But Sharp resisted, this was Balthazar's power after all: persuasion. He could convert the most obstinate critic into a loyal follower just by the power of his voice. Yet, as far as Sharp knew, there had been one who defied him completely, so Balthazar had him killed. *Have to find the chink in the armor first, can't let him fool me.*

Sharp ventured, "so then would you consider the Bezerra Occupation more of a religious crusade than a land reform movement?"

"Oh most definitely. The Bezerras hoard their money, and their land, and use it only to further enrich themselves. While the Landless Workers suffer and starve. I find it deplorable!" He jumped out of the chair and sauntered over to the window. Staring out at the *usina* floor, he watched his workers as he spoke. "Thus, when I heard that the MST were planning on occupying the Bezerra Plantation I knew in my heart that I had to support it. Not from a distance, safe from any repercussions, but right there in the thrall of it. I had to be seen if this occupation was to have a fighting chance."

"And did you ever reach out to Minister Quadros about this? I hear he was very vocal about land reform."

Balthazar snapped his head to the side, the dark brown iris of one eye peered over his shoulder and trained on Sharp. "That is true, but no. Never had a chance to meet with him while he was Minister. But our paths did cross a few times before. He would have been a great help if he were still here today." His words rang false to Sharp's ear—not because he knew already that he was lying, but there was a hatred in his words that made it impossible for him to say them believably. Everyone had a limit, and Sharp might have found Balthazar's.

He pressed on, "If I may be so bold, do you think the Bezerras might have assassinated Minister Quadros? No doubt when he returned from his trip he'd come here to oversee the occupation, right? Wouldn't the Bezerras want to prevent that from happening?"

Balthazar shook his head as he turned fully around. "No."

"Then what of Senator Stedile? We heard that he was in the process of negotiating a peace deal between the Bezerras and the Occupation."

"Remind me again what your story's about." Balthazar deflected, a curious suspicion hung on his words.

"This occupation," Sharp fumbled to reply, realizing he had pressed harder than he should have.

"I thought so." Balthazar stepped forward. "Their deaths are a tragedy, but they are of no relation to this occupation."

"I understand," he relented, "But I wouldn't be doing my job if I didn't, at least, ask, right?"

One side of his lips stretched into a tight smirk. "I guess I shouldn't blame you for your interest," Balthazar dismissed him, then rounded back to his chair behind the desk. "Why shouldn't two Americans be concerned? But I caution you that if you allow this standoff to consume your every thought then you're going to start seeing boogeymen everywhere, making connections where there are none. And that'll make for a troubling recipe. See what I mean?"

Sharp glanced at Braasch. Her brows shifted slightly signaling him to play it easy. He got the message, but a growling faded into his consciousness. *If I don't strike now then I'll never know the truth.*

"Sorry," he said, "Though if I may, Quadros and Stedile were important figures for the MST and I saw personally the effect their deaths had on the MST in Brasília. Emotions are high right now, and someone wanted it to be that way. If you don't think it's the Bezerras then who do you think was behind their deaths?"

Sharp could see the veins in Balthazar's neck twitch as he listened, his austere façade cracking. He was silent for a moment before he opened his mouth to respond. "The best journalists are the most determined, and you certainly are determined." He pointed a finger at Sharp. "But I think you're asking the wrong person. My focus is on the occupation, and the management of my plantation," Balthazar added as an afterthought, "I don't have time to play detective in these matters. But I'm sure that is not an answer you want to hear." Though smiling, his eyes offered a challenge. "Perhaps you should search a little closer to home. Your country hasn't always been on the level, after all."

There!

"Are you suggesting that the U.S. government might have been involved here?"

"Oh don't be so obtuse with me. It's what they do when they feel someone has swayed too far from the 'Washington consensus.'" Sharp felt the heat in his words. "You see, Mr. Sharp, Latin America has been nothing but one big workshop for the United States ever since the Monroe Doctrine. Testing new imperial designs before applying it to the world at large."

"So what you're suggesting is that the United States wanted to plunge Brazil into class warfare, because you didn't follow this 'Washington Consensus'"?

Balthazar shrugged. "If Johnson can incite a military coup here, and Nixon can make the Chilean economy scream, then I wouldn't put it past them to do this."

"But why Quadros in particular?"

"Agricultural dominance," he spat out without hesitation. "Can't have any real competition on the global market."

"So then that must mean you approve of what President Rousseff is doing?" Sharp felt Braasch's hand press against his forearm and squeeze. He ignored it, staring firmly at Balthazar. But he couldn't ignore how tight his muscles had become in this rapid exchange.

"Senhor," Scharnhorst interjected but Balthazar lifted a hand silencing him. He, too, had grown rigid.

Focused only on Sharp, he licked his lips. "Now do I approve of how she's going about it? Not necessarily. But do I approve that she's standing up against the United States? Of course. Any proud Brazilian should stand behind their leader in times like these on principle."

"That's fair," Sharp relaxed, attempting to play at ease. "So then you'd consider yourself an integrationalist?"

Though unmoving like a stone, lightning bolts flashed across Balthazar's eyes. Then all was calm again. "What do you mean?" He inquired with an even tone.

But Sharp had seen it—the very word ignited something inside him. "Well, from what I understand there are those who want Latin

America unified under one coalition of nations. They call themselves integrationalists. Seems like a unified South America would better be able to resist the encroachment of the United States, wouldn't you say?"

Balthazar nodded slowly. "Yes, but I never gave much thought to that. I'm afraid I'm not too familiar with the subject. Too busy preparing for the harvest."

"And the occupation," Sharp amended.

"And the occupation," Balthazar repeated.

"I think we've got enough for today," Sharp declared, rising from his chair. "We better be off." He looked at Braasch and nodded. She went for the recorder and pressed it off. "Thank you for your time."

"Anytime." Balthazar rose and extended a hand to the Americans. As they exchanged handshakes, he said, "Please call again, and if this occupation succeeds you're welcome to attend the celebration."

"Of course." Sharp offered him a firm grip and a steely stare.

As the Americans walked down the stairs, across the factory floor, and out into the open air, Sharp knew he was on the right path and had already decided his next course of action. It was time to put into use a particular set of skills he had been trained in. He'd return to the *usina* later tonight under the cover of darkness, sneak into that office, and find the evidence that'll break this case wide open. He'll bring down Balthazar once and for all, and finally prove his worth.

THE *USINA* AFTER DARK

Sharp spent the rest of the day preparing for his late night excursion. He endured Braasch's reprimand of his behavior with Balthazar all the way back to the hotel, then appeased her by submitting to her conclusion that nothing of value was gained and thus they should return to Brasília as soon as possible. In his hotel room, he ruffled through his bag for his blackest clothes, set them out, then lay on the bed for a few hours nap. His alarm chirped to life at 8pm.

Across the street Sharp had himself something to eat at the strip mall and returned to his room to begin final preparations. He took a shower, changed into his black clothes, and mentally readied himself for what he was about to do. Then came the waiting, the most excruciating point when adrenaline rushes you forward to only discover you're ahead of the game. The next few hours felt like years, but, just like everything else, they soon passed, and Sharp bolted for the door.

The night sky was bathed in a starless black. Sharp walked the length of the hotel at a casual pace, looking around him for any obtrusive onlookers. Nobody was about. As he sailed past Braasch's room, he found her curtains drawn close. He whispered a silent thank you for that small fortune, then dipped down to one knee next to their car. Though Braasch had the keys, Sharp knew of other ways to gain access. From his pocket, he pulled out a tiny felt pouch. Unzipping it, the pouch fell open in the palm of his hands revealing a variety of small metallic tools carefully strapped into their respective places. They resembled dentist equipment, each one oddly shaped at the tip. Sharp ran a finger over them pondering his selection. He pulled one out and set to work.

In his younger days he would have jimmied it in seconds, but the skill had long turned to rust after a time of disuse. But the habit of keeping that pouch on him had remained seared into his brain. Ever since his father handed it to him, he refused to part with it, though in the last few years he carried it more as a burdensome reminder than anything else.

Click.

Sharp slipped into the driver's seat and unscrewed the panel beneath the steering wheel exposing the wires. He found the ones he wanted and played with them for a bit until the engine revved to life. "I still got it," he congratulated himself.

Sharp guided the car out of the parking lot and turned onto the main road heading towards the *usina.*

As he drove a thirsty growl bounded through his mind. If all went well then Sharp should find the hard evidence he needed to link Balthazar to the deaths of Quadros and Stedile, reveal his plan with the Bezerra Occupation, and thwart his integrationalist schemes. Thus confirming his abilities as a secret agent and earning him the respect and admiration of both Sir and Braasch. He'd no longer be a listless soul wandering aimlessly through life, he'll finally make something of himself: a distinguished agent, a proud father, and a worthy son. Then, when back in San Diego, Sharp will receive a well-deserved promotion and a choice of any assignment he desires. A smile spread across his lips at the thought, it'll be the start of a grand future—a future that began tonight.

Sharp killed his headlights, pulled off the road onto the dirt side, and parked. Getting out, he scanned his left and his right for any late night travelers, he was all alone in darkness. He walked the rest of the way to the *usina.*

Sharp approached the premises carefully, ever alert. He kept his ears open for the slightest sound that gave warning to another's presence, perhaps the crunch of gravel under a boot. His eyes welcomed the yellow-orange glow of the overhang lamps. As he crossed the parking lot, a strange tingling ran up his spine.

Where are the guards? He inquired. Sharp had expected tougher security; that most of his time here would have been consumed with him maneuvering through a line of guards just to get into the *usina*—especially with what happened the other night—but the place felt eerily deserted. *Perhaps off doing patrol or something,* he reasoned.

Brushing his concern aside, he scurried over to the personnel entrance and checked the lock; it seemed simple enough for him. He retrieved his pouch and twisted the necessary tools in the keyhole.

Click.

Sharp smirked at his accomplishment. *Almost seems too easy. I'll be in and out in no time.*

He pressed down on the handle slowly and nudged the door open a crack. Once wide enough he slipped through and examined the darkness for security. None were to be found inside as well. That eerie feeling crept over him like a spider walking across his flesh, it made his skin prickle. *They must be focusing their attention on the fields rather than the* usina. *Better hurry, before they show up.*

Sharp cut across the factory floor through the shallow pools of moonlight that drifted in through the windows. Ascending the stairs, he wrapped his fingers around the doorknob to the overseer's office and found it locked. But it wasn't for long.

The door swayed open as Sharp pulled out a flashlight. He flipped it on and entered the office. Advancing around the metallic desk, he inspected the filing cabinet first. It, too, was locked, that is until he did his magic with his tools.

He pulled the handle of the highest drawer and thumbed through the files. The tabs were marked in Portuguese but the simplicity of the phrases allowed Sharp to comprehend and fill in any gaps. They revealed nothing of value: mostly old harvest records and invoices. The second drawer offered pretty much the same mundane run of the mill information. As he leafed through the tabs, the gremlin of disappointment reared its ugly head. But Sharp refused to submit, the night was still young for him and his search had barely begun. He'll find something.

Bending down on one knee, he slid open the third and final drawer. It, too, threatened to wound his ego further, but the deeper into the drawer he went, he noticed a change in the tab markings. They shifted away from the daily operation of the plantation and began expressing more scientific language such as: 'Mosaic Virus,' and 'Sucrose Yield,' and 'Cane Variety 3X.' Sharp had no idea what this all meant, but the tabs had piqued his interest. He pulled out the last one and flipped through it.

From what he could understand, the document inside came from the Research Department describing their recent breakthrough in their development of an advanced strain of sugarcane. The words 'Cane Variety 3X' popped up several times throughout their summary. The further Sharp skimmed a picture began to form in his head, but it was still too blurry to fully make out. He placed the file back where it belonged once he reached the portion where an abundance of scientific jargon and equations dominated the page. As he did, a thought popped into his head:

Braasch would love this. She'd be able to decipher these files if she was here.

He felt the clump weigh down his heart.

Continuing his search, another file caught his attention. This one was labeled: "Occupation".

"What's this about?" He whispered as he pulled the folder out to examine it. Inside were bound pages describing the Bezerra lands, the operations and strategies of the MST, and the historical success of land occupations. All of it meticulously gathered and compiled into a short and easily digestible report of sorts. *Why does Scharnhorst have this?*

Outside of the report, a few loose papers dangled precariously in the folder. Sharp set the report aside and perused the papers. He found one where scrawled across the top of it in a mechanical handwriting were the numbers 12082011. *A date*, Sharp easily discerned. *What does he have planned for December 8th, a good six months from now?* Underneath the date were two columns, on the left a list of names and on the right dollar amounts. Though Sharp didn't recognize any of the names, he couldn't help but notice the generous sums they were to receive for their services—at least six digits.

A buoyant sensation coursed through his veins, Sharp knew he uncovered something important, he could feel it, but he couldn't celebrate just yet. He still had more of the office to search through before the night was over. Placing the report back into the folder, he set it alongside its brethren and closed the cabinet drawer.

Immediately, he hoisted himself up to full height and swung his flashlight around landing upon the computer monitor sitting atop the metallic desk. Turning it on, Sharp produced the flash drive Dr. Derek had given him and stuck it into the USB port, then pulled out his cell phone and dialed the R&D department of Sector Seven. It rang three times before someone picked up:

"Hello?" A familiar voice answered.

"Hello, this is Ian Sharp," he whispered softly.

"Oh, hello Ian Sharp, it's a pleasure to hear you! This is Dr. Derek," the voice announced suddenly exuberant. "I knew you'd call at some point. How's the mission going?"

Settling into Scharnhorst's chair, he replied, "It's going well, even had someone try to kill me the other day, but that's been taken care of."

"That's good to hear. And how are you liking Brazil?" Sharp heard something creak, perhaps Dr. Derek's chair as he leaned back.

"Listen Dr. Derek," he cut the small talk short. "I need you to hack into a computer. I've already inserted the flash drive into the USB port."

The creaking sounded again. "Ok, give me a minute." Through the receiver came the rapid tapping of fingers on a keyboard.

As he waited for Dr. Derek to work his magic, Sharp set the phone to speaker mode and rested it on top of the desk.

"This is a little harder than I thought." Dr. Derek muttered to himself. "Everything's in Portuguese. I've got to first get everything translated before I can do anything else."

"Fine, just hurry it up."

The clicking of the keys continued for another minute as he mumbled his actions to no one in particular. Finally, he spoke up again, "Alright I've got it."

Sharp leaned forward, eager to search Scharnhorst's computer. He put his fingers to the mouse and stared at the screen. Then he froze. Shifting his gaze to his phone, he asked sheepishly, "Um...Dr. Derek?"

"Yes, Sharp?"

"What should I be looking for?"

Dr. Derek chuckled. "You newbies. Was there anything in the desk that might help us out?"

"Well there were several scientific files in his cabinet, all from the research department."

"Ooohh Excellent," he cooed, "Then check that out first. I'd love to see what a Brazilian agricultural research department is up to. The flash drive lets me see everything you're doing on the computer here at headquarters. I'll help where I can."

Obliging, Sharp clicked through several folders on the desktop, searching for anything that sounded scientific. Most of them were filled with accounting ledgers, maintenance reports, and worker info. But the deeper he looked, he eventually stumbled upon a curious collection of Scharnhorst's interests. One folder titled '*foco* theory' caught Sharp's eye and when he clicked on it, he found a smattering of Che Guevara musings and other Marxist revolutionary literature of Cuba. He then clicked on another folder called 'Eldorado de Carajás.' That brought up a catalog of newspaper clippings, pictures, and news videos of the massacre.

He's definitely been doing his research.

Finally, he landed upon a folder he'd been looking for: 'Variety (Experimental).' Inside were about twenty to thirty videos. Sharp chose one at random and watched.

The shot opened on a scientist with a mustache reaching behind the camera, adjusting it. He appeared youthful with jet black hair though a few age lines began to crease the edges of his lips. A lab coat hung over his shoulders and a blue shirt unbuttoned at the top alongside a loosened tie exhibited his exhaustion. Once the camera was to his liking, the scientist sat back and looked into the camera lens. A laboratory of metallic tables with sugarcane specimens scattered about in wide pans played background. The specimens all varied in size, some growing as high as the ceiling while others wilted pathetically. The scientist opened his mouth to speak, his words drenched in weariness.

"Emílio Figueiredo, recording on March 29th. So far everything has gone exceedingly well. We were able to divide the cells of our Sugar Specimen A and splice them in with Sugar Specimen B. The newly mutated cells appear to be handling the reproduction process well and have currently taken over a third of the root." He wheeled around throwing the spotlight onto the pan of sugarcane closest to the camera, two different colored varieties encompassed it. "We expect it to successfully take over the entire sugarcane shoot in about two weeks to a month."

Dr. Figueiredo turned back and addressed the camera once again. "If it is able to pass the stage that all the other experiments have stalled at, then we can begin the next phase of our research." He shook his head unsure of how to proceed. "For now, this is just a waiting game. I've let the other members off early for the week and have set myself up temporarily in the other room." He shifted the focus of the camera to the left revealing a doorway leading into a small room where a cot had been set up, draped in a green bedspread.

When he brought the camera back upon himself, the creases upon his brows had deepened. Inhaling, he slumped in his chair and began to fidget. A worriedness entered his voice. "I know, Senhor Scharnhorst, you want to keep up to date on *everything* that goes on around here so..." Dr. Figueiredo looked around, hesitated, then forced himself to continue in a conspiratorial whisper:

"One of the other members of our little project has started to ask questions." He smiled timidly. "Dr. Neves believes we are focusing too much on Variety 3X and not spending enough time on the mosaic virus. I explained to him its importance, but he still continues to argue with me. So far he hasn't been too much of a problem, but in due time he may become too much to handle." Dr. Figueiredo paused. "I suggest giving him about a week or two off. I think his time in the lab has gotten to him. He needs to be out in the sun for a while. I hope you can arrange something for him, Senhor Scharnhorst. Well, that's all for now. Emílio Figueiredo, ending recording." Then the video cut to black.

Silence pervaded the office for a moment before Dr. Derek's voice broke the silence. "Well, that was interesting."

"What do you think it means?"

"For one, they're willing to have their lab boys video record their progress. Sector Seven doesn't even allow me to record my thoughts on a tape recorder. We've lost so many good ideas because we couldn't get to a pen in time."

Sharp rolled his eyes. "Dr. Derek, I'm talking about what he was saying."

"Oh yes, of course," he blustered then paused in thought. "I don't know."

"Thanks for the help," said Sharp.

"Click on another one. Let's see what else they've got."

Sharp obeyed.

The next recording opened to three scientists standing over a single table in the middle of the same lab seen in the previous video, except this time the view was positioned higher up like a surveillance camera. The scientists spoke over themselves while intently focused on whatever held their attention. That's when the door located in the far back opened and in walked Scharnhorst. The scientists went silent as they acknowledged his presence.

"And what progress do we have today?" Scharnhorst asked, stepping closer to them. The scientists backed away from the table revealing a pan of immature sugarcane. Leaning over, Scharnhorst inspected it.

Dr. Figueiredo broke away from the bunch and peered over the specimen, pointing at the sugarcane now in perfect view of the camera. As he detailed their success, excitement carried his words. "We planted the mutated variety on this side," he began, "and on this side the normal variety. As you can see, the mutated one has a whiter color than the rest. When we began, we planted only two seeds of the mutated variety. As you can see, the white sugarcane is now about a third of the pan."

Scharnhorst shook his head, unimpressed. "And what do you make of this?"

The smile on Dr. Figueiredo's face lessened a little and he became fidgety again. He stuttered out, "Ah...Well, we...um." He cleared his throat. "It means we've officially mapped out the mosaic virus on a genetic level. We can manipulate it however we want now. With this information we'll have no problem eradicating the mosaic virus on a genetic level."

Scharnhorst gave a nod of approval. "Good work. I'd like a more detailed report on my desk by the end of the week."

"Yes sir."

Scharnhorst turned to leave but when he reached the door he stopped, turned, and eyed Dr. Figueiredo. "And what about the Variety 3X? How is that going?"

The scientist shrugged. "Oh that. That one will take a little longer to produce results, but we did just plant a new batch that already seems promising."

"Alright, well, make sure that's in the report as well." He was about to leave when Dr. Figueiredo called him.

"Um, sir? Do you know when Dr. Neves will be back from his vacation?"

Scharnhorst shrugged his shoulders and left.

Sharp paused the recording. "Did you get all that, Dr. Derek?"

"I did, Sharp, and I don't like the sound of them messing around with viruses. Why don't you copy these videos onto the flash drive and let Braasch take a look? She's got a degree in biology, if I remember correctly. Maybe she'll be able to shed some light on it."

"That's a good idea. She might know what this Variety 3X thing is." Sharp slid the videos into the flash drive folder.

"Is there anything else that you need from me?" asked Dr. Derek.

Before Sharp could speak, the lights outside Scharnhorst's office flashed on, startling him. He whispered quickly, "Not anymore, I have to go, bye." He quickly hung up, shut down the computer, and placed the phone and flash drive into his pockets. *The guards finally arrived.*

Peeking out the window, Sharp scanned the ground floor, waiting to see who was there. Scharnhorst materialized from behind one of the machines and walked directly to the stairs leading to the office. Sharp's entire upper body fell in shock. *What is he doing here at this hour?*

Immediately, he tore himself away from the window and looked for a place to hide. The clanking of Scharnhorst's shoes on the metal staircase sent Sharp diving under the desk. He swallowed hard and listened carefully, his arms wrapped around his knees.

He heard the doorknob jiggle then the lights flashed on.

THE GERMAN, GERHARD SCHARNHORST

Sharp listened to the slow methodical clopping of Scharnhorst's stride. Each step exploded in his ears like a thunderclap. Inhaling deep, he attempted to swallow a soundless breath, but it lodged in his throat unleashing a strained gasp. He clapped a hand over his mouth to silence it. A bead of sweat sailed down his forehead. Closing his eyes, he prayed for Scharnhorst to do whatever business he had and leave.

In that moment an epiphany struck him: *That's why there were no guards. Scharnhorst knew.* Sharp's chest deflated at the realization. *I willingly walked right into his trap.*

The footfalls died just on the other side of the desk. And Sharp waited, anticipating. His pounding heart traveled up through his throat and settled in his ears, deafening him. Sweat matted the ridge of his hairline and a numbing sensation flowed from his fingertips down to his wrist. His throat went dry. Each passing second turned to hours, and little by little Sharp lost control of his faculties as he waited for the German to make his move.

But the German didn't move.

What is he doing? Sharp worried as the synapses in his brain fired off one plan of attack after another. All distilled down to four main options: fight, flight, posture, or submit. None sounded viable; he'd be easily outmatched, he'd be risking the mission, he'd be exposed as the fraud he is, or he'd be killed instantly. He sat scrunched under the desk mentally paralyzed.

Then Scharnhorst struck.

A hand wrapped around the desk and latched onto Sharp's collar. A scream lodged in his throat. Scharnhorst yanked him out from under the desk and laid him flat on top of it, knocking over the computer monitor. Sharp lay there stunned, staring into the dark and menacing eyes of Scharnhorst. His lips split into a twisted smile.

"Mr. Sharp. What a surprise it is to find you here," Scharnhorst welcomed, then sent a fist against Sharp's jaw. He absorbed the blow without any reaction, his neurons short-circuited disrupting any communications from his brain to the rest of his body. "Senhor Balthazar was right about you. Though I had my suspicions right from the start." A left hook collided into Sharp's cheek. A spot of blood blossomed from the newly split skin. "I can spot another military man a mile away. And you, sir, are a military man. A novice at that, or incompetent."

The German's words snapped Sharp back into consciousness. Regaining control of his being, he flailed wildly atop the desk, his arms and legs united in their solitary desire for escape. They thrashed about searching for a target when his knee made contact with Scharnhorst's stomach. He gasped and stumbled back.

Scharnhorst's eyes lit up. "So you do have some fight in you. Good. I've been waiting for a challenge." He wheeled his head from side to side and cracked his knuckles. Looking at Sharp with joyful anticipation, Scharnhorst charged forward, thrusting his arms before him. But the heel of Sharp's shoe connected with the bridge of his nose. A trickle of blood stained his upper lip. The German wiped it away with the back of his hand and sniffed hard.

Sharp floundered off the desk and crashed to the floor. Flat on his stomach he scurried on all fours toward the door as fast he could. However Scharnhorst seized him by the leg before he could get too far and hoisted him into the air upside down. Hovering inches off the ground, Sharp gawked in amazement, *How strong is this guy?* A powerful jab to his midsection knocked the wonder out of him.

Scharnhorst released him and Sharp fell splat on the floor. Wounded, he nursed his aching abdomen with his arms as he curled up into a ball. The contents of his stomach threatened to unload themselves, but Sharp tempered the sensation as best he could.

A cruel laugh escaped the German's lips as he stood over Sharp. "What's wrong? Tummy ache?" He mocked. Then, wheeling back his leg, he leveled a series of kicks and stomps upon Sharp's side. Not too hard, just enough to antagonize, like a child poking a sleeping bear with a stick. Sharp endured the assault unable to respond as water welled around the edges of his closed eyelids. Realizing his failure to awaken the bear, Scharnhorst stopped. He stared down at Sharp, his face twisted in disappointment at his prey. Sharp spat out a glob of spit and blood onto the floor.

Kneeling down on bended knee, Scharnhorst clasped Sharp's jaw between his fingers. He waited for Sharp to open his eyes before speaking. "I'm going to enjoy this. A good chance to dust off my... *advanced interrogation* skills." He savored his words. "First I will break you piece by piece until I have obtained all the information you have behind those beautiful green eyes of yours. Then, as you beg for me to kill you, I will satisfy—"

A backhand sailing across his cheek clipped Scharnhorst's words short. Surprised, he teetered backwards releasing Sharp's jaw, and stood there momentarily dazed. Immediately Sharp jumped to his feet and stumbled out of the office. He flew down the metal staircase, raced across the *usina* floor, and dashed towards the exit. Flight it was to be.

I have to get out.

The mantra rang through his head.

I have to get out.

Fighting against his pain, and the urge to vomit, Sharp focused all his attention on running. He willed his legs to move faster beyond their abilities and inhaled controlled gasps of air as his traumatized lungs pleaded for more. His left arm cradled his right arm which had suffered the bulk of Scharnhorst's antagonizing.

I have to get out.

Sharp reached out a hand ready to grasp the door handle. He felt its smooth surface on his fingertips…

I have to get out.

…But something wrapped around his waist and heaved him backwards. The force sent his legs out from underneath him and he crashed hard against the concrete. Defeat washed over him as his body collapsed in exhaustion. Staring up at the grated ceiling, tears flowed from his eyes.

Scharnhorst stepped into his vision and leaned over him. His face contorted into a tight grimace.

A jolt of lighting surged through Sharp's nerves, he immediately began scooting backwards, his right hand thrust out defensively. "Please, please, please. I'll do whatever you want. Just don't hurt me." He submitted. "I'll tell you whatever you want." Fear filled his eyes and a tremor shook his lips. "Please, don't kill me." His back pressed up against a wall of the *usina* but that didn't stop his retreat, he continued as if trying to meld into the wall itself.

Scharnhorst followed him, clearly enjoying Sharp's whimpering performance. "Don't worry," he soothed, "You'll tell me everything you know one way or another. I'll squeeze all the information out of you. Every little drop. Then, once I'm satisfied, that's when I'll kill you. The faster you tell me, the quicker your suffering will end." He unleashed a low chuckle.

"Now," he breathed out as he inspected Sharp's body, who lay there helpless and shivering. "What am I to do?" Sweeping a glance from one side of the *usina* to the other, Scharnhorst reviewed the machines at his disposal. "Could use the plainer first. Flay a finger or two, how does that sound?"

Sharp breathed heavily. His head bowed down.

Scharnhorst shook his head. "No, too messy. What about imbibition? I've always been a fan of water torture."

Sharp shuddered at the thought, but showed no signs of resistance. Instead, he appeared weaker than before, sniveling, hoping Scharnhorst would see this and take pity on him.

"I got it." Scharnhorst snapped his fingers as a light bulb went off in his head. He bent down to Sharp's level. "I'm going to dip you into a vat of boiling sugar. Inch by inch."

Sharp's body went rigid.

Noticing this, Scharnhorst smiled. "Bingo."

As Scharnhorst rose to his full height, Sharp quickly reassessed his situation and switched tactics. "You can't," he stammered, finding his voice nothing more than a squeak. He cleared his throat and repeated in a firmer tone. "You can't."

"And why not?"

Bracing the wall, Sharp staggered to his feet. He held his head up and chest out, and stared Scharnhorst dead in the eye. Time to posture. "Because if anything happens to me then my partner will release everything we know about what you and Balthazar are planning. All of Brazil will know."

"Is that so?"

Sharp nodded.

Scharnhorst shook his head. "I don't believe you."

"What?" Sharp faltered.

"If you were truly working with your partner—Braasch, right? If I remember correctly—then she'd be here. But she isn't. You're here alone. And besides, nobody will believe you. Balthazar has worked hard cultivating an image of saintliness. His followers will never turn on him no matter how much evidence you provide. They will be loyal to the end." He stepped forward. "Now, I have an evaporator to prep. Will you play nice and stay right there, or will I need to tie you up?"

Out of options, Sharp readied into a proper fighting position with bent knees and raised his fists before him. He swallowed.

Scharnhorst let out a throaty laugh. "You're persistent, I'll give you that. But persistence can only take you so far, Mr. Sharp. You have to be committed as well—no half-measures—if you want to get out of here alive. So, come on—" He gestured for Sharp to come at him "—show me what you've got."

Sharp didn't move, a hesitancy locked him in place.

"I thought so." Scharnhorst sucked at his teeth. "They didn't train you right. What are you? Coast Guard? Air Force? You fight like one. You're no SEAL or Marine." He took one step forward. Sharp's muscles tensed as the German approached. "But I can tell you're holding back. Why? What's stopping you?" Sharp glared silently at him. Scharnhorst advanced another step. "I'm curious to know how much fight you have in you. So I'm going to offer you the same chance I give my students. Three hits. If you can knock me down in three hits then I'll let you go. But if you fail then you better be ready to defend yourself fully. I'll hold nothing back."

Sharp saw in the German's eyes a melding of two overlapping desires: honest curiosity and gratuitous pleasure. Scharnhorst was milking this for all its worth. But Sharp had no other choice, he knew his only chance of survival was to play his game, so he lowered his fists and closed the gap between them.

He mentally readied himself then swung his first jab right across Scharnhorst's cheek. The German barely reacted, all he said was, "One."

Sharp's second punch received pretty much the same response. Scharnhorst barely flinched when his fist made contact. "Two," he declared with a widening smirk.

He wheeled back and put all his strength into his final hit, a mean uppercut that clipped Scharnhorst's chin. The German stumbled back a few steps. As he massaged his jaw, he peered at Sharp, impressed by his growing vitality. "Three."

Revved up on adrenaline, Sharp tempted another attack and charged. However Scharnhorst sidestepped his advance easily, causing his motion to propel him farther than anticipated and lose his balance. The palms of his hands broke his fall. While crouched on all fours, Scharnhorst used this opportunity to kick him square in the chest. Sharp gasped at the impact and toppled onto his side.

Scharnhorst preened around the fallen Sharp laughing. "Is this the best the Americans have to offer? Are they just taking anyone off the streets these days who sign up? No matter their qualifications? Pity."

Sharp suppressed the pain in his chest and struggled to get to his feet. Shaking out his hands, he cleared his mind; his close quarters combat training returned to him. He wiped the sweat off his brow and cleared the tears from his eyes. He went into his fighting position as he inhaled one deep calming breath. Then stepped into the German's reach.

Scharnhorst unleashed the first punch, Sharp blocked it and countered with a jab to his solar plexus. Scharnhorst gritted his teeth.

He let fly another fist aimed for Sharp's nose; he grabbed it just in time and twisted the arm into Scharnhorst's back. "Now things are getting interesting," the German remarked, freeing himself from Sharp's grasp and pivoting 180 degrees to face him again.

Next came a dance of skill and luck. Nothing Sharp did managed to break through the German's defenses. Every punch was immediately blocked and countered. While he, in turn, dodged Scharnhorst's attacks, but those that did hit their mark sent shockwaves through his body. As the dance progressed, Sharp's breathing became much more constrained and his energy evaporated. It grew harder for him to hold his arms up. At this rate, it was only a matter of time before he'd succumb completely to Scharnhorst's brute force. Sharp needed to shift tactics.

That's when he spied a metal pan lying on top of a nearby workbench located next to an evaporator. Sharp guided the fight towards it; for every one step Scharnhorst took, Sharp took two. Once close enough to the bench, he clipped Scharnhorst in the ear, momentarily stunning him, then leaped for the metal pan. He grasped it in his fingers and swung it at the German's head. The awful sound of metal colliding with skull reverberated through the *usina*.

Scharnhorst reeled back several feet before collapsing to the ground. As he lay there, he shook the stars from his eyes. Just in time he spotted a blurry outline coming at him. Instinctively, Scharnhorst raised a foot in the air and, when sole met chest, hurled Sharp over himself. Sharp performed a barrel roll and planted himself back onto his feet. The German got up and faced him.

The metal pan went flying towards Scharnhorst's face, but he watched it pass over his shoulder as he dodged it. And when he turned his gaze back upon his opponent, he found Sharp already in mid-sprint, charging at him like a bull. Sharp wrapped his arms around the German's waist and tackled him to the concrete. He wailed on him until Scharnhorst freed one of his legs and kicked Sharp off of him.

They both rose onto their feet, breathing heavily, and eyed each other. A brief respite before the fighting continued anew.

In a flash, Scharnhorst leaped at Sharp and shot out a hand for his throat. He swatted him away then drove a jab into Scharnhorst's stomach. Stifling the pain, Scharnhorst grabbed Sharp's neck and squeezed his trachea shut. Clawing at the German's fingers, Sharp flailed about, struggling to break free, but his hold was too strong.

Thinking quickly, Sharp resorted to the only measure he knew that would free him. He reeled back his right foot, then swung it as hard as he could between Scharnhorst's legs. The impact to his crouch had the desired effect. The German's eyes screwed up into his skull as a beastly howl escaped his mouth. He tossed Sharp aside like an unwanted rag doll.

Sharp slammed into the stack of shelves containing large bags of unprocessed sugar. The stack rocked back and forth as Sharp collapsed to the ground. And, before he had a chance to react, the contents of the top shelf came tumbling down upon him. Bags full of sugar lay across his body, pinning him to the ground. He grunted and groaned trying to move his limbs, but all was in vain.

A hunched over Scharnhorst staggered up to him, grabbed a sack of sugar, and commanded, "Don't move."

Scharnhorst stalked off out of sight, but Sharp no longer cared at that moment. The pressure from the pile of bags dug into the sore spots left over from Scharnhorst's kicks and punches, and obscured any other thoughts that might have penetrated his mind. Closing his eyes, he lay there defeated like a captured animal awaiting its terrible fate.

The clump of guilt roiled through in his thumping heart while the gremlin of disappointment combed its talons through his hair. Sharp had failed; he had failed Sector Seven; he had failed his family; and, worst of all, he had failed his father. The only solace was that, perhaps, death might be a welcome reprieve after all; that death might not be a thing to fear, but rather celebrated as a godsend; an escape.

Yet, even as this idea swirled in his head, a desire to live within him refused to budge. Like a flower long deprived of sunlight, it might have withered over the years but, miraculously, it had never lost its potency. It still drove Sharp's actions, no matter how foolish they might be. And somewhere deep inside him there was still hope that he could rectify his failures. A ray of light shone upon the flower. Clenching his fingers into a tight ball, Sharp held out hope that he could still survive the night. He banished the gremlin to his subconscious and tossed aside the clump in his heart.

That's when he smelled boiling sugar drift into his nostrils and heard the rhythmic churning of the evaporator. Sweat consolidated along the ridge of his hairline. Opening his eyes, he surveyed the space around him. He couldn't see Scharnhorst fully, all he saw were his shoes at the top of the catwalk hovering over the evaporator. A stream of white sugar flowed out of the bag and into the vat. When the bag was empty, Scharnhorst tossed it over the railing and descended the grated stairs.

Approaching Sharp, the German grasped him by the armpits and, with one hard tug, pulled him out from under the pile of sugar sacks. Sharp allowed himself to be dragged across the concrete all the while maintaining a tight fist, waiting for his chance. Scharnhorst carried him up the stairs and positioned him right over the ledge. The heat rising from the evaporator felt like lava on his skin.

Just as Scharnhorst bent down next to his prisoner to speak with him, Sharp raised his balled fist before Scharnhorst's face and flicked a puff of sugar into his eyes. Scharnhorst screamed in pain and retreated, tending to his eyes.

Sharp, meanwhile, scurried away from the lip of the catwalk and crawled towards the stairs. But Scharnhorst was right on top of him. He jumped on Sharp, trapping him between his thighs, and began thrashing at Sharp. His eyes were red and watery as he blinked rapidly like a hummingbird in flight.

Sharp retaliated with a series of jabs of his own. Scharnhorst brushed them off with a grunt, then resumed wailing upon Sharp blindly. As he did, his grip upon his prisoner loosened just enough for Sharp to squirm a few inches out from underneath the German and free a leg. He propelled the sole of his shoe right into Scharnhorst's chest.

Forced off, Scharnhorst stumbled back, and his right leg slipped off the edge of the catwalk dangling over the evaporator. Panic instantly seized the German; he flailed his arms trying to correct his balance. But gravity got the better of him. The loud revving of machinery and the swoosh of churning sugar drowned out the splash of Scharnhorst as he fell into the vat.

Sharp quickly scurried to the edge and watched as Scharnhorst manically struggled against the tide of the twirling sugar. He screamed, an unnatural scream. Reaching out a hand, bits of molten sugar seared into his skin, it peeled away from the bone and plopped into the whirlpool, where it disintegrated entirely. Scharnhorst melted before Sharp's eyes.

As he watched, a strange feeling bubbled inside of Sharp, growing in intensity the closer Scharnhorst came to death. And when the screaming finally ceased and the limp body disappeared beneath a torrent of sugar, a smile crossed Sharp's lips.

Just as quickly as it had formed, the smile vanished. The exuberance he had just felt replaced with disgust. Disgust with himself for feeling such pride after just killing someone. It jarred him.

Turning away from the churning vat, he descended the stairs, though not of his own volition. He didn't feel like himself anymore, instead he felt as if someone else were manipulating his movements. His vision grew hazy and unfocused. His stomach roiled in pain and horror till it couldn't stand it anymore. At the bottom of the grated stairs, he keeled over and vomited. He wiped away the remains from his mouth.

His feet carried him back up into the late Scharnhorst's office. He collected the files from the third drawer and, without a second glance at the evaporator, walked out of the *usina*.

LATER THAT NIGHT

A heavy banging jerked Braasch out of her sleep. Instinctively, she bolted upright, her heart fluttering, and searched the darkness around her. No intruders. No immediate threat. All was silent. She probably only heard something in her dream that felt so real to her it shocked her awake. *That had to be it,* she reasoned.

Bang! Bang! Bang!

Her muscles tightened.

"Braasch let me in," Sharp yelled on the other side of the door.

Braasch exhaled, relieved. Then checked the clock on the nightstand; well past two in the morning. She groaned, now feeling a groggy irritation consume her.

Bang! Bang! Bang!

"Wake up, Braasch!"

She shuffled out of bed, walked to the door, and opened it a crack. But before she could peer through, Ian Sharp burst in, letting out a hand to announce his arrival. His other hand was full of files. He tossed them carelessly on the nearby table propped up underneath the window.

"I've got these things for you to look at," he slurred. His head bobbled some as if it had grown too heavy for his neck and his stride faltered as if he were still only learning how to walk. Alcohol hung on his breath.

Everything had become a haze to Sharp since escaping the *usina*. His memories of the last few hours were nothing more than a string of unfocused tableaus: the hotel viewed through the car windshield—the waitress's pretty smile—a medkit positioned next to his drink of choice—the sting of hydrogen peroxide on his cheek—the rabble of a lively bar. Sharp couldn't even be sure if what he was remembering even happened, all of it felt like a dream.

"Where the hell have you been?" Braasch confronted him.

"Out," he spat with a sneer, then plopped into one of the chairs next to the table. "I found something in Scharnhorst's office."

"What were you doing there so late?" She took a seat across from him.

"It's not I who was late, but poor old Sherburthold." He choked out a laugh, rubbing his face with one of his hands. But if it had been nothing more than a dream, then it was a vivid one that sparked a very real reaction of his senses. The worst of which were the lingering stench of sugar in his nostrils and the haunting death rattle of Scharnhorst in his ears. No matter how much he drank, those two sensations refused to dissipate.

"And it's all subjective anyhow," Sharp deflected. "I'm late for yesterday, but quite early for tomorrow." A trumpet blow of a laugh exploded from his lips, causing his whole body to scrunch in on itself, expelling the last of his intoxicated mirth. Lifting his head, he glanced at Braasch as if seeing her for the first time—a lovely image much better than the swooshing of the German's limp torso. He tilted his head to one side and teased playfully, "you should take a look. It's quite marvelous what I've found." He slapped the stack of files with the palm of his hand and slid it over to Braasch. "And I did it all by myself."

"I will, but not tonight. Right now you need some water and some sleep."

"No!" he barked out, the flirtatious smile disappearing and reappearing instantaneously. "Don't tell me you're not curious. Even a little bit."

"Fine," she relented. She was up anyway, so why not? "But first you need to drink some water."

Sharp rolled his eyes, then got up and staggered to the bathroom. He filled one of the complimentary glasses with tap water and swallowed it down in one gulp. "Happy?"

"Another," Braasch demanded.

Sharp huffed like a temperamental child, but did as he was told.

Satisfied, Braasch began to shuffle through the files. "Seems like they've been experimenting. Probably engineering a greater variety of sugar cane."

Sharp nodded his head as he returned to the table.

She picked up one folder with the tab heading: Mosaic Virus. An eyebrow arched fully in curiosity. "This...doesn't make sense."

"What doesn't make sense?" asked Sharp. He had his cheek slumped on the knuckles of his left hand with elbow propped on the table.

Without looking away from the folder, Braasch explained. "According to this the research department has been experimenting with the mosaic virus."

"What's that?"

"It's a common viral disease that affects over 150 different types of plants. It has no cure. The only way to get rid of it is to make sure it doesn't spread in the first place."

"Well, good thing I'm not a vegetable, or a mineral, or a modern major general." He stated overtly proud of that fact. "I'm an animal."

Braasch flashed a glance his way then returned to the report tucked inside the folder. "In the 1950s and 60s Brazil experienced a horrible breakout of the mosaic virus among their sugar crop. Whole harvests were destroyed by it. And the agricultural sector poured millions of *reales* into researching some type of antibody that could combat the virus. They were desperate to save their crops. At one point they even resorted to spraying the fields with milk hoping it would slow the spread, which was actually successful."

"Wow, protects against osteoporosis, hinders the spread of the mosaic virus, and gets elected to office, what can't Milk do?" He chuckled.

Braasch ignored him. "But what's strange here is that Balthazar's department doesn't appear to be researching some sort of antibody to fight the mosaic virus. No, the numbers are increasing." She flipped through the pages. "They're genetically enhancing it, making it more powerful."

She looked away in thought. Concern splashed across her face. Continuing on, she put that file aside, then picked up another, this one marked: Cane Variety 3X. She scanned it for a long moment before releasing a soft, breathy "Oh my God."

Sharp snorted awake, having fallen asleep. "What? What?" he asked, disoriented.

"They've also been experimenting with Cane Variety 3X. Do you know what this means?" She didn't wait for a response. "Cane Variety 3X was a new type of variety widely used in the 1940s and 50s. It grew at a faster rate than any other variety, which elevated sugar yields to unprecedented levels during the harvest season. Every sugar plantation was planting Cane Variety 3X. That was until they discovered that the sugar content of successive ratoons—leftover roots they replanted to grow new shoots—decreased faster than the older varieties. The amount of time and money it took to prepare the field and plant new stalks of sugar went from every two to three years to every couple months; it took a heavy toll on the Brazilian sugar industry.

"And now here's Balthazar's scientists tinkering with the variety. And, according to this, they're busy manufacturing a larger quantity of Cane Variety 3X seeds. But why?" The dots were slow to connect in her head, but when they did Braasch glanced at Sharp with an awestruck worry on her face. "Ian, do you see what's going on here?"

Sharp opened his mouth to speak, but quickly closed it and shook his head.

"If I'm correct, then Balthazar might be planning on unleashing a much more powerful incarnation of the mosaic virus. The results would be devastating. Entire crops would be destroyed and need to be replaced. And, if I don't miss my guess, Balthazar's going to make sure they replace them with Cane Variety 3X. It's a one-two punch. The sugar industry wouldn't be able to recover from such misfortune."

"A series of unfortunate events," Sharp quipped, knowing full well Braasch wouldn't get it.

"It's ingenious." She marveled. "This very well could be an act of biological warfare."

"Be-o-lee-hi-cal?" Sharp slurred.

"Many people think that biological weapons are meant to attack humans. In actuality, the most effective biological weapons target animals and crops because they have the largest repercussions, even larger than the diseases themselves. Balthazar is going to disrupt an entire food source."

Sharp bolted up out of his chair and yelled commandingly, "We must alert the masses." He then stumbled forward a step and collapsed onto the bed.

Braasch rolled her eyes and got up. "Not tonight. You might have uncovered something big here. But it's still all speculation. And there's no connection here with the assassination of Quadros."

"Yeah there is!" Sharp countered, the sheets muffling his voice. "It's all connected. Scharnhorst planned the occupation. He had a whole file prepping for it."

"I didn't see one here."

"What?" Sharp sprang to his feet and rummaged through the files. Sure enough there was no tab marked, 'Occupation.' His shoulders slumped in disappointment. "Damn it," he exclaimed. "I have to go back and get it." He went for the door, but Braasch charged him and blocked it with her body.

"Oh no you're not. You're going to stay here and get some sleep. We can continue looking over this tomorrow."

"No, Balthazar's behind everything. He's the one who killed Quadros. And Stedile."

"And how do you know?"

Even inebriated he couldn't go against the howling. In truth, he only came to Braasch with these files because he needed her expertise to unlock the information hidden within. Now that he had it he refused to spill any further.

"Because I'm sure of it," was all he could say.

"No." She put her foot down. "You need to sleep. Take off your shoes and get into bed."

His jaw tightened as anger coursed through his veins, but ultimately he relented. "Fine."

Taking off his shoes, he slipped under the covers while Braasch took a seat at the table, her eyes attentive.

Sharp rolled his eyes. "Oh you don't need to watch over me," he grumbled. "I don't need a babysitter. I'll go to bed. Come on. You'll need to sleep as well.' He gestured towards the rest of the queen sized bed. "And the bed's big enough for the both of us."

Without a word, she gave in—she, too, was still very much tired—and returned to her spot on the bed. She positioned herself on her side with her back facing Sharp.

Underneath the covers, as Sharp settled in, he shuffled around a good bit until he successfully undid his pants and threw them on the floor. Then eased into a comfortable position. A silence followed as both attempted to drift off to sleep, but found that they couldn't. Unspoken words lingered between them.

Minutes passed before Sharp couldn't stand the silence anymore and finally blurted out: "Scharnhorst is dead." His voice cracked. The alcohol steered his emotions down a different path. "I didn't mean to. It just kind of happened." A knot formed in his throat. "I just never thought that...that I could..." Something inside him prevented him from finishing the sentence.

"So I assumed," Braasch replied, her voice sympathetic. "I figured that the cut on your cheek wasn't from paper. And you don't get blacked out drunk to forget the good times. No, I've seen my dad get drunk often enough to recognize when one drinks to celebrate and one drinks to forget. He did a lot of forgetting." She repositioned herself a full 180 degrees and locked eyes with Sharp. "Tell me what happened."

Sharp hesitated, unsure how he could put what he had experienced earlier that night into words. "After our meeting with Balthazar, I couldn't shake off how he reacted when I asked him if he was an integrationalist. He, clearly, had no love for the United States. So I knew I couldn't just leave it at that. I needed more information, and that office seemed the best place to start. So I snuck into the *usina*. However it was a trap. Scharnhorst was there waiting for me.

"Next thing I knew, I was being kicked and punched around by Scharnhorst, I didn't want to fight him, I tried to run at first, but he cornered me. Then..." he thought hard, trying to piece together exactly how he felt in that moment, "...I got a few good hits on him, and I started to really think that I might have a chance here. That if I knocked him out, I could get out of there alive. And I was loving it. For some reason—I don't know how to explain it—but I think I saw this as a competition, a test of my abilities, and I was loving it."

Braasch laid a comforting hand on his shoulder. "It was the adrenaline, you were experiencing a combat high."

Sharp nodded and continued. "That's when everything I learned in training flooded back into my body and I was perfectly dodging Scharnhorst's attacks and laying a few punches on him as well." He let out a little laugh and shifted closer to Braasch. "I carried myself a lot better than I thought I would against Scharnhorst. But, somehow, he pinned me underneath a pile of sugar and I couldn't move. That's when he started up the evaporator. He was planning on boiling me alive!"

A pregnant pause filled the room as Sharp mentally girded himself for what was coming. "Luckily, I was able to get a little bit of sugar in my hands and…and…I only meant to distract him," he pleaded, tears welling up in his eyes. "You have to understand, that's all I meant to do."

"It's okay, it's okay," Braasch pacified as she hoisted herself into a sitting position. Then wrapped her arms around Sharp, cradling his head in the nook of her shoulder. "Just tell me what happened."

Sharp stammered. "Scharnhorst dragged me up the catwalk and, before he could throw me in, I threw the sugar in his eyes and booked it down the catwalk. But he caught me and I pushed him. That's when he slipped and fell into the vat. I pushed him into a vat of boiling sugar. I watched another human being melted alive. I listened to his screaming as he slowly died. But that wasn't the worst of it." His lips trembled. "I enjoyed it. I enjoyed watching him die." The dam broke and tears streamed down his cheeks. "What is wrong with me?"

"There's nothing wrong with you," Braasch consoled him. "That is a perfectly natural response. Your brain perceived this as nothing more than a victory, an achievement, thus releasing the necessary chemicals to allow you to celebrate. We all feel that guilt soon afterwards, wondering if there's something wrong with us. But that'll pass, and you'll find that taking another's life is as easy as riding a bike once you get the hang of it."

"But I don't want it to get easier," Sharp confessed.

"Then you have to find a new line of work, Ian. You knew the risks going into this, what piece of you you'd eventually have to sacrifice, and it was going to happen sooner or later."

Sharp murmured, "I failed."

"No, you didn't. It was either him or you. There are no half measures here, there never can be. And tonight, you learned that lesson the hard way." Braasch wiped the tears away from Sharp's face. "It'll get easier, but carrying that burden never will. I know what it's like: I've only eliminated three targets so far and the weight of it is something I'll never easily be able to shove off. I know that pain—trust me, Sharp—I do."

"But was it worth it?" Sharp shook his head. "I should have been the one swirling around in that vat. End all my troubles right then and there."

"Yes, it was worth it," Braasch affirmed. "You succeeded in getting us this information. Valuable information. This might just break the case. And that wouldn't have happened if you hadn't snuck into that *usina*. And, though this is a clear violation of several orders if not downright insubordination, I'm proud of you, Ian. I am. You've come a long way."

Even though this was the recognition he'd been hoping to hear since arriving in Pernambuco, it fell flat to Sharp's ears. The clump of guilt outweighed any pride he could muster inside himself. Even the howling failed to lift his spirits.

Instead, he retreated further into misery. "I thought I'd never have to do what I did, I could get by through incapacitating my opponent, you know? Much good that did me." He sighed. "Didn't even need a gun. I figured if I never held one then I'd never have to use it. They always felt so heavy in my hands—reminded me too much of my father."

Braasch remained silent. She tightened her grip on him and began running her fingers through his hair.

He put a hand on her knee and began. "I looked up to my father—I still do—but it hasn't been the same ever since...I was in middle school when it happened. We were walking through the local shopping center, it was a busy day, crowds everywhere. When, suddenly, this one guy bumped into my dad and kept on walking. I thought nothing of it, but after a few steps, Dad realized his wallet was gone. That guy had pickpocketed him, and Dad wasn't going to allow that to happen. He was a cop after all and it wouldn't look good if someone was able to pull a fast one on a cop. So he told me to wait at the food court while he started after the guy. Naturally, I didn't listen and ran after him. Here was my chance to see my dad in action.

"We ran for a long time. And at one point we got outside and were running down the sidewalk; that is until the pickpocket took a turn by the library and boxed himself in. You see, the library was built next to the reservoir and the parking lot butts up right against it. There's only one way in and out. I hung back and watched from afar as my dad confronted the pickpocket.

"I don't know what they said to each other, but the rest is all a blur. The pickpocket pulled out a gun and fired. My dad dropped to the ground. The pickpocket booked it immediately. And I saw it all."

Sharp sniffed. "My dad survived the gunshot, it had grazed him in the temple. But the impact of it and him hitting the ground knocked him unconscious. He hasn't woken up since. Now, he spends his days sleeping in a hospital bed. And it gets harder and harder to see him after every visit." A new track of tears sailed down his cheek.

"I'm sorry," Braasch whispered. "I'm sorry for everything you've been through. You're too good of a guy for all this to happen to you. You deserve so much more."

Sharp looked up into Braasch's eyes. He hadn't noticed how brilliantly they shined in the moonlight; or how her red lips curved gently when she bit into them with her teeth. Or how soothing her fingers were in his hair. As they stared into each other's eyes, his heartbeat quickened a pace as a new desire flooded his being. Letting it consume him, he pressed his lips upon Braasch's. And she kissed back.

THE MISSION MUST GO ON

Sharp woke up with a pounding headache and a staleness in his mouth. An alcohol induced haze obscured his memories of the night before. Opening his eyes, he blinked the grogginess away and immediately felt that something wasn't right. The room looked like his but he was sure the generic picture hanging on the wall was supposed to be a river landscape not a still portrait of a flower pot. And the sheets were a wavy blue though Sharp was certain they had been stripped earlier. *What's going on?*

Bending over, he found that his duffle bag wasn't where he'd laid it down when he first arrived, instead there rested a large suitcase—the one Braasch had brought if Sharp remembered correctly. As he attempted to make sense of his situation, a hazy recollection of last night crept along the border of his consciousness while an inkling of worry poked at his heart. He swept a hand across the bed and found nothing but a pillow. He exhaled relieved, knowing he was alone.

Click!

Sharp's body shuddered at the sound. Lifting his head, he saw Braasch walk out of the bathroom, perfectly dressed in a blue shirt and a black skirt. He sat bolt upright at her appearance, his mouth agape. Without looking at him, she crossed to the door and opened it. Then turned her head and locked eyes with Sharp. Though her face seemed no different, Sharp could tell by her demeanor that something caused it to droop a little; and that it wasn't weariness. *Shame, perhaps?*

"I'm making a trip to the Subdivision office," she stated flatly. "Get some information I need." Sharp opened his mouth to speak, but Braasch cut him off. "I can do this on my own. You need some time to recover from last night. Drink some water, and I'll have the hotel bring you something to eat. I don't expect to be back until late." Before Sharp could say anything she ducked out of the room and closed the door behind her.

Sharp fell back, his head hitting the pillow, and exhaled. Staring up at the ceiling, he shifted the pieces of last night around in his mind, trying to make sense of it all. He hadn't been blacked out drunk since college, but now that he was older and had a lower tolerance than his wilder days, it took a heavy toll on him mentally and physically. He knew he should drink water but even the thought of it made him want to throw up. And food was beyond the question.

Why am I here?

Glancing to his right, he found the table littered with files. A puzzle piece clicked into place: *I'm here cause I wanted to show these off... Oh god, Scharnhorst.*

The German's unnatural screams struck him like a jackhammer. A wave of nausea suddenly overpowered him, forcing him out of the bed and into the bathroom where he dry heaved stomach acid. It left an awful burning taste in his mouth.

Back on the bed, he sat upright, willing himself to think past his confrontation with Scharnhorst. It came surprisingly easy now that a bigger concern of his had eclipsed it.

That's when snippets of the conversation from last night formed in his mind, he began to remember. Braasch had unveiled Balthazar's plan; *she claimed it was an act of biological warfare.*

Perhaps he wasn't as blacked out as he thought he was if he still had vague memories; perhaps he just wanted something else to take the reins for a while and, thus, surrendered complete control.

But if it was just to show off what I found, then why am I still in Braasch's room?

A knock at the door interrupted his thoughts. Answering it, a hotel employee carried a plate of breakfast—a traditional American breakfast of eggs and bacon. Sharp thanked them and took the tray. Then he braced himself and bit into the first forkful of egg. He chewed it to paste before finally swallowing. It stayed down. As he ate, his nausea dissipated. And the more water he drank, the more the pounding in his head lessened. He was slowly recovering.

But when he nearly finished his meal, he froze, a piece of bacon hung inches from his mouth. He remembered.

I kissed her.

That's all he remembered, but things never end with just a kiss. And knowing the pent up desires he had suppressed, or refused to acknowledge, when he first saw Braasch, there was no doubt they seized upon his absence. They had sprung loose like a troop of mischievous monkeys, wreaking havoc in their wake. And here, they succeeded in inflicting the worst damage possible.

No longer hungry, Sharp tossed the piece of bacon aside and collapsed backwards across the bed.

Oh god, what have I done?

Panic seized him.

"Oh god...What am I going to do?" He asked aloud. "What am I going to tell Katelyn?"

A thought popped into his head, *She doesn't have to know.*

"Yeah," Sharp seconded. "There's a lot I can't tell her already, so why would this be any different." The clump of guilt practically bounced in his heart and landed with a hard thud. He shook his head. "No, this is taking it too far...Damn it!" He exclaimed, then searched the room for a solution. None was to be found.

"I can't...I can't..." He wavered, "Not now...I can deal with this later." Relegating his marital crisis elsewhere in his mind, he turned his focus elsewhere. "I've still got to stop Balthazar. I don't want to think about it."

Impulsively, he ruffled through his pants for his phone and brought up a number. It rang once before someone answered:

"*Olá*," announced a feminine voice.

"*Olá*," he replied, feigning calm as best he could. "This is Ian Sharp. Is Mayor Brizola in?"

"Yes, I'll tell him you're on the line."

The wait was excruciating. He had no idea what he was going to say to the Mayor, he just dialed him on a whim. He wanted a distraction, an outlet, but now that he's found one he wasn't sure if he wanted it anymore.

"Hello, Senhor Sharp," Mayor Brizola chirped. "How's Pernambuco treating you?"

Sharp inhaled a breath, then began, "Not so good, I'm afraid."

"Really," his tone grew concerned, "tell me, what is it?"

Sharp decided to just dive in head first. "Braasch and I came upon some interesting information from Balthazar's research department. Have you ever heard of Cane Variety 3X?"

A pause. "Why yes, I'm familiar with it. My dad complained about it for years before he died. Said it ruined us financially for a long time. Why?"

"I'd like to talk to you more about the Variety—determine the impact it had on the sugar industry."

"Sure, I'd love to. But I have an upcoming meeting I must attend. Why don't you come down to my office and we'll talk face-to-face, what do you say?"

"Sure," He said lamely. "However Braasch won't be able to make it, she's busy with other business right now. Which means she has the car, so I wouldn't know how to get to you."

"I'll send a car to pick you up, say around four. Does that work?"

"Fine. Thank you for your time."

Sharp said his good-bye, then hung up and tossed the phone across the bed. A debilitating case of lethargy consumed him. All he felt like doing was dipping under the sheets and wallowing. He had no taste for the rest of his meal, which went untouched. And he lacked the energy to take a shower and get ready for this spontaneous meeting he thrusted upon himself. Another stupid rash decision. He wanted nothing more than to be alone…on his own deserted island.

Oh Katelyn…Susie and Beth. How am I going to face them? How many lies am I going to have to tell them? This was all a mistake.

Massaging his forehead with his fingers, he agonized over what could be done to rectify this. But every path he took led him to the same destination: the loss of his family. Yet, there was one way he could prevent this. If only…The clump grew bigger in his heart. Sharp clutched his chest and soothed the discomfort away. *No, they have to know. I have to tell them.*

"But, right now, there's nothing I can do about it." Sharp reasoned aloud. "I have to finish this first. That's all I can do."

He broke away from the bed and collected his belongings. Returning to his own room, he stood under the cascade of hot water in the shower for a long time, till his skin felt raw and cleansed. Then he shaved the stubble from his jawline and changed into his suit. After another hotel meal, Sharp felt relatively decent, now that his hang-over was gone.

When four o'clock arrived, the government car showed up and carried Sharp downtown to City Hall.

Sharp's eyes filled with wonder the moment he entered Mayor Brizola's office. Spinning around, his jaw hung loose at the impressive display of books covering every inch of wall space. Sharp found that they were all properly categorized; the Mayor had history books, science books, law books, fiction, fantasy, philosophy, classics written in English, Shakespeare transcribed in Portuguese, cultural analysis, political affairs, sociology, agricultural, and, not to mention, a plethora of biographies on Antônio Conselheiro, Eva Peron, and Archbishop Oscar Romero. One shelf was even dedicated to the MST alone. And this seemed only the tip of the iceberg as Sharp perused this veritable library of the world contained in the printed word.

So lost was he that he completely forgot himself, and the world melted away. Even his melancholy retreated to the shadows of his mind. Perhaps this wasn't as bad a distraction as he thought. Marveling, he muttered, "What an amazing collection you have."

"Thank you, I've read every book here." The Mayor's soft nasally voice ventured cautiously into pride. "I had them install the shelves when I became mayor. I wanted to display to the public my education, and convey an understanding that I will use what I have learned from these books to help improve our dear city." Mayor Brizola switched gears. "Now, you've met Acting Minister Geisel, right?"

Sharp spun around and finally acknowledged the other two gentlemen in the room. Mayor Brizola sat at his desk while Minister Geisel occupied the couch.

"Oh Minister," Sharp said, surprised. "I wasn't expecting you."

"I came in yesterday." His arms were flung out across the backrest, his legs splayed out before him, as if he were trying to encompass the entire couch with his compact frame. "I wanted to observe the occupation on the ground. So I flew up to see how things were unfolding." Waving a hand before his face, he inquired, "What happened to you?"

Sharp touched the cut on his cheek. "Oh I cut myself." he shrugged. "Stupid mistake." He sat in the last available chair in the room. "I hope I'm not interrupting anything."

"Not at all," the Minister made a throw away gesture. "When the Mayor told me you were coming to see him, I inquired if I could join you. He said you had some questions you'd like to ask about Cane Variety 3X."

"Yes, but first..." Sharp glanced up at the ceiling, a logjam of questions silenced him a moment. He struggled to unplug the blockage and reestablish a steady logical flow of questions. But, failing, he let loose the first one his tongue could release. "How important is Balthazar in the sugar industry?"

The Minister adjusted himself on the couch, leaning forward. "He's very important. Brazil is the largest producer and exporter of sugar in the world. We account for 28 percent of the world's sugarcane production and 25 percent of the world's sugar exports. The Northeast is a large chunk of that: exporting around..." He bobbed his head, racking his brain for the information, "...70 to 75 percent of their product. Domestically, about half of our sugarcane production is converted into ethanol—fuel for our cars. Balthazar's *usina* is a leader in both aspects. Without him, we'd be struggling on the world market and wouldn't have fuel for our cars."

"And how important is sugar to Brazil?"

"It's essentially our life blood. When you add up everything, the sugarcane agro-industrial system brings in more than 86 billion American dollars annually. That's not something to shirk at." The Minister's lips scrunched together and his gaze drifted away from Sharp. A hint of antipathy tinged his words. "However, we've been forced to institute deindustrialization in order to achieve that, thus reducing Brazil to a level of sub-imperialism."

"Sub-imperialism?" Sharp asked.

As if pulled out of a trance the Minister shook his head and forced a smile. "Oh, that's right, you're an American. You wouldn't have ever studied Latin American theorists, let alone know their names."

Sharp nodded, accepting the validity of his assumption, though wishing he had put it into kinder words.

"Sub-imperialism refers to the effect globalization has had on Latin America. In our case, we've willingly trapped ourselves between the developed and underdeveloped world in order to best serve our international relations."

"In essence," the Mayor interjected, "we've restricted or reduced our high-technology industries and research so that we may have a stronger competitive advantage on the global market elsewhere."

"Someone needs to be the agro-business powerhouse that feeds the world," the Minister declared. "So why not Brazil?"

"And let me guess..." The haze dissipated from Sharp's head as he fit this new information into the larger picture. "The main country that forced you into this subservient position has been the United States. Am I correct?"

The Minister nodded. "After our debt crisis in the mid-1970s, Brazil was forced to submit to a complex web of outside interests and pressures—especially from Presidents Reagan and Clinton. And there was nothing we could do because once we opened our markets to foreign investments, the Americans swooped in and became our main source of direct investments. So we followed their lead."

"And Karma is a patient woman." Sharp mumbled, a saying his father used to recite from time to time.

"What was that?" The Mayor leaned over his desk curious.

"Oh, nothing." Sharp brushed it away. "So getting back to Cane Variety 3X. From what I understand, this variety was a popular sugarcane variant that produced large yields of sugar per harvest."

"Yes," the Minister answered. "And required less fertilizer and irrigation. In less than a decade, Pernambuco was using the variety for nearly 80% of its harvest, and experiencing an increase of sucrose yields of 40%. However, it was a very persnickety variety. Cane Variety 3X was a slow-maturing cane. Which means if you wanted the maximum yield from your crops you had a very short window at the end of the harvest season in order to gather it all up. Not so easy to do on a large plantation, nor when trying to maximize overall tonnage. Then there's the fact that its ratoons, when replanted, produced a significantly reduced amount of sucrose in the next harvest."

"And if an entire country were to plant Cane Variety 3X, what would happen?"

The Minister huffed incredulously at the question. "Why would a country ever do that?"

"Just asking, hypothetically."

The Minister thought for a second, then answered, "It depends on the country. Sugar is an important commodity for several countries. Latin America basically survives off sugar revenues. But, depending on the severity, it could be devastating."

"How so?" Sharp slid forward to the edge of his chair.

"Well, Sharp," The Mayor explained, taking on a professorial air. "Almost every food product has some level of sugar in it: soda, snacks, candy bars, even so-called health food. Sugar has redefined eating in general. Once upon a time people actually sat around the dinner table three times a day and ate breakfast, lunch and dinner. Now because of sugar, there are meals between meals, new concepts of eating, new timetables. Sugar has become the foundation of eating. It's the only agricultural commodity that has revolutionized how human beings survive. I have a book on the subject." He rose from his seat and searched his bookshelves.

"I think that's alright, Mayor." Minister Griesel proclaimed. "He doesn't need a whole history lesson here."

Mayor Brizola turned back. "Oh," his excitement faded as he returned to his seat.

"The food industry would collapse if sugar was suddenly scarce." The Minister got to the point. "Whether that will be good or not depends on how a country reacts to it. Hell, we might need a sugar shortage just for the sake of reducing our dependence on it. Take the Indians for instance. They've been using sugar as a sweetener for their teas to such a liberal degree that diabetes is the fastest growing health concern in India. Yet, the demand in India continues to climb despite rising sugar prices. Imagine what a shortage would do to them."

"How about the United States?" Sharp inquired. "What would happen to us?"

"The United States has had an interesting connection with sugar. Since the Civil War, your desire for self-sufficiency and regional development eventually grew into a concern for national security. You even established an American Sugar Kingdom, comprising Puerto Rico, Cuba, and the Dominican Republic, just to ensure there'd never be a shortage. World War One confirmed your fears and, by World War Two, sugar had become a staple in basic raw materials. Alongside iron and tin, your factories used sugar as an acetone for building bombs and bullets. For America, sugar is more than just a food product—it's a war material. Should sugar disappear, the political implications could be devastating; a sign of national weakness and compromised security."

Sharp leaned back in his chair. "And, I'm assuming, if the United States can't produce its own sugar, then we'll turn to Brazil in order to compensate."

The Minister nodded. "I believe so."

Sharp put the final pieces into the puzzle. "So that's what he's planning."

"What?"

"Sow economic mayhem in the United States, then reap the benefits." But something in the puzzle didn't make sense. "How does this relate to the Occupation?"

"What are you talking about?" The Mayor asked.

"Mayor Brizola." The Minister jutted forward as if suddenly remembering something. "Speaking of the occupation, I believe you've got other matters to attend to there. You should probably get going. I'll stay here and talk with Sharp a little longer."

Caught off guard, the Mayor stammered out. "You're right. I am supposed to meet with Silva today. But he can wait, I'd like to hear more—"

"Please, Mayor, I insist. We'll be fine here." He stared down Mayor Brizola.

"Of course." He wilted. "Shouldn't be so rude. I should go. Sorry to cut this short."

He shook their hands good-bye then hurried out the office.

"Now, what was it you were saying?" Minister Griesel leaned back, his gaze inspecting Sharp carefully.

Sharp continued uneasily, the exchange had brought forth prior suspicions formed during his first interaction with Minister Griesel. They had laid dormant, forgotten because of the deluge of events these last few days, but were now awoken. "I was saying that…" he swallowed, then steeled himself. "We know what Balthazar is up to. He's manufacturing a stronger version of the Mosaic virus that he'll unleash on American sugar crops. Once those are wiped out, and the American farmers are scrambling for a new batch of cane, he'll ship out millions of Cane Variety 3X. They'll unwittingly sow their eventual collapse. And then what?" He asked pointedly.

"I don't know what you're talking about," the Minister said coolly, perhaps too coolly for someone who would have been hearing this for the first time. *Unless…*

"You do." He countered, jumping out of his chair. "You've known all this time. You're in on it. You're a member of the *Santidade*."

"Now, please, Mr. Sharp." Minister Griesel bolted upright into a standing defensive position. "I think you're making wild assumptions here."

"No. It's all coming together now. But what's the connection?"

"If you'll just—"

Sharp grabbed him by the lapels and held the Minster close, their faces inches apart. "What's with the occupation? How does this tie into his other plan? Tell me!"

Just then he heard the office door swing open. Turning, he found the man himself enter, followed by two guards wearing suits and dark sunglasses. "Sorry if I'm late," Balthazar declared with a beaming smile. "I hope I'm not interrupting anything."

THE SANTIDADE

Sharp didn't move, he simply stared at Balthazar. Neither of them saying anything for a long moment, until the Minister interrupted:

"If you would let go of me now, please." He tugged at Sharp's fingers, freeing his lapels, then shoved them back at Sharp.

He barely registered the gesture; too busy silently berating himself for once again lowering his defenses and walking right into a trap. *I can't be so trusting, it's too dangerous in this line of work.* Sharp hoped he lived long enough to learn the lesson.

Walking a straight line through Sharp and Minister Griesel, Balthazar leaned against the desk, folded his arms, and asked, "What did you find out?"

"Mr. Sharp knows everything." The Minister replied as if he were merely relaying to him that a kitchen appliance was acting up. He plopped down onto the couch cushion. "He knows you've enhanced the Mosaic Virus, he knows you're producing Cane Variety 3X, and he knows where you'll unleash it."

Balthazar inspected Sharp, who stood defiantly despite the overwhelming sense of failure roiling inside of him. His first response was to blame it on the alcohol, it had diminished his abilities to think clearly and properly assess the situation. He was still suffering the consequences of letting those monkeys loose.

"Anything else?" Balthazar inquired.

"Before you walked in, he wanted to know what the connection was with the occupation."

Nodding his head, Balthazar spoke directly to Sharp. "I must admit you are a tough one, Mr. Sharp. You and your partner have been more trouble than I thought. However, I'm not going to let you escape this time."

"What are you going to do to me?" Sharp finally spoke up.

"You'll see," Balthazar declared, then sighed. "I had hoped at first that you two were truly journalists, but Scharnhorst did his research and found that neither of you are on the staff for the New Yorker. You could have at least done a little more due diligence on your cover stories."

His rebuke stung Sharp. Everything he'd done up to this point had been so amateurish, messy, and capricious. And he also succeeded at dragging Braasch down with him. He shouldn't have been sent to Brazil in the first place, he wasn't ready.

But, yet again, he had made it this far and uncovered a real threat against the United States. None of that would have been possible without him. And so Sharp decided to focus on the positives, and that gave him strength.

"You killed Minister Quadros," Sharp pronounced bluntly, "So that you could get your little toady here into a position of power. And Stedile was competition for you. With him out of the way then the MST was all yours. But why, Balthazar? I get your hatred for the United States, but what good is this occupation to you?"

Balthazar rubbed his tongue against his teeth. "The United States is only part and parcel of a global reconfiguration. You see, Mr. Sharp, there's a seismic shift occurring here that's bigger than you, bigger than me, and bigger than Brazil. Many will never see it coming until it's already upon them, and by then it'll be too late. Change is in the air, Mr. Sharp. And I will see to it that it is so.

"You think the Mosaic Virus and Cane Variety 3X is a means to an end? No, it is but a beginning—that spark that'll set everything into motion. And I can't have someone like you messing it up."

"A beginning?" Sharp parroted, trying to fully understand its meaning. "What exactly is this *global reconfiguration* supposed to achieve?"

Balthazar smirked. "The restoration of my family's glory."

"Glory? You make sugar. What are you trying to eliminate? FDA requirements?" Sharp prodded.

"No." Balthazar replied through clenched teeth, refusing to rise to his insolent needling. However, his face betrayed a trace of annoyance hinting that the remark had struck a raw nerve. Noticing this, Sharp decided to strike again:

"Corner the market on children's cereal?"

"No," he strained to say, holding back.

"Well," Sharp said, his tone dismissive, "It couldn't have been that glorious if your—"

Balthazar slammed his fist against the desk. He exploded, "You have no idea what my family has done for this country!" Fury consumed him. "And how are we repaid? My grandfather was brutally tortured and murdered by the military, my father stripped of his titles and exiled from the seat of power, and I was shunned by those who once revered the Balthazar name. Our family has suffered horribly. But I will soon rectify that. Soon everyone will remember the sacrifices we Balthazars have made for Brazil. I will follow in my ancestors footsteps and lead this country into a new era of Order and Progress." He inhaled deeply, calming himself. "That is the purpose of the *Santidade*."

"And what exactly is the *Santidade*?"

Another mischievous smile spread across Balthazar's face, "A religious sect devoted to building a better and brighter future for those oppressed. And I am its Pope."

"Your Minister here mentioned something like that," he glanced at Minister Griesel. "Said that it had been wiped out."

Balthazar shook his head. "Oh no, it is still very much alive and has been for centuries. We merely prefer secrecy—no one can tear you down if they don't know you exist. It was the only way the African and Indian slaves had a chance to overthrow their Portuguese masters. Yet..." He amended reluctantly, "...the Portuguese did once nearly destroy the *Santidade* entirely with their 'war of extermination.' They razed villages, captured runaways and sent them back to their masters, and sold free Indians into slavery. But the Word of *their* God protected us. We saw the Jews of Egypt as ourselves, and knew that their God was not on their side, but on ours. So we bided our time. We waited for the plague to descend upon our oppressors and a Moses to emerge and lead us to the Promise Land."

Sharp suppressed a great temptation to roll his eyes. *Oh great, I'm not dealing with a megalomaniac billionaire here, I've got a religious fanatic.*

"Then came the Glorious Incident in 1857." Balthazar continued, baring his teeth as if reminiscing fondly about the good old days. "The English interloper Samuel Balthazar had connived his way into the ongoing feud between the Paises and Barretos—the largest agricultural families at the time. He ended the feud by marrying the only daughter, and child, of João Pais Barreto."

"So this is where you come from?" Sharp mocked. "A shifty opportunist. That's quite an ancestry."

"He's not my ancestor," he stated coolly. "He is but a tragic figure who made the fatal mistake of sleeping with the wife of an easily angered Indian. In a fit of rage, the slave killed Balthazar and fled for his life. When Balthazar's body was found the next day, the blacks and Indians discussed what they should do." He leaned forward, lowering his voice into a whisper. "That's when they turned to my real great-great-great-grandfather, Paublo Paranhos, for advice. He had been nothing more than a common field hand at the time, but he had visions, strong visions, that would leave him laid up in bed for days. And they asked him what should be done. That night he had a vision:

God had reached out to him, telling him that he should take the place of Samuel Balthazar and care for his flock, for Paranhos was the only one who could do it. So that's what he did. Paublo Paranhos died that day and Samuel Balthazar was resurrected."

Balthazar wrung out his hands in rapturous joy. "To commemorate our good fortune, the first thing he did as 'Samuel Balthazar' was change the *usina*'s name to *Santidade através do trabalho celeste,* thus ridding the plantation of any remnants of our horrid oppressor. We were our own masters now.

"You see, Mr. Sharp, I come from a strong lineage of powerful popes. Starting when Paranhos feigned a sudden bout of reclusion to hide his identity, and used the political clout Balthazar had already cultivated to spread the *Santidade*'s message. Soon we would dominate Brazil, pulling the levers of government from behind the curtain, and no one the wiser."

The words flowed out of him like a waterfall. After years of being dammed up deep inside of him, Balthazar relished the rare occasion when he could open up the floodgates and let his history—the real history—stream out of him. He continued, uninhibited:

"When Paranhos's child was born, he was formally baptized as Edgar Balthazar, the next in line as Pope."

Sharp eyed Balthazar cautiously, unsure how much of his story to believe. Balthazar spoke with such strong conviction, like an itinerant preacher espousing the eternal damnation of the unrepentant sinner, that it was nearly impossible not to be captivated by his words. But Sharp resisted as best he could by applying cold dispassionate academic expertise in order to assess the veracity of Balthazar's words. *He's nothing more than a master charlatan,* Sharp thought, *who has successfully fooled even himself into believing his own words.*

"Under Pope Edgar," Balthazar preached, "the *Santidade* freed the slaves, then brought down Pedro II and established a rightful democracy. A free nation devoted to 'Order and Progress.' And that's how it would be for the next forty years.

"When Pope Edgar died in 1897, his son, Pope James Balthazar, sought to create a destiny of his own, but an intense personal flaw would bring him ruin. Early in his papacy, he commanded newspapers across the country to vilify the burgeoning 'holy city' known as Canudos, led by a man known as Conselheiro. Pope James didn't want any competition that might threaten the *Santidade*'s supremacy. But the ploy worked too well. The President sent in military forces to crush Canudos—it turned into a massacre. Their sacrifice sparked sympathy and public outcries against such heavy handed measures. Conselheiro became a revered martyr. It was a colossal blunder for Pope James, one he'd spend the rest of his reign trying to amend."

Balthazar paused and lowered his head. Closing his eyes, he lamented his ancestor's plight. As he did so, Sharp glanced at the only exit available to him aside from jumping out the two story window. Both guards stood before the door. They were muscular, perhaps ex-military. Sharp was no match for them, and he knew it. Even though he might have taken down Scharnhorst that was but a fluke, and Lady Luck was surely not to favor him twice. Turning back, he listened as Balthazar resumed his impromptu sermon:

"Despite his setback, Pope James oversaw an era of social and economic growth unmatched in the world. He turned Brazil from a third world country into a modern civilized nation that rivaled any other in Europe. But the taint of Canudos prevented him from achieving his ultimate goal: a *Santidade* utopia. It sowed enough resistance in those in government to actively hinder Pope James's influence and power, and challenge his authority. Some, in time, even conspired to overthrow him entirely. But Pope James would beat them to the punch.

"He noticed a change in the wind and changed with it. Throwing his support completely behind the rising *tenente* movement, Pope James oversaw the military coup that ousted President Washington Luís and replaced him with Getúlio Vargas as president in 1930. The *Santidade,* once again, lay at the center of power stronger than ever before and unquestioned. But, like always, Pope James's paranoia flared up and he worried that others might usurp him. So to forestall that he urged Vargas to transform his presidency into a dictatorship, which he willingly obliged. Under the *Estado Novo,* Pope James stepped up the suppression of dissidence and purged any government official who refused to pledge loyalty to the *Santidade.*"

I thought we had it bad with the conspiracy theories, Sharp quipped silently. The more Balthazar went on, the more rallied up and frantic he became, growing less like a refined preacher and more like a talk radio commentator. Balthazar accepted without question the made-up history of the *Santidade* and propagated it fervently like those who broadcast the wildest rumors of the Freemasons and the Skull and Bones society back home. In some way Sharp began to pity him. *He'll soon be wearing a tinfoil hat.*

Balthazar noticed Sharp's face screw up into an expression of ardent skepticism and smiled, misinterpreting it as astonishment.

"In any case, the war against the Nazis took a heavy toll on his delicate psyche. Pope James feared that Nazi sympathizers were everywhere and that his most trusted allies were out to get him. The end came when he received word that the military had overthrown Vargas. That's when he snapped, and suffered a debilitating mental breakdown. Pope James was institutionalized and died in isolation three years later.

"Stepping into his shoes was the unimaginative Timothy Balthazar. He tried tirelessly to return Vargas to the presidency and succeeding in 1950—if it worked for his father then why not for him. Yet, any hope that the *Santidade* was once again in control were dashed four years later, when Vargas committed suicide right before the military stormed the presidential mansion.

"Once great allies, our relationship with the military grew strained during and after the war, and only worsened from there. The next ten years witnessed a struggle between us and them trying to wrest control of Brazil from one another. We were evenly matched, but then in 1964, the inevitable happened: the military, with strong support from the United States, successfully established a dictatorship. Once again we were forced into submission, and Timothy Balthazar let it happen."

"We lost many great people during that time, especially when the tyrant General Médici governed over Brazil. One day in 1969, military agents showed up on the plantation and took Pope Timothy away; and tortured him to death." A sadness filled his voice. His story was no longer some distant history passed down from generation to generation but now a living memory etched onto Balthazar's soul. "Though I was merely a child when it happened, I still remember that day they dumped his body in front of our *hacienda*. How bruised and broken he was. Horribly discolored in shades of black and purple. They didn't even have the courtesy to wipe off the blood—he was covered in his own blood."

Beneath the sadness, an anger began to burble furiously. He clenched his fist as he relived the ghastly sight of his grandfather. But before it could burst forth Balthazar suppressed it; a ripple contorted his neck muscles as he did. An effort that expelled his enthusiasm too quickly. Sharp could see the verve drain out of him.

"Robert Balthazar, my father," he went on, stooping a little, "Was pope during the *Abertura*. However, instead of using the moment to reclaim our rightful position of power, he decreed that the *Santidade* would no longer participate in politics and, from now on, we shall focus only on the betterment of our community. He refused to ruffle any feathers—never took any risks—because he was still afraid of what the military might do should he step out of line. I, on the other hand, am not so afraid. And I know that the *Santidade* will one day return to its former glory. And I know that its message will reach the hearts and minds of those all across the continent. And I know I will be the one who does that. With the help of my..." He searched for the right word, "…associates, I will unite all of Latin America under the *Santidade.* Soon everyone will know the true history of the Balthazar legacy and the glory of the *Santidade.* They will remember forever what I did for Brazil. And it will be beautiful."

Balthazar paused and narrowed his gaze at Sharp. "But first I must eliminate a little bothersome fly who has already done a significant amount of damage."

Sharp tensed, his fight or flight hormones positioned at the ready waiting for the order.

"I'm amazed you even stood a chance against Scharnhorst. He was a fine soldier, and the enhancements made him undefeatable. Well, nearly," Balthazar amended.

"Enhancements?" Sharp repeated.

But no explanation was given, instead Balthazar diverted the discussion elsewhere. "He was to train an army for me. One ready for the revolution to come."

"The MST," said Sharp. "Why them?"

A smile crossed Balthazar's lips. He leaned back on the desk, his arms propping him up. "Because they already have *mística."* His hand twirled in the air with a flourish. "An army of loyal soldiers already indoctrinated to obey their *militante* leaders; trained not to fear death nor cower from violence; and instilled with a purpose and a spirit that'll keep them fighting till the very end. If they were to rise as one, a revolution would be all but certain. And all they need is a little push in the right direction. Occupations have their success, but the reward is so paltry compared to what they could truly gain. They lack vision. Now a revolution, on the other hand…" He left the sentence unfinished, letting it dangle for Sharp to fill in the rest—and nothing that came to mind set him at ease. "The Bezerra Occupation is the push the MST needs. It will be the catalyst that sets off a chain of mass protests all across Brazil. Together, the poor landless farmers, and their equals oppressed in the cities, will rise against the injustice of the world and rid this country of unfettered capitalism. Then from there we'll reach out and tear down the world order and rebuild without boundaries, without war; one human race sharing resources, celebrating unity, and overcoming tribalism." Balthazar closed his eyes and envisioned the future. "Imagine a world where there is finally peace in the Middle East, or Africa wiped clean of warlords and poverty, or even an America who no longer has to assert its dominance through brute force. A utopia."

As he listened, Sharp, ever subtle, shifted his body slowly into an attack position. He might not have the strength to incapacitate his opponents, but he didn't need to. All he needed was surprise and speed. If he could stun the guards long enough then he could just maybe get out of there alive.

Balthazar sighed pining for that future, then opened his eyes. "But to get there we first need a revolution. Society has been stuck in the same place for ages now, old concepts founded on the American and French Revolutions are starting to wear thin. We've done nothing but go in circles for centuries: destroying countries, creating new ones, and reconfiguring the old ones. Nationalism and patriotism no longer matter in a world where globalism has destroyed barriers once thought insurmountable. We can communicate and travel freely like never before. Why be loyal to an arbitrary border for the rest of your life just because you were born within its confines? Let's broaden our horizons." He glanced at Sharp. "That is what we plan to do. And it all starts here, Mr. Sharp."

Balthazar flashed his gaze from Sharp to one of his guards and, before Sharp realized what happened, something smacked hard against his head. Robbed of his advantage, a dizziness suddenly consumed him and he collapsed to the floor. As the room faded to black, he heard Balthazar say, "Too bad you won't get to see it."

BLAZING CANE

Sharp stirred. His head throbbing, his vision hazy, he groaned softly as the sensation of his body returned to him. His fingers and toes twitched mechanically. Then the muscles in his forearms tensed tight for a second and relaxed, his thighs did the same. His shoulder blades bent back together, his chest expanding without resistance: all seemed good. Sharp still had use of his limbs and felt no pain except for a particular ache near the back of his head.

He lifted his head, but, before he could even get an inch of the ground, his neck collapsed under its weight. His head crashed against a hard sturdy surface sending a bolt of lightning through his skull. He winced. And the world spun around him.

Reflexively, he raised his hands to nurse the wound, but something tugged at his wrists halting their motion entirely. Sharp peered to his side and saw that a length of old rope held his wrists to planks of wood. So too were his legs clamped down to their own piece of wood. Each piece nailed firmly to one another restraining his movement.

A voice from the haze snapped his attention elsewhere. "Good, you're awake." Sharp couldn't see who it was at first, everything was clouded in darkness. But the smell that wafted into his nostrils gave him a clue. The air was fresh, a slight breeze, and it seemed to carry a scent of nature. But then came an odor he had never experienced before—it wasn't good or bad, just strange. Sharp didn't know what it was.

Shuffling his body from side to side, he tested his constraints. As he did, he heard the crunching and felt the sloshing of...sand?...against his back. Yet it was coarser than sand...*Dirt!* He was lying down on dirt, Sharp was sure of it.

He blinked the clouds from his eyes and the world around him shifted into focus somewhat: a dark blue sky hung over him and a sheet of green surrounded him. This sheet rippled in the breeze. Sharp didn't comprehend it at first, but as the pain in his head subsided, it gained greater definition and detail. The sheet of green morphed into a ragged bunching of thin stripes, like a patch of uncut grass, each one individually waving in the wind.

Sharp took it all in, the smell in the air, the touch of the ground, and the sight of green stripes. That's when his brain snapped into clear focus. He was tied down somewhere in the sugar fields.

Beside him was the man who spoke, Balthazar. Bent down into a squat, he glided an eye over Sharp's constrained limbs, inspecting his captive like a big game hunter marveling at his trophies after a successful hunt. His face alight in triumph. Locking eyes with Sharp, he said, "Tonight, we are celebrating. It's the last night of the *safra*, which means we must deliver an offering to God. A tribute for his protection. We do this by setting fire to a hectare of our harvest, and letting it lie fallow until the next season. And it is quite a marvelous sight to behold: a hectare of sugarcane consumed in red and orange flames billowing into the night sky. And tonight, Mr. Sharp, you are going to be a part of our celebrations."

He reached a hand down to the soil between his legs and caressed it tenderly. "Sugar is an amazing gift from God. Once rare, kings sought it out as a precious symbol of their power, but as the white gold reached the masses it lost that reverence. But never its importance." He dug his fingers into the soil, clenching a ball of dirt in his fist. He held it out in front of him. "Even when burned the sugar remains untouched within the scorched cane. In a wake of destruction, there is still life beneath the ashes. A glimmer of persistence, and a will to live. An opportunity for renewal. Not unlike the *Santidade*. The Military sought to burn us out completely in the 1960s, destroying our way of life. But now the Balthazar name is stronger than ever and will continue to grow stronger as the *Santidade*'s influence expands across this continent."

He stared at the soil in his hand, rotating and examining every speck of earth that nourished his sugar cane. Then he tossed the rest onto Sharp's chest.

"Nothing will stop me from becoming Balthazar the First, the emperor of the *Santidade*. From the ashes of the past we will reap the benefits of the future. And your ashes will be the first upon which we will reap in order to rebuild this world anew. A world my ancestors have strived for."

Finding his tongue, Sharp quipped, "Doesn't sound like much of a world I'd want to be a part of anyway."

Balthazar chuckled. "I see you haven't lost your sense of humor." His features turned serious and his voice grew harsh. "Well listen to this then, Mr. Sharp. In twenty minutes, we will light the first wave of fires over there." He pointed to his right. "It will then spread slowly, engulfing every stalk of cane until it reaches you. Once it engulfs your whole body, all that will remain will be ashes, beautiful ashes that my lovely sugarcane will use for nourishment. You can scream if you want but it will be of no use. The crackling and popping of the cane will easily drown you out for several yards. You will die tonight, Mr. Sharp," he reveled, "There is no doubt about it. All that is left for you is to think about what you have done and wonder where you went wrong."

Though powerless, Sharp challenged Balthazar with a defiant stare, refusing to display any weakness in his final moments. He tightened his hands into fists and held a proud chin as high as he could. Tears threatened to well up at the corners of his eyes but he blinked them away.

Balthazar offered one last grin, showing all of his white teeth, then rose to his full height. "You have twenty minutes, Mr. Sharp. Make it worth it."

He turned his back to Sharp, walked to the row of sugarcane, and disappeared. Sharp listened to the sound of shoes crunching down dirt till it faded into nothingness. Then his injury unleashed another volley of lightning bolts through his head.

His body jerked from side to side, the ropes dug into his wrists. He hurled himself up and an unseen rope snagged around his neck. Sharp gagged and collapsed. Drained, he lay there panting, his eyes closed, mouth agape, brows scrunched together. All was futile.

As this realization came to him, somewhere deep within his being he felt one last innate animalistic thrash for survival surge through him and he unleashed a full throated scream. But only the stars up in the darkened sky could hear him, and they were there not to provide rescue but only to watch. Sharp was alone, and he was to die.

The scream weakened as he squeezed out the last of the air from his lungs, then all was silent except for the waves of sugarcane in the breeze. Lying there, Sharp appeared calm, finally accepting his fate. Yet inside, the scream had torn down the barrier surrounding his heart and unleashed a frenzy of emotions that fed upon Sharp's captive state. All at once Sharp felt everything.

A mournful howl reverberated through his skull as the gremlin danced joyously. Its traps had been an overwhelming success. Sharp had walked into every one of them and, bit by bit, his confidence cracked. Soon a mist waded in filling all his thoughts with doubt, and Sharp had no idea which way to turn. This diverted him to that miserable island within him that was completely devoid of any hope. He sought refuge, but fell only into another one of the gremlin's traps. Sharp never stood a chance. The gremlin couldn't help but gloat.

It stroked one of its crusted fingernails across Sharp's chest. It had been playing cat and mouse for so long that its hunger had grown insatiable. Saliva fell from its lopsided mouth as its splintered tongue caressed its jagged teeth. Disappointment had taken so long to devour its prey when there had been so many opportunities before now. Sharp's life had been one constant disappointment.

But the worst of them was the clump that weighed down his heart. A cold clump of guilt that just sat there as a reminder of those he's hurt. It had been so easy to ignore but over time it had grown to such a size, and rattled violently with every thump, that it became impossible to do. *Beth... Susie... Katelyn.*

A whiff of smoke drifted into his nostrils; his twenty minutes were up. But Sharp didn't care anymore, it was over anyways. He resigned to his fate.

Closing his eyes to the sparkling night sky, he exhaled a breath, and thought of his wife and daughters. *I'll never see them again. Never get to kiss Katelyn, or cuddle with her in bed. I'll never get to grow old with her... but after last night I could never look her in the eyes again and pretend nothing was wrong. Oh god...* "Where did we go wrong?" he whispered as if the cane themselves would provide an answer.

Susie, Beth. I'll never know what they grow up to be. If those ballet lessons will ever pay off, or if they'll become scientists, politicians, artists, athletes... I would have been proud of them no matter what they become, or who they love... I won't be there when they need me the most. I hope they remember me.

Sharp swallowed down the knot forming in his throat. A tear escaped his eyelid and sailed down his temple into his hairline.

As he dwelled on the future, he also reflected on the past. *I'll leave them with six years, six wonderful years. And eight years with Katelyn. Oh all the things she has put up with. If only I had a chance to pay her back for everything she's given me: a supportive wife, two extraordinary daughters, and a scrapbook of cherished memories. I hope she remembers the good times. I hope she finds someone who can make her happy the way I couldn't, especially in marriage.*

The popping and crackling of sugarcane grew louder as it inched closer towards him. It roared like a fourth of July fireworks display. Sharp closed himself off from the outside world and retraced his steps that lead him to this very moment.

I should never have left them, I should be home right now, putting the girls to sleep—dancing with them...This had to be my mission. Why did I join Sector Seven? No, it's when I joined the Navy. That's when things began to fall apart...but was it?...Dad. The thought of him produced a melancholy sigh. *I should have visited you more in the hospital.*

"But I couldn't," he confessed to the world, setting free the words he had kept bottled up inside himself for years. "I couldn't bear seeing you the way you are now. It hurt. God, how different my life would have been if you had just woken up. I held out hope for a long time, but it never happened. And at some point I gave up. I gave up on you, dad. I guess this is what I get, huh?" He turned his head to his right. "I needed you."

Sharp could feel the distant heat wash over his arms. Sweat formed across his hairline. Opening his eyes, he spotted the tower of black smoke billowing over the sugarcane, the flames still hidden out of sight. Which meant he still had plenty of time left to wallow a little longer before the end. Sharp inhaled deep through his nose, then exhaled through his mouth.

How beautiful the stars look tonight, he marveled. They twinkled like distant diamonds. "Don't get a view like this often in San Diego," muttered Sharp. "Hope the girls get to see a night like this one day." An old promise he'd long forgotten about popped into his head. "Never did get to take them camping. Just us four out in the woods away from all the distractions. That would have been fun."

That's when an epiphany struck him. *All this time I'd been looking for adventure, running from one thing to the next, till I found something that scratched that itch, filled that void, when I had it all along. My family, the grandest adventure of them all. I just refused to see it. God, how stupid I am.*

Just over the stalks of cane a tongue of flame came into view. Small at first, barely a flicker of orange, but it grew and expanded the width of Sharp's vision. Like an advancing horde charging down a mountainside, it morphed into a solid wall of flame that incinerated everything in its path.

The smell of roasted sugar swirled around Sharp and sweat droplets cascaded down his forehead. A loud pop shook the ground beneath him. The moisture in his throat evaporated. With the flames bearing down upon him, Sharp remained calm—he was ready.

Like matchsticks the stalks of cane nearest Sharp's side burst into flames. Their leaves chewed away till they were nothing more but embers wafting in the breeze. And those embers then landed upon a neighboring stalk, marking it next for immolation. So the cycle went, one stalk after another, creeping ever closer to Sharp.

The embers floated in the air like a revelry of fireflies, dancing merrily, oblivious to the destruction they left in their wake. Some flickered mid glide before evaporating into nothingness, while others ventured farther and birthed a whole new flock of fireflies. Sailing over Sharp, they danced with the twinkling stars.

He swallowed.

Instinctively, he forced his body away from the approaching flames, but the rope held him steady to the wood. He could feel the heat singe the hair on his arm.

One flaming stalk bent as it succumbed to the fire. Sharp watched it carefully as it wilted and, with a slight tug of his arm, he repositioned the rope in its path. Nourished, the flower of hope within Sharp began to bud. Though tiny in stature against its other brethren, and fragile, it glowed brightly in the dark. Like a lighthouse, its presence brought reassurance to this wayward sailor.

The flames licked at the rope, catching a multitude of frayed strands. They sizzled like tiny fuses till they collided together and produced a puff of smoke, followed by a small amber spark that ate through the rope.

Sharp pulled as hard as he could. The rope went taut, then snapped under the pressure. He yelled out in excitement at his success.

The gremlin screamed and fled.

Immediately, Sharp slipped the rope around his neck over his head and rose into a sitting position. He went to work on freeing his other hand.

A firefly drifted around him and landed on his shoulder. He brushed it away before it could settle into his shirt.

A loud popping caught his attention. Glancing up, he saw that another fire had been lit at the other end of the field. He doubled his effort to get his hand free. If he didn't hurry then the two fires would soon engulf him. He worked his fingers around the knot, but it refused to loosen.

The gremlin remained defiant no matter how large the flower grew. It snarled and snapped its jaw at the flower. But when it tried to sink its teeth into one of its petals, it retreated into the darkness with several teeth now badly chipped and broken.

The knot slackened and Sharp slipped his hand out of its bond.

A wave of flames threatened to wash over him at any moment. The heat plastered his hair to his skull and matted his shirt to his back. It became a fight to breathe, Sharp panted for whatever little oxygen he could get. Wiping the sweat from his face, he went for the rope holding down his feet.

Suddenly, the sleeve of his shirt burst into flames. Sharp screamed and frantically patted the fire out. Once extinguished, he returned to untying the knots around his feet.

He was starting to feel lightheaded.

A howl encouraged him onward.

Shaking the rope away from his left leg, Sharp went after the one on his right. He lost sensation in the tips of his fingers, and his movement became sluggish. But Sharp willed them to obey and untie the final knot.

Free at last, he jumped onto his feet. A surge of blood to his brain offset his equilibrium, but Sharp couldn't wait to find balance. He stumbled woozy into the sugarcane. Everything teetered, except for the two giant plumes of black smoke carving out a pathway against the stars.

Through the crackling and popping, he charged forward with only seconds to spare before the two plumes met and sealed him away to his doom. Fireflies danced around him, spreading destruction wherever they landed. Sharp paid them no mind, his energy—his focus—all on putting one leg in front of the other without falling over.

His lungs gasped for air; his skin sizzled in the heat; his eyes burned from the smoke. Sharp ignored it all, he was determined to survive—to make it out alive.

And just when the two plumes threatened to deny him escape, Sharp leaped into the air. The flames leaped after him, but failed to grasp him. He sailed through untouched.

He continued running until he came upon a road. Only then did he collapse to the ground and inhale sweet oxygen. For minutes he lay there, collecting himself.

When he felt ready, he hoisted himself back onto wobbly legs and walked down the road. No cars passed by.

His salvation came when he spotted a parking lot in the distance. As relief flooded his body, he doubled timed it over to an old brown VW Gol Gti. He smashed through the window, slumped into the driver's seat, and fiddled with the wires underneath the steering wheel. It revved to life and an over joyous sensation consumed Sharp.

PART 3

BRASIL

Our Strength is a fight that calls
the triumph of hope that will come,
we will forge this fight with certainty.
a free country of peasant workers,
our star will finally triumph!
Come, let us fight fist raised!
Our Strength leads us to build,
Our country free and strong.
Built by people power!

- MST ANTHEM

A CHANGE

Black heavy bags hung under her eyes after a week of troubled sleep. Her skin sagged off the bone, her figure wilted in a worse for wear blouse. She hadn't bothered with her hair in days, and it was starting to resemble that of a rat's nest. Reclining in her chair, she heaved a defeated sigh then dropped the receiver onto its cradle.

Braasch believed in something called a life force: a spiritual current of sorts that provided energy for the body, but it was of limited quantity and couldn't be replaced. We were all born with a certain amount of life force; unfortunately we didn't know how much. Therefore, it was important to be conscious of how much one exerted on any given day, or during any given activity, to ensure that one didn't expel too much too quickly. However, since returning from Pernambuco, she could feel her life force drain out of her being, sapping twenty years from her allotment.

True to her word, President Rousseff levied sanctions on several American goods soon after her arbitrary deadline passed. To top it off, her speech declaring the sanctions contained a thinly veiled call to build up the country's military. She initiated a dangerous game of brinkmanship. But, so far, it seemed to have worked. Currently the American Secretary of State was in Brazil negotiating with her Brazilian counterpart for a possible resolution. Meanwhile, the full weight of this predicament landed upon Braasch's shoulders—though no one blamed her for this, she couldn't help but blame herself, and acknowledge her failure. It threatened to crush her.

Braasch exhaled again, staring at the blank gray walls of her office. Though it felt more like a prison cell to her now, a punishment.

Across from her sat Estrella. His fingers tapped against his inner thigh. A tacky brown suit covered his languid frame. Despite the melancholia in the air, his face exuded Zen. Nothing seemed to ruffle him; like water washing over a rock. Estrella opened his mouth to speak, "Didn't sound so good. What did he say?"

Braasch shrugged. "I'm not fired for one," she stated sarcastically.

"Always a silver lining," Estrella latched on boisterously.

"But I will be reassigned if I don't figure out a way to resolve all this soon. Sir's been reassuring the Defense Secretary that we're doing everything in our power, but if I don't hand him some good news soon then…" She shook her head. Worry arched her brows.

"That Sir," Estrella expressed exasperatedly. "What does he think we'll be able to do? It's not like we wanted all this to happen, it's not our fault. And he knows we have a lead right?"

Braasch rested her chin on her knuckles and stared off at nothing in particular. "Yeah, but all that's gone now. I told Sir what Balthazar was planning, but without any hard evidence, he dismissed it right out of hand." Despite how much she resisted, her mind forced her back to the day Sharp went missing:

Braasch returned to the hotel room to find her door cracked open. She approached cautiously, silently pushing it open wider and stepped through the threshold. That's when her assailant attacked, clubbing her right on her head. Braasch collapsed, dazed. The contents of her bag scattered across the floor. The assailant bent down, his gaze focused not on her but on the files now on full display. Noticing the gleam in his eyes, Braasch realized what they were after and went into defensive mode.

He reached for the files, but Braasch swatted his arm away. The assailant then lunged at her, using the full weight of his body to overpower her. They wrestled at the door of the hotel room. He pinned her down with a knee to her midsection while his chest clamped the left side of her body down. As he strained to shuffle the files into the bag, Braasch swung her free arm as hard as she could against his spine. It made a muffled thump, and his back caved slightly enough for her to pull her left arm out from under him. She squirmed away from her assailant, then jumped to her feet, the room teetered for a moment.

The assailant crammed the files into the bag and stood up. He went for his pistol. Thinking quickly, Braasch grabbed whatever she should get her hand on—the glass Sharp had used the night before—and threw it. It hit the assailant square in the forehead, knocking him back through the open door. He stumbled, collided with the second-floor railing, and sailed over. A car below broke his fall.

Braasch flew down the stairs, but was too late. The assailant had removed himself from the car and was already firmly planted in the driver's seat of his own. She went for the door handle but it wouldn't budge. The car revved to life. She quickly sought out her own keys only to realize they were in her bag, which now lay in the passenger seat next to the assailant. It peeled out of the parking lot leaving Braasch to watch helplessly as the car, the assailant, and all the evidence disappeared from view.

She shook the memory away, preferring to forget it altogether. But in the last few days that moment haunted her. She couldn't escape her failure at the worst opportune time.

She'd never felt so dejected or demoralized before in her life, and so powerless. Even in her own office, she felt trapped, like a bird in a cage, and all she could do was peer out and watch the world crumble before her. Braasch had tendered her resignation but, surprisingly, Sir rejected it. Instead, he harangued her on her sloppy investigation and demanded she do better, then hung up. His tone sounded more like a disappointed father than an irritated superior—and that cut Braasch right to the core.

"If only Sharp were here," she muttered lost in thought. "He knew better than anyone what was going on."

Estrella lowered his head. "Nobody in Pernambuco has seen hide nor hair of him. I'm afraid he's—"

"No." The word cracked like a whip out of her mouth. She lunged forward in her chair and spat out, "It's only been a week. He might still pop up yet."

That was the only thing left giving her a flicker of hope. Braasch clasped onto it like a life preserver and refused to let go, no matter how tenuous her grip. Her nights became filled with thoughts of him; she worried, she feared, she cried for him. All the while tossing and turning in the night unable to get a wink of sleep. Where was Ian Sharp?

Estrella didn't argue, what was the point? But he did try to prepare her mentally for the cold possibility of the worst. "We've talked to Mayor Brizola, inspected Balthazar's plantation, and questioned Silva. Nothing. It's like he simply disappeared into thin air."

She sighed, her whole being collapsed in on itself. "He was on the verge of breaking this case wide open. He figured everything out—he even got the evidence to prove it." She swiveled 180 degrees and glared out the window. A red horizon gleamed in the distance as dusk gave way to twilight. "We're back at square one," Braasch lamented.

"No," Estrella corrected. "Sir's completely clipped us, we're not even allowed to follow this lead anymore. We're in the negatives at this point."

"Then what's left to do? Just twiddle our thumbs and watch the world burn?"

Estrella hoisted himself up onto his feet. "Why not? Then we'll be able to make some s'mores before it's all over." He quipped, then said, "It's late. Perhaps a good night's rest will clear some of the cobwebs."

She waved him off without turning around. "You go on ahead. I'm going to stay here a little longer."

Estrella opened his mouth, then shut it. A lecture wouldn't do her any good right now, nor would she listen. So instead he said, "Okay, don't stay too late. Need you fresh for the end of the world."

"Will do," she breathed out.

Estrella exited the elevator and walked towards his car. As he did, he eyed the concrete floor of the parking garage, and thought, *Poor woman, never seen someone so destroyed by the world. If this doesn't kill her, then nothing will.*

"Manuel Estrella," a voice called out to him.

Thrown from his thoughts, he turned in the direction of the voice. He had recognized the voice immediately, but when he spotted the speaker he had no recollection of who it could be. It was a raggedy figure with days' long stubble and greasy matted hair—clearly hadn't showered in days. His clothes were heavily soiled and torn. His skin stained a dark brown, whether from filth or the sun Estrella couldn't tell. When he reached the emerald green eyes peering at him, that's when it finally clicked.

"Sharp?" He inquired hesitantly.

The figure nodded his head.

"Jesus," His shock gave way to relieved joy. "Didn't expect to ever see you again. Where have you been?" Stepping forward, a pungent smell struck his nostrils, repelling him back. "Oh. Okay. Yeah. Let's get you cleaned up first. Get in the car." He motioned for Sharp to follow. "Let me lay down a towel first. And roll down the window."

After making the necessary adjustments the both of them settled into Estrella's hatchback. As he pulled out of the garage, he stole another glance at Sharp. His face scrunched up, the smell hung in his nose. "What the hell happened to you?"

"Where do I start?" Sharp replied. "When I was nearly burned alive? Or when I infiltrated the sugar mill and shoved Scharnhorst into a vat of boiling sugar? Or what about the *Safra* celebrations where a bunch of gunmen crashed the party? So much has happened."

"How'd you get here?" Estrella specified.

Sharp shrugged. "Pretty much hitchhiked my way from Pernambuco."

Estrella gasped disparagingly. "Now you didn't need to do that. You could have gone to the Sector Seven division there."

"Yeah," Sharp concurred mockingly, "If I knew where that was."

"Well what about calling? You could have called one of us."

"My phone's gone, and I didn't memorize any phone numbers. Didn't think I'd have to."

"Well you do now!" He emphasized bitingly. "So how'd you get here?"

Sharp recounted his adventure, picking up right after escaping from the sugar field. He detailed how he had hotwired a car and booked it to his hotel only to find a police barricade surrounding the place and no sign of Braasch anywhere. Fearing she'd been taken, and Balthazar's men lurking about, he hightailed it out of there. Lost in a foreign country with no resources at his disposal, he did the only thing he could think of: he set out for familiar territory, namely Brasília.

It proved to be easier said than done, for hotwiring cars along the way only got him as far as the amount of gas available in the tank would take him. He then hitched rides with a few charitable drivers who were on their way to Brasília—his Spanish a serviceable bridge across the language gap. He even spent a good length of time in the back of a poultry truck. And there were times when there was no car available to hotwire or any driver to hitch with, so he walked. It had been a grueling journey that left him nearly starved, both physically and mentally, and yet he had made it. He had survived.

"I still think there was a better way to handle that," Estrella remarked when Sharp finished telling his story. "Didn't need to take the trek from Pernambuco to here."

Sharp turned his head slowly so as to glare fully at Estrella, his face an emotionless husk. "I'm sure there was," he said flatly. "But let's drop you off in the middle of nowhere, with no money, no means of transportation, and no common language with the locals, and see how you do."

"Okay. Okay." Estrella brushed Sharp's severity aside. "I was only joking. It's just good to have you back. Once we get to my place you can take a shower. I'll lend you some clothes. Then we can really have a chat."

"Thanks," Sharp said, relief flooded his voice.

After a time Estrella pulled into an apartment complex and parked in his designated spot. They took the elevator up several flights, then walked down the hallway to his apartment. As he inserted the key, Estrella glanced at Sharp. "It'll be a bit tight, you might have to fight my other guest for the couch."

"Other guest?" Sharp repeated, his brows arched in curiosity.

The door swung open and Estrella waved his hand gesturing for Sharp to enter. When he did he noticed someone sitting on the couch watching television, their back to them.

"I brought company," Estrella announced, closing the door behind him.

The person turned her head and locked eyes with Sharp. Her mouth fell open and her eyes widened dumbfounded. Sharp halted in mid-stride, he, too, was shocked to find her here.

Ian Sharp and Anir Quadros stared at each other in silence, both too stunned to speak.

"Good," Estrella stepped between them. He threw the keys onto the counter. "You know each other." Then pointed down the narrow hallway and said in the same breath, "Bathroom's that way. Leave the door unlocked; I'll slip you some of my clothes."

Sharp didn't move, he stood there transfixed in Quadros's gaze. Estrella rolled his eyes and nudged Sharp out of his trance. "Come on, get going," he shooed, "You can marvel at Anir after you've taken your shower. Come on." He practically had to shove Sharp into the bathroom as he regained his powers of speech and stammered out the beginning of a question. Estrella closed the door on him before he could finish.

"Well, he took that well," Estrella sighed, then made his way into the small nook that was his kitchen. Opening the fridge, he rummaged through it for the ingredients he planned to use for that night's dinner. As he did, Quadros jumped out of her spot on the couch and approached the countertop that divided the kitchen from the living room.

"What is he doing here?" She whispered.

"He's taking a shower." He said into the fridge. "Which, by the way, can you go into my closet and pull out a set of clothes for him? Sweats should work until we get something more his size."

"You know what I mean."

He laid the last of the ingredients down on the counter next to the fridge, closed it, and turned to face her. "He's alive, that's all I care about right now," his tone turned defensive. "And right now I'm relieved that he is. I brought him here because you saw what state he's in. He's been traveling for the last week, and right now what he needs most is a shower and some rest. We can grill him later. Okay?"

Quadros bit her tongue, merely letting out a clipped 'fine,' then huffed off into the bedroom to do what was asked of her.

Estrella shook his head, then set to work making dinner. First he sautéed some onions and garlic until they became translucent. He added some tomatoes to soften them and, as they cooked, shredded up chicken breast, olives, peas, and corn. For an added taste, he threw in a touch of parsley, some salt and pepper, and other seasonings. When finished assembling and cooking the filling, Estrella set it aside and began prepping the crust.

Cooking was Estrella's distraction, his happy place. Just him and his food. Though he wished he could afford a place with a larger kitchen, he enjoyed the intimacy of this little nook. Over the years he had created so many fond memories here. As well as a few he'd like to forget. And, just like all the other times crammed away in the kitchen nook, as he poured the flour and stirred in the egg yolks, he found a moment of Zen.

Alone with his thoughts, he worked out the details of this new development, and adjusted his plans accordingly. He set the pie into the oven and turned around. There was Sharp standing at the lip of the kitchen. Estralla jumped back, spooked. Not because he seemingly materialized out of nowhere, but because he looked...different.

Though at first glance he didn't look too different: the sun had kissed him several shades darker than Estrella remembered and, running along his left arm, a tender discoloration marked where hair had once been—an injury that had begun to heal over. However, it was in his face that Estrella noticed a change. His features were harder, perhaps a little more pronounced due to the lack of food on his travels, yet a kindness, a playfulness, had definitely disappeared. *He's no neophyte anymore,* Estrella realized. *He's been broken in.*

"That felt fantastic," Sharp exclaimed. "Thank you."

Estrella brushed him away. "It's no problem, you'd do the same if I had risen from the dead. Here, why don't you take a seat." He gestured to the small dining table placed where linoleum tiles meet carpet. "Would you like a drink, or something?"

"Water would be fine, thank you." Sharp plopped himself into a chair and rested an elbow on the dining table.

"Sounds good." Estrella filled a glass full of water and handed it off to Sharp. "Anything you need, let me know. You'll spend the night here and tomorrow we can let it be known that you've returned from the wild."

"No," Sharp declared—perhaps a bit too forcefully. Estrella froze, taken aback. Sharp explained in a milder tone. "I don't want anyone to know that I'm alive. At least not right now."

"Why?"

"I've had a lot of time to think of my next move these last few days, and it'll be easier to do what I need to do if everyone thinks I'm dead. The Pope of Sugar won't be expecting me that way."

"You've got a plan?" He went to check the oven, opening it a crack. Satisfied, he nodded and focused on Sharp. *Those eyes…*

Sharp swung his head from side to side unsure of himself. "Something like that. The Pope built himself an empire; one that will not be taken down so easily. First we've got to do something about the *Santidade*."

"Oh God," Quadros groaned, making her presence known. She switched off the television and stood up. "That cult of his?"

Sharp's brows knitted together. "You know about the *Santidade*?"

She nodded her head. "Of course I do. He's not as subtle as he thinks he is about it. He read one little thing about the *Santidade* years ago and it got into his head. Remember my husband was an activist before he got into politics. He'd share with me what he had heard while traveling. One was about how Balthazar was trying to revive the *Santidade*. Luís brushed it off as nothing but the antics of a crazy billionaire, but that changed when he became Minister of Agrarian Development."

"Well he was right to be concerned," Sharp commented, "The Pope's done it. And his goal for the *Santidade* is integration."

The Pope? The way Sharp said it caught Estrella's attention. He mulled the words over in his mind. *Is he even conscious of what he's doing?*

"Not just uniting the nations together," Sharp continued, "But razing them to the ground and building an empire atop their ashes. With him in charge. Then he'll seek revenge on the United States."

"And how do you plan on stopping him?" Quadros asked, taking a seat at the dining table.

"He might have formed a cult of personality around him, but that won't protect him in a court of law."

Sharp's tone didn't match his demeanor, Estrella could tell right away, and understood immediately that what he said wasn't meant to convince them of his plan, but rather to convince himself. He had another idea percolating somewhere deep within his brain that he refused to acknowledge, though it hung on his hardened eyes. *Trying to maintain a semblance of humanity.* Estrella lowered his head, sympathetic for what Sharp was going through—having to fight the demons within himself, alone. *But in the end we all lose.*

He turned away from the conversation between Sharp and Quadros and scanned the kitchen. After twenty years he had seen enough of the world corrupting young, bright, able-bodied men till they became nothing more than tools meant to destroy each other. He had grown tired of it. Estrella didn't want to see it happen again, especially not here in his own home. Best not to be a part of it.

Slipping on oven gloves, he reached in and pulled out his dish. He let it sit on the stove to cool a little before slicing into it and cutting out a piece. Once he loaded up three plates with *Empadão de Frango,* he joined the conversation.

"Dinner's ready."

"Let me check," Quadros went on, merely nodding a thank you Estrella's way when he set a plate down in front of her. "There are still a few people I might be able to reach out to who don't particularly like Balthazar. They might be willing to help."

"That'll be great. I need everything I can to build a case against him." Sharp glanced down at his plate. "This looks delicious, like a chicken pot pie."

"This is the Brazilian version," said Estrella as he retrieved forks for everyone. "A recipe my mother used to use."

"I can't wait to eat some real food." He marveled, then dug in hungrily, shoving a mouth load of pie into his mouth. He leaned back savoring it. "This is great. Thank you, Estrella."

Estrella nodded, saying nothing. He took a seat at the table.

"And what are you going to do?" Quadros asked, returning to the matter at hand. She swallowed down her morsel.

"Me?" The fork before his lips hovered in the air a moment before he set it down on the plate. "I'm going to see what I can do about the Bezerra Occupation. If I can end it before December that'll put a wrench in the Pope's plan for a bit. Hopefully undo it entirely before it can get completely off the ground."

"If we're not at war by then." Estrella muttered into his *empadão.*

Sharp continued without hearing him. "That's plan A. Tomorrow, though, we begin preparing for plan B." He glanced over at Estrella.

Unsettled, Estrella asked, "What's plan B?"

"I need you to train me. Probably won't need it, but best be prepared, right?"

Estrella sank. He should have seen it coming, that he'd be roped into partaking in Sharp's corruption. Being entrusted to nurture and maintain an obvious, yet unspoken, lie. But he couldn't say no—he knew what was riding on this—and duty came before anything else. So he nodded, feeding into Sharp's unconscious obtuseness. *If you don't name it, then it can't haunt you.*

Estrella bit into his *empadão,* it tasted bland in his mouth.

AT THE OCCUPATION

"Very troubling," Silva exclaimed after listening to Sharp's story, "What you're saying." He sat in a makeshift chair before a polythene tent. "And difficult to believe."

The sun beat down a hot August heat upon the occupation. Clothes clung to skin and beads of sweat crowded foreheads. Everyone moved at a slower, lethargic pace with less talking and more relaxing. A lazy day for the occupation free of worries and free of work.

"But it's all true," Sharp defended. A white button down shirt and brown slacks covered his frame courtesy of Estrella. Perspiration discolored his armpits. "This occupation is in danger. The Pope's planning to light a powder keg here and, when it explodes, it's going to be bigger than Eldorado."

A dull clatter of camp noise surrounded them: women rattling cookware against pots, children frolicking in their recess games, and men chewing the fat in huddled circles. Someone passed by where they sat, too close for Sharp's comfort. He lowered his voice, tempering his urgency for confidentiality:

"If you don't act soon, then people will die."

The white-haired Silva rubbed the back of his neck with a handkerchief, his face a mixture of consternation and distrust. As he thought out his next words, he stared silently at the scene before him, without really looking at anything in particular. A moment passed before he replied as diplomatically as he could, "And you're saying this is

Balthazar's doing?" Failing to completely remove the skepticism from his voice.

Sharp nodded. "He's going to use this as a flashpoint for revolution. Incite the MST to overthrow the government."

"I think the sun has gotten to you," Silva dismissed. Reaching down he picked up a water bottle and held it out. "Your mind's melting. Here, have a drink."

Sharp deflated, his head fell to his chest. He hadn't made any progress since returning to Pernambuco. Silva refused to listen. "He's tried to kill me twice now. And I wouldn't be the first."

"Quadros and Stedile."

Sharp nodded.

Silva fell back in his chair as if a wave were crashing over him. "Balthazar has supported us since the beginning. He's supplied us with food, tents, protection, and so much more. He's a savior to these people." He threw out a hand gesturing to the rest of the occupation. "You know how it'll look if I were to say that we couldn't trust him anymore. I'd be run out of here in a heartbeat."

"I know, I know," Sharp conceded. "What I'm asking of you is not going to be easy. I'm just saying it might be better to—" He scrambled for the most neutral word he could find "—pause this occupation until Balthazar has been taken care of."

"And when would that be?" Silva inquired.

Sharp shrugged. "It's hard to say. He's well protected. We can't conduct a full on assault against him, gotta chip away at his support structure till he's got nothing left to stand on. If we want to bring him to justice then it can't be rushed." Though he spoke it aloud, reiterating his intentions, an undercurrent of Plan B wafted through his thoughts. He'd been making progress with Estrella, overcoming those mental barriers that prevented him from pulling it off, but this was merely precaution. Sharp was confident he wouldn't need to enact Plan B. *Though it is the easier route to take.*

Silva scoffed, pulling Sharp away from his thoughts. "So in other words it might never happen." Sharp opened his mouth to speak but Silva cut him off. "December is a long time from now. If we hold off till then, it'll be impossible to remount a second occupation here, the momentum would be gone. The Bezerras will have their victory. I can't allow that. And, frankly, I don't know if I can listen to any more of this." Silva motioned to get up, but Sharp let out a hand to stop him.

"At least give it some thought," Sharp suggested desperately, he couldn't afford to let Plan A crumble before his eyes. "I know this is a lot to take in, but—"

Silva spat out, "Balthazar has done so much for us, I can't just turn my back on him because of what you say. I barely know you. Just because the Mayor trusts you, doesn't mean I should. You've given me nothing."

"I know," Sharp flailed as one does when refusing to listen to the inevitable death knell. "All I have is my word right now. But in time I will have more evidence. I've got people—"

"Even if what you say is true, we can't be so easily evicted. We're prepared to take on an army."

"So you think. But this is going to be so much more ruthless. Blood will be spilt and a lot of it. Worse than Eldorado."

"Sharp," Silva stated sternly, on the verge of bursting. "We are already putting our lives at risk by being here. Every day the Bezerras threaten us with death. They harass us every chance they get. Those gunmen out there are a constant reminder of what we are up against. We're not afraid of what they can do to us, because we know that at the end of all this we will finally have a chance at Paradise. And Balthazar right now is the only person supporting us. He will guide us through the worst of it. Should the Bezerras attempt to evict us forcefully then we'll be ready. We will not give up."

Sharp breathed an exasperated sigh. "You're making a huge mistake."

Silva stood up. "I think you should leave. We're done here."

Sharp jumped out of his chair to counter, "Silva, I know how much this means to you. But this isn't just about the Bezerra land anymore. It's about all of Brazil, and Latin America, and the World. The Pope's fixing to set the world on fire."

"Then maybe it should be!" Silva unleashed, delivering the death blow.

Taken aback, Sharp stared into his eyes, they had turned hard as stone. His confidence wilting, Sharp didn't know what to say. Probably best to just cut his losses and leave before he could cause any more damage. He might have lost the battle here, but not the war—he still had time, he could still make Silva see the truth before it was too late. That alone kept Sharp's resolve alive. As he turned to leave, Sharp muttered one last refrain, "I'll be back." Then, like a wounded animal, he scampered away through the tents.

Traveling through the labyrinthine path between the haphazard tents, Sharp calculated his next move. Plan A was not entirely dead, not yet. And Sharp shouldn't have expected it to unfold exactly the way he wanted it to so easily, that was a foolish thing to believe. It just needed to be adjusted to developments on the ground.

An idea popped into his head: Luís Stedile. Balthazar had murdered him for intervening between the occupation and Bezerras, perhaps if someone were to take up that mantle—in secret, with greater security, of course—and negotiate a resolution, then this'll blindside Balthazar and undercut his plans. Sharp perked up. *Quadros should know someone who'd be willing to play the part.*

As this new strategy took form in his head, a subtle change in the air nudged at the corners of his consciousness. Sharp stopped in the thoroughfare, close to the giant cross where Balthazar had given his speech, and scanned his surroundings, nothing appeared out of the ordinary yet something felt off. Even others around him began to take notice, a few stopped what they were doing and looked around unsettled.

He tried to brush it off as merely the heat getting to him, but he couldn't shake it. Something was troubling him, and the feeling wasn't his alone. Those around him felt it too, and it seemed to spread, more heads popped up over the tents to share in their collective unease.

Looking down, he could swear that the earth was trembling beneath his feet. *An earthquake?* He wondered.

Then someone nearby shouted, catching his attention, and pointed into the distance. Sharp followed the person's outstretched hand to a point in the road that broke over the horizon. There a small puff of brown smoke bubbled in the air.

Soon that puff of smoke grew into a storm cloud of dust with what looked like a small black insect at its epicenter. As it charged forward, the insect split into several others and started to take on a uniform shape: big rectangular creatures bearing their metallic teeth with hungry wide reflective eyes. A frenzied horde came to feast.

Before Sharp realized what was coming, the campers were already shouting commands and scurrying about hurriedly, panic stuttered their movement and alarm rang in their voices. The occupation sprang to life—the blazing heat no longer a match for their call to action. Men retreated to the polythene tents while women and children charged forward and fell into formation before the barbed wire fence. They held pots, pans, utensils, whatever was close at hand when they heard the call.

Sharp watched this unfold unsure what was happening. Bewildered, he didn't know what to do, but had the good sense to find a safe place to hide. Keeping his eye on the commotion before him, Sharp stepped backwards till he found himself pressed up against the base of the cross. He dipped behind it, leaning his head out to observe.

Silva appeared from the line of tents, his face tight as he scrambled across the campsite yelling out orders. To Sharp he bounded about like a general overseeing the placement of his soldiers before enduring the assault of an invading army.

The insects scurried across the dirt road on the other side of the fence, and came to a stop one after another. A white streak ran across their bodies bordering the word "*Policia.*"

Sharp's eyes went wide. *No, what are they doing here? They can't be...*

A ramp descended from the back of the vehicles and a flock of police officers poured out of them. Their boots pounded a heavy rhythm drowning out all other noise. They fell into formation mirroring the women and children; only they were dressed in heavy armor and visored helmets not loose gowns and T-shirts; and held pistols and automatic rifles in their hands. A patch of Velcro ran across their left breast where a name tag should have been.

From the blur of black faceless officers one stepped forward carrying a megaphone. The insignia on his helmet designated him as the Commander-in-Chief. He lifted the megaphone to his visor. It whined to life before he spoke:

"This is your first and only warning to peacefully gather your belongings and leave the premises. As ordered from the state of Pernambuco, I have been given full authority to do whatever in my power to end this illegal gathering once and for all. I do not want there to be violence. Do as I say and nobody will be harmed. However, if you have not shown signs of leaving in ten minutes then I will have no choice but to use force. You have ten minutes to decide."

The megaphone whined out and a hostile silence descended upon the occupation. The Commander-in-Chief dropped the megaphone to his side, looked to his left then his right, then settled in to wait.

Nobody moved a muscle. Men, women, and children of the occupation stood their ground as was drilled into them months in advance. All there was to protect them was their ragged worse-for-wear clothing. The rocks, frying pans, sticks, whatever they held, were no match for the weaponry and riot gear of the police. Though the campsite comprised over 10,000 people, the small number of the police had superior—and lethal—methods at their disposal. A confrontation could lead to a bloodbath.

Sharp gawked at the two ad-hoc armies, his mind struggling to understand: *Is this Balthazar's? But it's too early. No, I was supposed to have time... I had till...* Reflexively, he glanced at his watch. And, though he did not expect it to provide any comfort, the gesture merely instinctual whenever time was invoked, it did stun him to the core, revealing his simplest, yet most consequential, mistake. The way Americans write dates they place the month before the day while the European system swaps the two. So when Sharp read the numbers 12082011, he assumed it meant December 8, 2011, yet Scharnhorst was German and would have meant 12 August 2011. And today was August 12, 2011.

Before he could berate himself, Sharp kicked forward toward the row of tents and huddled men. Adrenaline coursed through his veins and his heart thundered against his ribcage. He searched those assembled for the white hair of Silva, but he couldn't find any trace of him. Panic began to overwhelm him.

Sharp received a bevy of confused looks as he dodged in and out between the staggered rows of men. Sharp didn't care, he pushed on hoping to correct his mistake before it was too late.

But the longer he searched in vain for Silva, the more his hope drained away from him. *Why can't I find Silva?* His search took on the difficulties of trying to find a kid in a carnival; always spotting him in the corner of his eye only to discover they weren't there or tricked by someone who looked faintly similar. Silva was nowhere to be found. *It's like he's disappeared completely.*

An explosion of gunfire proclaimed that time was up. However, it didn't come from the police officers on the other side of the fence, it came from the other side of the camp where the barrier of trucks were. The gunmen were attacking!

Sharp joined the collective of men who whipped their heads around to the sound of gunfire. Gunmen stormed through the nearest tents, tearing apart the polythene, smashing possessions, and upending furniture. They left nothing untouched in their wake. The occupiers who had taken refuge when the police arrived fled from the new threat that had descended upon them. Sharp watched the chaos rage with shock plastered against his face.

That's when he heard a whistling fly above him. Looking up, he saw a stream of smoke sail through the air. A gas canister thudded against the dirt and hissed out its white phosphorus contents. Several of its brethren soon followed, and doused the line of women and children in a thick mist.

A chorus of wood snapping punctured the hiss of gas, quickly replaced by the coordinated stomping of heavy boots. Through the shifting gaps in the smoke Sharp could just make out the wail of batons and the thrust of riot shields. A cry of terror emanated from the smoke.

Sharp stood watching as the police horribly abused the women and children like a pack of farm animals meant for the slaughter. He couldn't move, couldn't react; the atrocities he was witnessing shut him down. All he could do was observe as one officer flung a girl into the dirt and proceeded to beat her mother with the butt of his pistol, indifferent to their pleas for mercy. Getting up, the daughter grabbed a rock and threw it. It thundered against the officer's helmet making him stumble for a moment. In retaliation he raised his firearm and fired. The mother screamed bloody murder and scrambled to her fallen child, cradling her body in her hands as tears cascaded down her cheeks. Her child was the first to die.

The gunshot snapped Sharp out of his paralytic state and he quickly assessed the situation. He had to get out of there. He had to make it to his car.

The frontline broke completely, women and children retreated into the labyrinth of polythene tents while the police pressed their advantage.

One officer turned towards Sharp, his visor made his head look like a giant metallic orb. Then readied his rifle and pulled the trigger.

Sharp jumped to the side just in time, a spray of bullets whizzed by him. Without hesitation, he kicked forward into a run and disappeared into the maze of billowing white smoke and black tents. The faceless officer went into pursuit.

A burst of bullets exploded behind Sharp, but none came close to hitting him. Whether the officer aimed to kill or just to scare didn't matter, the blatant tactic achieved its purpose. Sharp the helpless prey fled, panicked, frightened, from his ever vigilant predator.

All around him was pandemonium. A frantic stampede of ten thousand occupiers no longer united as one, clambering to escape, to survive. It was every man, woman, and child for themself.

Sharp forced his way through a crowd of hurrying occupiers headed in the opposite direction. He butted elbows and shoulders, pushed away those directly in his path with little regard, and yelled at them to make way—though none listened. They couldn't listen, fear had clogged their ears and panic had stifled their reason. They'd been reduced to nothing more than wild beasts whipped into a frenzy.

Sharp dipped behind a still standing tent and caught his breath. Looking over, he found no sight of the officer. He breathed out a sigh of relief, then immediately assessed the situation. From what he could tell the police had advanced deep enough into the campsite causing them to spread out their forces and leave an opening wide enough for Sharp to slip through and get to his car.

Taking his chance, Sharp kept his head low and weaved through the carnage of ransacked tents, smashed tables and chairs, and the occasional body prostrate in the dirt, their moans the only means of separating the living from the dead. Soon the smoke grew thicker obfuscating his pathway and confusing him. Sharp nearly landed in the middle of a skirmish between occupiers and evictors before catching himself in time to retreat. Backtracking, he realized he had no clue where he was going, the scenes around him looked all the same throwing off his internal compass. He didn't know which way to go.

But then he glimpsed the top of the giant cross peeking over the plume of smoke. Using that as his guide, he sprang forward, careful not to attract the attention of the officers and the gunmen. He shut out the sound of war raging around him and kept his mind focused on his main objective: escape.

He nearly reached the clearing, freedom nearly within reach, when suddenly a figure stepped before him blocking his path. Sharp skated to a stop and eyed the man, an empty holster hung at his hip; dust plastered his jeans and shirt; and his mustache bent upwards tracing the smile on his lips. Sharp's eyes widened in recognition. *The bomber!*

Sharp swallowed down the dust in his throat as the gunman raised his pistol. His finger squeezed the trigger, but Sharp was faster. He swatted the pistol aside and the bullet went wide of its mark by an inch. He then darted back into the labyrinth of tents. The gunman on his tail.

He jumped over a body and diverted into a neglected tent. All that was present was a green cot and a rickety table. On top of the table sat a frying pan. Grabbing it, he waited by the entrance. When the gunman entered Sharp swung with all of his might. It hit his shoulder causing him to flinch, an angry cry escaped his lips. Bent over, nursing his newest injury, the gunman leveled his pistol and fired. It ripped through the tent wall and a death cry sounded outside.

Before he could get another shot off, Sharp reeled the frying pan back over his shoulder. But before he could swing, the gunman let fly a fist with his other hand, catching Sharp right in the gut. A gasp escaped his lips as he stumbled back. The pan fell to his side.

Then the gunman rushed at him squaring his good shoulder right into Sharp's ribcage, the two toppled over onto the cot. The metal sidebar banged against Sharp's shoulder blade. He let out a cry as his hand lost its grip on the frying pan. It thudded onto the dirt floor.

Holding him down, the gunman's eyes had a glint to them like a hunter about to bag the most sought after game. But Sharp refused to go down without a fight. He swung his head forward smashing his forehead against the gunman's nose. Sharp heard something snap upon contact.

A banshee wail exploded from his mouth as blood oozed out of the gash across the bridge of his nose. Sharp pushed the gunman off and scrambled to his feet. The gunman remained on the cot rocking from side to side and nursing his nose between his fingers. Sharp stood over him watching him writhe in pain, then a glint of metal just below him caught his eye. He had dropped his pistol right beside the flying pan.

Sharp went for it, swooping it up into a tight fist, and took aim. The gunman shouted something in Portuguese, a curse from the way it sounded, before opening his eyes a fraction and noticing the weapon pointed at him. He stopped fidgeting and stared up at Sharp. His eyes welled with water, the lower half of his face covered in blood.

Sharp's finger wrapped around the trigger. That's as far as it went before an image of his father flashed through his mind. But this image was different from the others. Usually Sharp saw his father as his father, the man he looked up to for moral guidance, yet now he stood before Sharp in his uniform, as a police officer, as a defender of the law. And though he had been too young at the time to know the awful things his father had seen and done while on patrol, the things that keep him up at night, his mother eventually relayed them to Sharp when he was old enough to understand. Sometimes drastic measures had to be taken in order to secure peace.

Only now did Sharp see with clarity. Only now did he stop resisting the ultimate truth. His father had carried a heavy burden on his shoulders every time he put on that uniform. Every day he had to determine the lesser of two evils and follow through no matter how much it tore away at his conscience. That was the sacrifice he made for the law. And yet he still turned out a decent man, and a loving father. Perhaps the same could be true of Sharp.

But it would be on his terms: no needless bloodshed. The gunman wasn't the one who deserved to die—at least without due process first. *No,* Sharp realized, *he's only following orders. It's the man giving orders that matters. And the moment he used his influence to cause harm to others that's when he surrendered his own rights. The law no longer applies to him.* Justification enough for Sharp to feel at ease for what he knew he needed to do next—Plan B.

His mind made up, Sharp stepped forward, bent over the gunman, and smacked him across the forehead with the butt of the pistol. The gunman collapsed like a sack of potatoes.

Pocketing the pistol, Sharp cautiously peeked outside; the pandemonium had moved elsewhere in the camp giving him a clear path to his car. Darting out, he ran across the open thoroughfare and bounded over the torn down wire fence. He jumped into his car and sped away.

About a mile away he finally let out a sigh of relief and relaxed. But the anger and guilt still swirled deep inside of him, motivating him into action. But since the Pope would be surrounded by guards and followers and, therefore, impossible to approach, Sharp decided it was a good alternative to expend some of his energy instead with a little visit to City Hall.

LATE NIGHT CHAT

Mayor Brizola unleashed a yawn as he reclined in his chair. His tie was loosened, his sleeves were rolled up, and his suit blazer hung over the back of his chair. He looked physically and mentally worn out. Swiveling around in his chair, he was surprised to see it dark outside his window. A cityscape before him protected from a pitch black sky by the illumination of the streetlamps.

Checking his watch, he found it later than he expected. He slumped exasperated and stared unfocused at the computer screen, all his energy sapped from his body. These last few days he'd been burning the midnight oil longer than he wanted. He knew he should go home and finish up this proposal another day when he was better rested, but it couldn't wait. Mayor Brizola needed to get this finished so that he could finally present it to Balthazar and earn his acceptance.

But his arms refused to move, his back refused to straighten, and his mind refused to concentrate. He was all tapped out, and it was time to listen to his body. Letting out a heavy sigh, he turned around, moved the mouse, and clicked the save icon. Then proceeded to shut down his computer. Like hoisting a sack of potatoes, Brizola carried himself out of his chair and shrugged into his suit blazer. Drooped over he ambled to the door.

Opening it, he flung his hand out and slapped the light switch. Darkness consumed his office. He stepped through the doorway, but before he could cross completely, a hand materialized in his peripheral and latched itself upon the lapel of his blazer. Mayor Brizola squeaked like a mouse caught in a trap. He hadn't expected anyone else to still be here so late. Whipping his head to the side, Brizola glimpsed only an outline of a figure faintly obscured in shadows.

"Who are you?" the Mayor gasped startled.

The figure pushed him back into the office. "Forgotten me already?" He said, the voice sounded familiar. He flipped on the light switch, closed the door, and thrusted Mayor Brizola against his desk.

Standing face to face, the Mayor now had a good look at the man but didn't recognize him. The beard, the green eyes, the dirty blonde hair, it painted a faint possibility, but it couldn't be. *He had a boyish look to him,* Mayor Brizola remembered, *this guy looks stone cold. It couldn't be the same guy.* Yet the more he studied his features the more likely his notion became. Finally, he ventured aloud. "Ian Sharp?"

"So you do remember me." Sharp smiled, approaching ever closer, their faces mere inches apart. The Mayor braced against the desk. Sharp's piercing gaze burrowed into the Mayor's panicky brown eyes. Unable to withstand it, he shirked his head away and wilted as if trying to disappear into his suit.

"I wondered where you went," he sputtered. "They just told me that you'd gotten everything you needed and had headed back to the States." His body shook. He didn't understand why Sharp was acting so terrifying, but he knew if a struggle would ensue that he'd be no match for Sharp's greater build. "I'm glad to see you're back. But why are you trying to frighten me?"

Sharp placed the palms of his hands on the Mayor's double padded shoulders. "Because I wanted to talk to you," his tone grew friendly, too friendly. Internally, Mayor Brizola shuttered. His heartbeat quickened and his fingers became clammy. He darted his eyes around refusing to make contact with Sharp's. But with a good solid shake Sharp rattled him into submission. "I want to know everything you know."

"Know about what?" He could barely control the panic in his voice. One wrong slip and who knew what would happen. *Sharp wasn't himself, this isn't the same man.*

"Don't play dumb with me." Sharp barked.

"I'm not!" Mayor Brizola cowered. "I don't know what you're talking about."

"The eviction! And don't lie to me, I was there. I barely escaped. Now tell me!"

"Honestly, I don't know what you're talking about," he pleaded.

Sharp forcefully bent him over the desk, yelling. "You expect me to believe that the mayor of Limoeiro knows nothing about the Pope's plans for the Bezerra Occupation!" He pulled him off the desk and dragged him to a bookshelf. The Mayor stumbled over his own feet trying not to fall over. "That you aren't in on it!" Sharp pinned him against the wall of books, a wooden shelf dug into his spine. "Are you seriously that incompetent, or what?"

"The Bezerras wouldn't dare evict," the Mayor whimpered. "They wouldn't risk that kind of press coverage."

"Exactly, just the way the Pope would want it."

"What?" The Mayor exclaimed, taken aback. "Alex? No. He left me in charge of that. I'm writing up a proposal as we speak about how to resolve the occupation."

"Don't lie to me!"

"I swear!" Brizola shouted defensively, his sniveling turned to flailing resistance. "He wanted me to be the one who settled this standoff because he trusts me. I've known Alex for a long time and he'd never do anything to endanger his supporters. You saw him at the *Safra* celebrations."

"Probably staged like everything else." He hissed through gritted teeth.

"No, he's a good man. He wouldn't harm a fly."

"Yeah!" Sharp volleyed, his anger matching Brizola's obstinacy, "Then tell that to Senator Stedile and Minister Quadros. He had them killed, and he wouldn't bat an eye at the hundreds who died today."

"No! No! No! No! NO!" Mayor Brizola thrashed about. His hands swung wildly. A leg kicked out as if succumbing to some uncontrollable spasms. He struggled to break free, but Sharp held him tight in his vice-like grasp against the bookshelf.

"Mayor Brizola, get a hold of yourself," Sharp strained to hold him down. "It's time to quit fooling yourself. The Pope is nothing more than—"

The hardcover smacked Sharp right on the cheek. His head whipped to one side, but his hands never loosened from the Mayor's lapels. Realizing his mistake, Mayor Brizola dropped the book and braced for whatever might come next.

Recovering, Sharp eyed him with fury burning within them. He pulled Mayor Brizola off the bookshelf and swung him around like a ragdoll, then let go. He sailed through the air, tumbling over the desk—knocking over the computer monitor—then crashed into his chair. It collapsed to the ground with Mayor Brizola cradled in its armrests dazed.

Sharp was on him, towering over Mayor Brizola. Terrified, he raised a hand to stop him and pleaded for mercy. "Please! You have to believe me! Alex is a good man! It must be a misunderstanding, whatever you think he's done!"

Hoping to sooth a raging bull, Mayor Brizola had unknowingly waved a red cape before Sharp's eyes. His words only further infuriated him. In a blur, he snatched Mayor Brizola out of the chair and foisted him onto his feet; then, with a hand, smashed his face against the glass window pane.

"What do you think would happen to you from this height?" Sharp inquired. "Don't think it'll kill you, but I would say it might hurt a lot. Don't you think?"

His face pressed against the glass, Mayor Brizola rasped out, "Don't." This wasn't the same man from before, he was a crazed lunatic.

"Then tell me what I want to know!"

"I already—"

"No!" Sharp cut him off. "Surely, you must know what's going on. You can't be that big of a fool."

A tear welled up at the edge of the Mayor's eyelid and sailed down the crease of his nose to his lips. The tension in his body left him and his frame visibly sank. Defeated he whispered, "Alex has never approved of me. Never liked me. I'm sure he wishes I never even existed." His voice filled with sorrow. Like reciting some magic spell, his words cast away a veil revealing a truth he had buried deep within himself and had preferred left unspoken. "He doesn't involve me in any of his plans. Doesn't tell me anything." He sniffed back a tear. "It's all been a lie."

"What are you saying?" Sharp's voice softened, his hold loosened.

"I believed him because I wanted to believe him." With face still smashed against the window, Mayor Brizola stared out overlooking the beautiful nighttime glow of Limoeiro. "I've bit my tongue so many times because I wanted him to like me. And whenever he threw crumbs at me I leapt at them, thinking this was my chance to finally prove myself worthy."

Sharp eyed the Mayor, uncertainty arched a brow. Silence pervaded the room as the anger within him suddenly dissipated and he released the Mayor.

Rubbing at his cheek, Mayor Brizola stepped out of range from Sharp's immediate reach. And watched carefully as Sharp bent over and righted his chair, perhaps as an act of remorse, then plopped onto the couch. He sat there still, slumped forward, his head in his hands. Sense seemed to have returned to him. But the Mayor wasn't about to let his guard down, especially not after receiving a taste of what Sharp was capable of.

What happened? He wondered. *He was like some wild beast. A journalist wouldn't act like this.*

Licking his lips, Mayor Brizola broke the silence. "You don't work for the New Yorker, do you? Who are you? What are you?"

Sharp raised his head, balancing his chin on the tips of his fingers. "I'm an agent for Sector Seven, a secret government agency tasked with investigating and preventing foreign and domestic attacks on the United States. And the Pope is a threat to the United States."

The Mayor shook his head. "He can't be." But the moment the words escaped his lips he lowered his head despondent. Another truth revealed itself. How many times had Balthazar rebuffed him, ignored him, or just plain bullied him, while Mayor Brizola willfully turned a blind eye to his more aggressive nature or made excuses for his actions? It was time to stop lying to himself and face reality. Balthazar was capable of anything.

And what of the occupation? The thought steeled him, rallied him. Setting his jaw tightly against his teeth, he straightened. A powerful resolve fueled him.

"Sharp, tell me what happened," Mayor Brizola demanded sternly. "Everything. What is my brother up to?"

"Brother?" Sharp repeated, stunned.

"Half-brother," He amended. "Same father, different mothers. My mom never mentioned my father until she was on her deathbed. That's usually when big secrets are revealed, isn't it?" He paused rubbing his tongue across his teeth as he re-lived that moment. "Well I was late into my teens when she told me, and we had been outcasts most of my life. If it wasn't for the library I wouldn't have had any form of education. The librarian took pity on me; she was the closest thing to extended family I ever had. But when I found out I had a real family, and even a brother, I was so excited. But Alex wasn't. He saw me as nothing more than a bastard when we first met—a liar." As he recounted his story, he drifted over to his chair and sat down. He scanned the office for nothing in particular. "Then one day I got a call from out of the blue, and it was Alex, calling to make amends. Next thing I know I'm running for Mayor of Limoeiro and he's supporting me all the way…wonder how many votes he bought," he muttered thinking aloud. Then shook his head and focused on Sharp. "Anyway, here we are." He let out his hands. "Now tell me what my brother has done."

It took Sharp half an hour to brief Mayor Brizola on what he had discovered during his investigation. He did his best to leave no details out, starting from the assassination of Quadros and ending with his escape from the eviction of the Bezerra Occupation. Mayor Brizola listened silently, only piping up to ask a question or two for clarification from time to time. When Sharp finished, all the Mayor could do was whisper, "My God."

Sharp concurred with the sentiment with a nod of his head. "He has a personal vendetta against the United States, and this group he's a part of has given him the means to exact revenge. The Pope needs to be stopped."

Mayor Brizola reclined back, cupped his chin in the palm of his hand, and let out a sigh. "And all this time I believed he wanted nothing more than to revive the *Santidade*. Was it all a lie?"

"The *Santidade* is nothing more than a cult led by a madman."

"No!" Mayor Brizola unleashed defensively. "That's not true! The *Santidade* is a symbol of hope, founded on the slaves' desire for freedom. We might have broken those physical chains that bound us centuries ago, but there are so many new chains—invisible chains—that hold us down. That's why the *Santidade* needed to be reborn—so that those chains could be broken once again." His words gushed out of his mouth like a waterfall and with the same intensity. "Alex gave that to me—a purpose. That's what I ran on. I refuse to give that up." Only when he finished did Mayor Brizola realize he was breathing heavily. He had been shouting.

Sharp stared at him, a look of surprise washed across his face before a smile twisted his lips and his eyes beamed excitedly. "You are related. You sounded almost like the Pope himself right there." Mayor Brizola scoffed, but Sharp went on. "It's true. If only he listened to you. I'm sure you noticed what he's done with the *Santidade*. That with him in charge he'll only bring destruction to your cause and to this country. People are going to die."

"But it doesn't have to be," The Mayor urged. "I was hoping to convince Alex to make the Bezerra Occupation something bigger than just land redistribution. We need to shift the paradigm completely. If we wanted change—real change—then our actions have to be bolder than what they've been. We've got to think bigger. That's why I've been working on this proposal to present to Alex and to the leaders of the MST."

"What proposal?"

The Mayor licked his lips eagerly, he grew as giddy as a boy about to present in front of the class during show and tell. "I want to establish a municipality!"

"What?" Sharp asked, his disappointment inversely correlated with the Mayor's level of enthusiasm.

Undeterred, he continued, "Not necessarily a new idea, it's been done before, but we have the opportunity here to do it on a bigger scale. Even if we appropriated only a fraction of the Bezerra lands, it'll still be enough land for the occupiers to develop. We could build houses, schools, police stations, fire departments, and what have you. Create a government based on the ideas of the *Santidade*; and it'll all be on the level. Limoeiro and this new municipality will demonstrate what's possible. Show Brazil that a utopia can exist. Plus with Alex's backing it'll get the financial support it'll need to grow, as well as the press attention it deserves."

"And you really think this could work?"

"Yes," he declared unequivocally. "The more attention we get the more people will learn of the *Santidade*. They'll see a government acting on good faith, proposing and implementing real reforms, and producing concrete results. They'll be inspired by us and motivated to enact change themselves. Soon one municipality after another will adopt our programs, followed by the big cities till, hopefully, the national government does so too." The light within him dimmed some when reality reminded him of events currently unfolding. "But none of this could happen without that spark, and the Bezerra Occupation was supposed to be that. But now, I guess, it'll never happen. Alex chose a different path to take. Had I known I would have done everything I could to stop it. He's been playing me all these years, and here I've been bending over backwards to get him to accept me.

"And yet I can't fully hate him." Mayor Brizola said as he reminisced about his past. "He's the one that introduced me to the *Santidade*. And by doing that he gave me something I've always wanted."

"What?" Sharp asked.

He swallowed, water welled at the edge of his eyes. "A family. The *Santidade* has become my family. When I had nobody, they embraced me. Showed me love, and cared for me. They made me feel wanted. The happiest day of my life was when I became Mayor." He laughed, a tender laugh. "To think how far I've come. I would do anything for them."

"Then fight for them. The *Santidade* needs you now more than ever."

"How? I can't go against Balthazar."

"You'll have to. You can help me expose him for who he is and what he's done. Together we can bring him to justice."

Brizola shook his head. Defeat already settled in his heart. He knew nothing could be done, but to watch helplessly as his beloved *Santidade* crumbled before him. "That's very noble of you, but very naïve."

Sharp narrowed his eyes. "What do you mean?"

"You can't just believe that once you hand this off to the system that it'll handle everything the way it should—meting out just sentences to the guilty. Because oftentimes it's an unjust sentence for the innocent. Whenever humans are involved you have a faulty system. It's impossible to account for their emotions, their ideologies, their desires, and their beliefs. There's a chance that this could backfire."

"But once the evidence is out there then everyone will have no choice but to take action against the Pope."

"Sharp," Mayor Brizola sighed. "Alex has thousands of landless works behind him. They think he's the next coming of Jesus Christ. Do you really believe that showing them the facts is going to change their minds? It's not, because they've already developed an unshakeable image of him in their heads. They'll dismiss anything that even remotely contradicts that image. Create any excuses, no matter how wild, just to protect their worldview. All you'll do is further inflame the passions of the MST, and they'll rally behind Alex even harder. Is that the risk you're willing to take?"

Sharp lowered his head in thought. Then mumbled aloud, "There's another way to save the *Santidade*."

"There is?" Mayor Brizola inquired. He could see the gears turning in Sharp's head, formulating a new plan right there on the spot.

Leaning forward Sharp whispered conspiratorially, "You'll do anything for the *Santidade*, right?"

"Yes."

"Good. This'll require your cooperation."

His tone unnerved Mayor Brizola. He asked hesitantly, "What do I have to do?"

"Better left unsaid." Sharp jumped up from the couch, getting ready to leave. "All you have to do is be ready to act when I give you the signal."

The Mayor narrowed his eyes. "Signal? What's it going to be?"

"You'll know..." He walked to the door and right before exiting he repeated, "You'll know."

THE SIGNAL

A sea of red ballcaps, signs, and MST flags flooded through the *Eixo Monumental* leading to where a stage had been erected in the center of the *Praça dos Três Poderes.* Thousands of angry landless Brazilians gathered there to protest the horror of the Bezerra Occupation eviction, and champion sweeping land reform once and for all. Enough had been enough.

Since the eviction, news of the Occupation spread like wildfire throughout Brazil. Media outlets ran nonstop discussions, held deeply opinionated debates, and blasted the call to action. In the days to follow the masses poured out into the streets to protest. They first started as small gatherings where supporters and detractors spontaneously sparred outside local government buildings and hurled insults at each other, while the police stood aside maintaining the peace.

However that changed when a small group of newly radicalized *militantes* decided to take matters into their own hands. In the dead of night they stormed the premises of the Bezerra plantation, barged into their hacienda—murdering security guards and two Bezerra members in the process—and took the household hostage. National troops were called out to handle the situation, prompting 24 hour nonstop coverage that glued the nation to their television screens. As the standoff ensued, Brazil split even further: half the nation hailed the actions of the *militantes* while the other half vilified them. There no longer was any room left for compromise.

Meanwhile the cry for agrarian reform reached its crescendo as an ear shattering roar. Yet, government officials resisted the people's cries for as long as they could and that only further inflamed their passions. So the landless and their supporters cried harder and louder. And the man who led this chorus was none other than Alexander Balthazar.

Balthazar was ubiquitous, appearing on every news program that would have him and offering full-throated praise for what the *militantes* were doing. He made speeches at protests and rallies, and demanded the government to act on agrarian reform. He shook hands with the newly minted Minister of Agrarian Development for a photo-op, and joined President Rousseff for a sit down emergency meeting behind closed doors.

As for the standoff, it came to a rather lackluster end. The *militantes* eventually surrendered peacefully—no exciting final showdown as had been anticipated. Nevertheless, Balthazar jumped at the chance to decry the federal government's involvement and their close relationship with the wealthy class. Surprisingly the Minister of Agrarian Development publicly agreed with him and pushed forth a radical piece of legislation that closed "social function" loopholes and increased regulator powers for INCRA. The MST immediately announced its support for the bill, and thousands—if not millions—of Brazilians voiced their agreement. Thus now Congress found itself trapped between a rock and a hard place. They had hoped to delay passage of it until cooler heads prevailed, but Balthazar had other plans in mind.

"...For too long you have been unable to speak." The tinny echo of Minister Griesel's voice reverberated through the loudspeakers. He stood on the stage behind a podium, gesticulating wildly. Several cameras scattered amongst the protesters captured his movements and broadcasted it on a jumbo screen just off to the left of the stage. "Nearly fifty years ago it had been the Military dictatorship who planted their boots on your throats, but now it is the inaction of this Congress that threatens to suffocate us once again. Deny us our voice so that we may never yell again. And I say no longer! If they will not hear our words then let them hear our actions!" The masses exploded in a round of applause and cheers.

Just off stage, hidden behind a long tall black partition, Mayor Brizola and Alexander Balthazar stood watching the Minister's performance. A thin stack of notecards hovered before Balthazar's chest as his lips mouthed silent words. Periodically he glimpsed down and scanned the hastily handwritten words, then continued to mumble quietly to himself.

The Mayor could feel Balthazar's nervousness emanating off of him despite his statuesque demeanor. The cards never waved in his hands, sweat never materialized along his forehead, and his behavior never turned cagey. He exhibited nothing but calm.

He, on the other hand, was a ball of anxiety. Though the Mayor wasn't scheduled to give a speech today, he had received a letter that morning. Someone had slipped it under his hotel door and all it said was: 'Today.' That was enough to send him on edge; the anticipation alone threatened to undo him.

"Quite a big crowd gathered," Mayor Brizola commented for the simple sake of saying something to distract himself. "And I'm sure there are millions all over Brazil watching all this on television. Certainly has snowballed quickly, wouldn't you say?" He glanced at his half-brother who wasn't listening, too focused on his speech. Mayor Brizola continued on as if he had replied, "Yeah, and to think just a few weeks ago our objective had just been to get the Bezerras to redistribute some of their land. Now we're pressuring Congress to do that on an unprecedented level. Strange where fate should take us, huh?"

Balthazar didn't react, he merely muttered a few indistinguishable words under his breath.

"It's just a shame how we had to get here, don't you think?" He prodded, baiting Balthazar to react. "A repeat of Eldorado, but on a much grander scale." Brizola knew exactly what he was doing. He wanted to be caught, let his brother know that he knew what he shouldn't know, and thus prove that it was foolish to underestimate him. Yet as much as he tried to lure him into his trap, Balthazar either failed to take notice or just didn't care. Brizola looked directly at Balthazar and emphasized, "It's as if someone had planned it that way."

That caught his attention. "What? Did you say something?"

"Oh, just saying what good this bill would do for the *Santidade*," he let out whimsically, pleased with himself, then turned his attention back to the Minister on stage.

"Oh, yes. Of course," Balthazar expressed absentmindedly.

"Father would be so proud." Out of the corner of his eye, Mayor Brizola could see Balthazar leering at him. He never could hide his disgust that he shared a father with Brizola.

"Yes, I'm sure he would be." He tempered the contempt in his voice.

The two barely spoke about their father—it had become an unwritten rule between them, mainly enforced by Balthazar—so Brizola used that knowledge to needle Balthazar a little. He pressed on. "What do you think he would say about what you've done with the *Santidade*? He would surely be astonished."

"Doesn't matter what he would think." Balthazar brushed the thought aside. "All he cared about was the status quo, and never stepping out of line in case the military returned. The thought of that paralyzed him—and made him do stupid things," he exclaimed pointedly at Brizola. "When he died, I wondered what my purpose would be as the new Pope. I was afraid for a time—afraid that I'd be just like him. But as you can see, I'm not. You on the other hand..." He buried the rest in heated silence. "I refused to make the same mistakes as him. And look at where I am now."

"Oh, I'm sure he wasn't as bad as you think," Mayor Brizola countered. "I never had the chance to meet him, but from the stories I've heard he was always a gracious and gentle person. People of Limoeiro still talk about him fondly."

"He was a simpleton, a coward," Balthazar bit back. "I made it my mission to never be like him. But the more you try not to be like someone, the less you're trying to be like yourself. I had boxed myself in and I couldn't get out. That was until I got the phone call."

"Phone call?"

"The call that changed everything. They offered me retribution." A smile spread across his face and his eyes lit up. "And how could I resist? It's taken seven long years to reach this point, but it's finally here and soon I'll taste sweet victory."

This was the most Balthazar had ever opened up to Brizola, and Brizola wasn't about to let it end. "There's more to life than retribution, Alex. So what if you exact revenge on the United States. Will that really solve anything?"

A rapid succession of emotions flashed across Balthazar's face from surprise, to wonder, to concern, to anger, to acceptance. He finished with a laugh. "If you thought this was just revenge then you have no idea what this is all about."

Mayor Brizola declared bluntly. "You're just using the *Santidade* to fulfill your own personal vengeance. That's wrong."

"No," he barked. "I'm ushering the *Santidade* into a new era, you weak-minded fool. You lack vision. But I...I see a continent where people prosper in the name of the *Santidade*. Working day and night, night and day, every day. Soon, where Latin America once stood will be a string of provinces of modernization, industrialization, and cultivation. Underdevelopment will be a thing of the past. Memorials will be erected to honor the *Santidade*, and streets will be dedicated to my namesake. A magnificent revolution tearing down capitalism and nationalism so that the *Santidade* can rise from the ashes. All because of the triumphant leadership of Alexander Balthazar, the Pope of Sugar. Everything will praise my glorious achievements. Newspapers, movies and wonderful, wonderful murals stretching as far as the eye can see. My God, it'll be beautiful."

Brizola's eyes widened in shocked disbelief. He was speechless. But before any more could be said between them, Minister Griesel's shouting caught their attention. "Now, it is my pleasure to introduce you to the man who made all this possible. Please welcome to the stage, Alexander Baltahzar."

The crowd erupted in applause as Balthazar jumped the stairs and emerged onto the stage. He waved his hands in the air greeting the masses. Mayor Brizola watched him go, his whole worldview crumbling before him. He had suspected Balthazar to be zealous, but he hadn't expected the depth of it to be so deep. And now that he had taken the plunge, he couldn't ignore what he saw. *He's a fanatic,* Mayor Brizola reflected sadly, *and a dangerous one.* Rubbing his temples with a finger, he berated himself for having blindly followed this man, latching onto his every word like an obedient lapdog and waiting for praise that would never come.

"Oh, Sharp," he uttered under his breath. "Whatever you're going to do, do it quick."

Balthazar strode to the podium and stood there a moment basking in the crowd's revelry. His pearl white teeth beamed through a wide triumphant smile. Then he thrust out a hand and gestured for the masses to quiet. When they did he began:

"Amazing, simply amazing." He scanned the crowd from left to right, then glanced down at his notecards. "We are on the precipice of a new era here in Brazil. Once upon a time it was we, Brazilians, who guided our future: we ended slavery, took down a king, built a republic, and prospered. However with the dawning of the twentieth century our future was snatched away from us and passed around, like some game of hot potato, from one authoritarian regime to the next. Starting with Vargas and ending with Figueiredo...or so we thought. When democracy returned we rejoiced, but now the veil has been removed revealing our true authoritarians, the true puppet masters: the landowners who backed these dictators. Men working behind the scenes to ensure their survival and your suppression." A hiss spread through the crowd. "But today we end that forever. Today we take back our power and make Brazil the nation it was always destined to be."

Mayor Brizola listened to his speech, though really only half listened. Subconsciously, his mind was elsewhere, mentally preparing a speech of his own. He pulled from the ether lines he had jotted down a long time ago and spliced them together. Sentences he had created during flights of fancy and never expecting to have to actually speak them aloud, but the moment had finally arrived. Sharp had told him to be ready for when he gave the signal, and the letter he received that morning told him he was running out of time to prepare.

An inkling of what the signal will be crept into his thoughts—he had to be ready.

Taking a breath, he returned his attention back to Balthazar.

"…The last few months have not been kind to us. With every advance we make, they seek to rip it away. We elevated a champion of reform and he was brutally assassinated on a goodwill tour in the United States. And still his killer has not been found—the United States refused to give that man up. And our weak-willed President has done little to force their hand. It's as if they're waiting for tides to turn, till we've forgotten and moved on to other things. And, boy, were there other things…'

Mayor Brizola turned away entirely as Balthazar delved into the events of the last few months. He couldn't bear hearing all the deeds that he himself had orchestrated. The lie was too much to bear. Instead, he called out to a nearby stage hand and asked for a piece of paper and a pencil. When he got them, he began to write down his speech and make the necessary corrections where needed.

This one speech had to be perfect, it couldn't be some perfunctory gesture or empty words of motivation. It had to come from the heart. Only then will his words have an impact. Yet, it also had to be a difficult balancing act. In one speech he had to offer a eulogy, a revelation, and a promise.

His hand shook and his heart fluttered as his anxiety rattled his nerves, but he continued to write. He refused to submit; he refused to bow down; and he refused to be the fool anymore. *For the Santidade.*

He shook his head, clearing his head of any distractions and wrote on while Balthazar continued to speak.

"...Now is our chance," he blustered proudly. "The coming days will decide whether we will continue with the status quo or march proudly into a world reborn. And if you do not speak up now then I fear it will choose the former. We cannot let that happen. We must raise up our voices together as one so that we are heard. Who here amongst us wishes to see this world—so long debauched—burn so that a new world full of hope and promise could rise from its ashes?"

A wave of uproarious applause washed over Balthazar. He closed his eyes and raised his hands in complete submission to the crowd's jubilation. Pure nirvana on his face.

But then, suddenly, he jerked back, as if a strong gust of wind had slammed against his chest. A sonic boom echoed over the heads of the masses. Mayor Brizola whipped his head up to find Balthazar flying backwards and crashing to the floor. Immediately a horde of stage hands rushed the stage and gathered around the fallen.

Balthazar gurgled out a rivulet of blood from his lips that oozed down his chin. His body shivered, his face grew pale. A stagehand peeled the blazer away to reveal a pool of red spreading across his white shirt. He'd been struck in the chest. Balthazar thrashed weakly for life as his consciousness departed his body.

A team of paramedics pushed through the huddled group and began doing all they could to resuscitate the Pope. But the life behind Balthzar's eyes dimmed till it blinked out completely. His body went lax.

Remaining where he was, Mayor Brizola watched Balthazar be lifted and carried offstage. He knew whatever they did, it would be hopeless. He'd be dead in no time if he wasn't already. Lowering his head, he put the final touches to his speech. He knew he should have felt remorse at what just happened, but the tears never reached his eyes. Now was not the time to cry, he'd have to save that for later, when he could truly shed a tear for his late brother—his only family, and connection to his father.

Finished, he folded the paper and placed it into his pocket. He sighed, expelling his anxiety. *Time to stake my claim.*

Mayor Brizola waited for the confirmation of Balthazar's death before he put his plan into action. In the waiting room of the hospital he assembled the head council of the *Santidade,* made up of the principle administrators of the usina, eight men Balthazar trusted, conferred with, and delegated responsibilities for all things *Santidade.* But Mayor Brizola had a suspicion Balthazar didn't tell them everything, which worked to his advantage. It'd be a lot easier to unroot any plans Alexander Balthazar might have sowed during his reign—*thank God Scharnhorst is dead.* And if he could convince them to support his elevation to the papacy, then the battle would already be half won.

"Pope Balthazar is dead," he said sadly. The collection of men lowered their heads all as one. They tried their best to stifle their cries, but sniffles gave them away. Before the moment of silence could linger for too long, Brizola spoke again. "Take this time to cry. This is a moment worthy of tears. But we can't mourn for too long. Balthazar might be dead, but we can't let his vision for the *Santidade* die with him." A few heads nodded in agreement.

Mayor Brizola scanned the group carefully for any hint of them knowing Balthazar's true intentions. A sideway glance, or a flick of the eyebrow. He spotted none. They'd been left out of the loop just as he had been. *Good, let it stay that way.*

Mayor Brizola went on, "It's what he would want. With that, the press is waiting outside and we need someone to put on a brave face and speak to them." The group of men glanced at one another, apprehension clear on their faces. "I believe I should do it." Their heads whipped towards him. Then he declared proudly, "I am Alexander Balthazar's half-brother. And since he never married and had no children, I am his last relation left on Earth. If you need proof I have it, but for now I ask for your trust, and your approval to be the one who speaks for the *Santidade.* Do I have it?"

A spirited debate consumed the council with Mayor Brizola chiming in occasionally to defend himself, or provide further clarification. It lasted for roughly ten minutes before the council agreed to a vote. It was unanimous. Mayor Brizola would speak to the press, then at a later date they would discuss the matter of his legitimacy and possible elevation to the papacy. Mayor Brizola accepted this without complaint.

With that done, he walked out of the waiting room and into a flurry of snapping lights and shouting reporters. He approached the hastily propped up podium where several microphones stood at the ready. Atop the podium lay a single piece of paper. Eyeing it curiously, he unfolded it and read the scrawl: "The Pope is dead! Long live the Pope!"

Without emotion he folded it and put it into his pocket, then retrieved his speech. He laid it flat, took a breath, and opened his mouth to speak.

HOME

Sharp tore his eye away from the sight of his rifle and observed the pandemonium he had just caused. From this height, it looked like thousands of ants below scattered across the *Eixo Monumental,* fleeing as if some giant beast had upset their anthill.

Turning away from the view, Sharp packed away his sniper rifle into its case then slipped it into a duffle. As he did, the clump in his heart weighed him down heavier than ever before. *It had to be done,* he told himself, *This had to be done.*

Sharp flew down the stairwell, the wide rectangular case jostling at his side. When he reached the first floor he emerged into the lobby and joined the panicked crowd. Keeping his head down, he adjusted his ball cap low so that it covered his face. Panicked Brazilians scurried before him, but all he saw was their feet pass through his limited vision. He couldn't risk looking anyone in the eye, he couldn't handle the thought of it; not with what he's done.

He made his way outside where the scene surrounding Sharp reminded him of an apocalypse movie. Swarms of people racing through the streets in one direction hoping to escape the blast range or something like that. The sight of it produced a pain in his chest. He rubbed his left breast with the palm of his hand trying to ease it some, it had little effect. *You're exaggerating,* he reasoned, *it isn't that bad.* Yet no matter how hard he tried to put what he saw into perspective, his conscience refused to listen. Hundreds became thousands, heavy panting became screams of terror, and curious concern became panicked flights.

At the corner Sharp turned and approached a white nondescript car. He threw the case into the backseat, planted himself behind the steering wheel, and sped off into Brasília's traffic.

He pulled out his cellphone and searched for a particular contact, it rang twice before Estrella picked up.

"Hey, this is Sharp. It's been done."

"Good," Estrella replied. Sharp could hear the melancholy in his voice. Over the last few weeks Estrella's usually laid-back demeanor had grown increasingly downcast for some reason, and every time Sharp asked him about it Estrella brushed him off. "Don't get too comfortable with other people cleaning up your messes," he quipped, but it lacked any real mirth.

"I won't. But my time here is over. Watch over him, okay?"

"I will," Estrella replied. "From here on out João Brizola will have the full backing of Sector Seven. I see a long reign in his future as long as he doesn't step too far out of line."

"He won't," Sharp confirmed. "His radicalism is more incremental, more manageable. He'll be a fine Pope, and might even be a great man one day. Thank you, Estrella, for everything."

"It was no problem. And Anir appreciates all you've done for her. Now she doesn't need to look over her shoulder every second. She's free to do whatever she wants. Though she is still sour over having to conceal Luís's real assassin."

"It has to be done. The Pope's still a hero to many and it has to stay that way. He gave them hope and, maybe, his death will motivate them to build his utopia, but through more constructive means. His message has to endure. Anir understands that, right?"

"She does," he sighed. "But that doesn't mean she has to be happy about it."

The clump bounced to the beat of his heart. "Gotcha. Also, remember that this was Braasch's plan from the beginning. She suffered the abuse last month so that I could conduct my investigation in secret. All the credit goes to her."

"I got it, I got it. Don't worry."

"And thanks again for the training. Who knew the sniper rifle would be my weapon of choice."

"Like I said you needed distance, both physically and psychologically, and a sniper rifle does both."

"Yeah." Sharp reflected on his time at the gun range, the series of weapons he had held but couldn't bring to fire. Then Estrella handed him a sniper rifle and something just clicked inside him. The barrier shattered and all his hesitancy seeped away. Sharp couldn't explain what it was, at least not to himself, but he was satisfied nonetheless, Plan B was a go, now he could become a real Sector Seven agent.

Returning to the phone conversation, Sharp closed, "Alright, it's time to go home. It's been great working with you."

"Same here," Estrella said flatly. "Whenever you're back in Brazil, give me a ring."

"Will do. Goodbye." He hung up the phone.

Before arriving at the airport, he made a quick stop at a post office where he dropped a letter into the mailbox. One addressed to Heather Braasch, and meant for her eyes only. Sharp bit his lip as he let go of the letter reassuring himself that this was the right thing to do. Then returned to his car.

At the airport he grabbed his luggage, minus the duffle bag which was to be collected by a Sector Seven agent at a later time, and hurried through security. Sharp got a bite to eat before his flight and boarded the plane when it was time. He was finally heading home back to San Diego.

As the plane took off Sharp closed his eyes and reflected on his time in Brazil. *It could have gone so much better. Less sloppy. But I did what needed to be done. And it had to be done. Like Truman and the atom bomb I had a choice to make; one life to save millions. I hope it was the right choice. Was it ever this hard for you, dad?*

Sharp shook his head, stopping his train of thought from traveling any further down that road. What's done is done, and that's all that matters.

Instead, he turned his sights onto the immediate future and thought of Katelyn, Susie, and Beth. It had been weeks since he last saw them, last spoke to them. They're going to be so surprised to see him. Sharp smiled at the thought of it. But the feeling didn't last long. His infidelity soured his mood. Another secret he'd have to keep locked away in his heart right next to the clump of guilt.

But that didn't mean he wasn't going to make up for it. No, Sharp was determined to give Katelyn what she wanted, what he promised. First chance he got, he planned to march over to Sector Seven Headquarters, look Sir right in the eye, and demand to be transferred to some sort of desk job, anything that kept him landlocked. And if Sir didn't comply then he'd resign. He owed that much to Katelyn.

The sun was on the descent by the time the plane touched ground in San Diego. Sharp grabbed his baggage from the overhead compartment and booked it straight out the airport. He found his car where he had left it several weeks ago and, fortunately, it still had enough juice in the battery for it to start up. Cruising out of the airport terminal, Sharp breathed a sigh of relief. His adventure was finally coming to an end.

About an hour later through rush hour traffic, Sharp pulled into the driveway. He picked at his wedding ring in the cup holder with his fingers and slipped it on. Something felt off about it—as if this ring wasn't meant for him. It fit just fine, and yet Sharp couldn't shake this feeling that it didn't belong. He swiveled the ring around his finger for a moment then gave up, concluding that he just needed time getting used to wearing it again.

He reached for his belongings in the backseat, then walked the pathway to his oddly deformed house. Nothing had changed about it since he left and Sharp wanted to keep it that way. After a few seconds fumbling with his keys he finally slipped it into the lock and turned. As he crossed the threshold Sharp shouted, "I'm home," and slammed the door shut behind him.

He heard no patter of little feet as he expected, or smelt any cooking wafting from the kitchen. All was still. The house was completely silent.

With the wind gone from his sails, Sharp dropped his baggage by the door and shouted again, "Hello? Anybody here?" He passed through the dining room and into the kitchen. Empty as well, but noticeably more put together than last time he was here. All the moving boxes were gone.

Sharp checked his watch. *Must have gone out to get something to eat. Got a knack for poor timing, don't I?* Yet, when he peered into the garage he found Katelyn's car was still there, worry filled him. *Maybe they went for a walk somewhere,* He speculated. *I should call her.* But he also didn't want to spoil the surprise so he decided against it. He'll wait till they come back.

In the meantime, Sharp proceeded to the little alcove where the washer and dryer lived and dispensed the contents of his baggage into the washer. As it filled with water, he scooped out a cup of laundry detergent and poured it across his dirty clothes, then lowered the lid.

Next, he ascended the stairs and entered the master bath, where he turned on the shower. Staring at himself in the mirror, he leaned in close and combed his fingers through his beard. Then ruffled through the drawers for his electric shaver and got down to business. Once trimmed down close to his skin, he took off his clothes, grabbed a razor, and jumped into the shower. He finished the rest by touch. The water felt nice and hot, exactly how he liked it.

Fifteen minutes later, he stepped out and toweled himself dry. Glancing at the mirror, he looked like his old self again. He smiled.

Once in comfortable night time attire, Sharp headed downstairs where he'd wait for the return of his family. He plopped down onto the couch and switched on the television.

He did very little watching, his mind too busy reflecting and predicting for him to be a captive audience. From time to time he'd glance at his watch and wonder where they were. Surely, Katelyn wouldn't keep the girls out this late.

When darkness took over the outside world completely, Sharp's anxiousness grew too much to bear. He decided to call her. He brought up her contact and, the moment his phone connected with hers, he heard a barely audible ringing coming from somewhere in the house. Sharp looked around, listening carefully, as he pinpointed its location. His brows arched in confusion. *She might have forgotten her phone.* But the reassurance failed to still the quickening pace of his heart.

Getting up from the couch he moved to the foyer. The ringing was still distant but he locked onto a direction. He turned to the landing above him. *Yeah, she must have forgotten it, that's all.* As he shuffled up the stairs he redialed Katelyn's number after it went to voicemail. And though he expected the ringing to come from the master bedroom, probably lost somewhere amongst the bedsheets, he was surprised to hear it come from above. Sharp whipped his head up and stared at the ceiling. It was coming from the attic.

Why is her phone in the attic? Sharp pondered as he went for the chord that brought down the narrow ladder. The moment it slid open the ringing grew clearer and more distinct.

Climbing the ladder, Sharp poked his head up through the opening. He didn't see it at first when he scanned the attic, but when he did the sheer shock of it sent him tumbling down the stairs. He crashed to the floor and, as he stared up at the dark abyss above, water flooded his eyes. *No, no!* Sharp refused to believe. His lips trembled. Short gasping breaths escaped from his mouth. A whiff of Katelyn's perfume floated into his nostrils.

Sharp forced himself onto his feet, his knees were wobbly and his stomach churned violently. Vomit rose through his throat. He braced the ladder and took the steps up one at a time. *I have to be sure…I have to be sure it's them.*

Firmly in the attic, the color from his face drained away as he stared down at the three bodies propped up against the attic wall. Katelyn sat in the middle with her arms wrapped around Susie and Beth while they snuggled in tight against her chest.

"Katelyn," Sharp called out softly. "Katelyn."

She didn't move.

He took a step forward, letting his cellphone slip from his fingers and thud on the wooden floor. With his next step, his knees gave out completely and he collapsed onto all fours, his head bowed low. He sniffed. "Susie...Beth." He glanced up hoping to see them react, but they didn't move either. The dam broke and tears cascaded down his cheeks.

"How?" He whined, then crawled forward on his hands and knees. Coming within a foot of Katelyn, Sharp reached out a hand and caressed her cheek. "Please," he whimpered, lifting her head up. Her eyes were closed. "Wake up. Get up." But her head only fell forward when he pulled away.

That's when he noticed the slip of paper planted in Katelyn's lap. He snatched it up and read it:

Congratulations Mr. Sharp on ending the glorious reign of Pope Alexander Balthazar. We took the liberty of paying you back.

Signed,

WHISPER

The slip fell from his hands as a torrent of tears fell from his eyes. The clump in his heart expanded across his chest, compressing his lungs and smashing flat the flower of hope. A mournful howl filled his ears. Sharp laid down his head into Katelyn's lap and brought his girls closer to him. "I'm sorry," he apologized. "It wasn't supposed to be like this. I'm sorry. I'm sorry. I'm so sorry."

ABOUT THE DESIGNER

Paul Beveridge is a brand designer, illustrator, and creative director whose work brings a broader perspective on how books must speak beyond their pages. Completing a book is a big endeavour, but also just the first step. A full-service creative partner, Paul's work extends beyond the cover, from book design to book launch, branding & marketing.

www.ingramcontent.com/pod-product-compliance
Lightning Source LLC
LaVergne TN
LVHW100519110826
845146LV00002B/705
* 9 7 9 8 9 9 4 5 8 4 4 0 8 *